Ancient Matriarchs:
Book Two

Into the Storms,
GANET WIFE OF
SETH

Angelique Conger

SOUTHWEST OF ZION PUBLISHING / LAS VEGAS

Angelique Conger/Southwest of Zion Publishing
7401 W. Washington Avenue
Apartment 1053
Las Vegas, Nevada 89128
www.AngeliqueCongerAuthor.com

Publisher's Note: This is a work of fiction. Names, characters, places, and incidents are a product of the author's imagination. Locales and public names are sometimes used for atmospheric purposes. Any resemblance to actual people, living or dead, or to businesses, companies, events, institutions, or locales is completely coincidental.

Book Layout © 2014 BookDesignTemplates.com

Book Title/ Author Name. -- 1st ed.
ISBN 978-1-946550-02-6

To Jack
Who always loves and forgives me.

CONTENTS

Prologue

W omen filled the meadow once more. They brought with them blankets to sit on and baskets filled with lunch, toys, and activities for their small children. They found comfortable places to sit, spread out their blankets, and got comfortable.

A chair sat on one end of the green, a seat of honor for their Matriarch and Grandmama, Eve. The day before, she shared her story. The hum of voices dwindled and silenced as Ruth and Ganet escorted their ancient mama across the meadow. Along the way, she reached out to touch a child's face, and comment on the beauty of a babe. Her love for them was palpable. None missed it.

No one felt frustrated by her slow progress; none encouraged her to hasten her step. Rather, they patiently stood, honoring her as she passed through the crowd. When Ruth and Ganet had tenderly assisted her to her seat, a low murmur again rumbled across the meadow.

Ruth lifted her hands to gain their attention. "Sisters, welcome! Yesterday, we enjoyed the words of our beloved Matriarch Eve, as she shared some of the events of her life. A treat awaits you again this morning. Ganet tells me she spent a sleepless night, thinking and preparing for this presentation. Like Eve, she is an honored Matriarch and wife of our Prophet, Seth. Her life has not been easy. There is much you can learn of obedience to Jehovah from her story. Now, listen, and appreciate her challenges and love of the Lord."

Ruth sat on the grass next to Eve, while Ganet rose. A slender, medium-height woman with blue eyes, she caught the attention of those waiting. Streaks of auburn brightened her long brown hair that curled softly around her ears. She inhaled deeply, glanced back at Eve and Ruth, then spoke.

Marriage to Seth has been a blessing. Our life has been filled with greatest joys and deepest sorrows. Among all these, living with Seth and watching him use his priesthood is wonderful.

After our sweet marriage, we followed Adam's example and Jehovah's command, traveling to distant communities to share the message of Jehovah with those children whose parents chose to follow the Destroyer, those who never heard of Jehovah's love. We traveled to many of these, with varied responses. A few were open to learning, while some were totally against our message and chased us away. With most communities, we had mixed results; some wanted to learn, most did not. Some had more violent plans for us.

We traveled in a generally western direction, stopping in villages as suggested by the Spirit of the Lord. Some of these we were warned to avoid, as their residents were deep into the worship of Lucifer.

Chapter One

Permission

My good friend, Seth, hurried toward me. The concern on his face caused me to wonder. Everyone in Home Valley knew his gentle nature. This unusual concern left me questioning myself. Had I done something to cause him pain? I sifted through my memories of the past few days, remembering.

We had met in the hills above Home Valley the day before. Seth teased and cajoled me, calling me Wild Woman, as he had for the last several months. "You never look before you move, Wild Woman. Have you not learned anything, yet?"

"No. Why should I learn when I have you here to protect me, Goat Herder."

"Why indeed?" He laughed and pulled me close. "I do love saving you, but one day I will not be there."

"Not here to save me?" I pulled back and stared into his face. "Why ever would you not be here for me. Do you love another?"

Seth's hands caressed my upper arm, his thoughts far away. "It is not that I love another woman, Ganet. I love you more than I ever thought was possible."

"But?" I folded my arms beneath my breasts and glared at him.

I waited for his reply, which did not come as quickly as I would have liked. I began to wonder if another woman did hold his heart more than me, before he finally responded.

"I do love another more than you, Ganet, my love. I love our God, Jehovah."

I heaved a great sigh of relief. "I know of that love. You worried me. You took so long to answer, I feared you love another woman."

"I do."

"I know. You love your mama. I do, too."

Seth laughed. "You guessed. I do love my mama. So does my papa. I love you."

"There is still something you are not telling me." I stepped away from him and lowered my eyebrows. "What?"

"I wish I could say, Ganet. I really do want to tell you. But, … but, I cannot. I have not been given permission to speak of it to anyone."

"When you receive that permission, will you share with me?"

"Oh, Ganet!" Seth closed the space between us and wrapped his arms around me. "That is one of the reasons I love you. You accept my inability to share, yet you expect me to when I can."

He kissed me, deep and long, a kiss I enjoyed and returned, until he pulled away and disentangled his arms from around me.

"What? Did I do it wrong?" I stared up into his startling blue eyes, so much like his papa's. "Did I—?"

"No, Ganet. You did not. I have to go. I have something I must do. I will find you as soon as I can."

With that, Seth turned and jogged away. I stood, rooted where I stood, watching him leave, wondering what I had done.

This had been the day before. Now he strode toward me with concern written across his face. Fear sparked in my innards, making me sick. Had our kisses offended Jehovah? Would he leave me to serve Jehovah and never return? Or, if he did, would he bring a wife from a far-off land?

"Ganet, my love!" He closed the space between us and grasped my hand in his. "What is wrong?"

"My thoughts, exactly. Why the look of concern? Did you find me to tell me you will be leaving Home Valley?"

His face fell. I knew it. I did not know whether to be angry or sad. Angry tears threatened to reveal my grief. I spun around, not wanting to see the joy in his eyes as he shared his leaving with me.

"Ganet?"

"You are leaving. I knew you were."

"Yes." I heard him swallow. "Yes. I am leaving in service to Jehovah."

A tear slipped from beneath my eyelid. I dashed it away, not wanting him to know how much it hurt.

"But Ganet." He gently dragged on my arm, turning me around with it, until he could look me in the eyes. I studiously stared at the earth beside his feet. "I have been given a commission to travel through the land and teach the love of Jehovah to my brothers and sisters, that is true. However, I am not to travel alone."

Seth touched my chin with his other hand and urged my face upward until I could not help but return his stare. "Jehovah desires that I take a companion, a wife ..., his voice dropped to a whisper, "if you will have me."

I twitched my head as though a mosquito buzzed in my ear. "If, I ...What did you say?"

"If you will have me. Ganet, will you be my wife and travel across the land in search of my brothers and sisters, so that we may teach them of Jehovah's love?"

I dug a finger in my ear. "You want me?"

"Yes, Ganet. I love you, more than anyone else, save Jehovah. Will you be my wife? May I visit with your papa?"

His words finally wormed their way through my fear and frustration. Seth did not plan to leave me behind, he wanted to take me with him.

"Ganet?" The concern returned. "Will you marry me—if your papa agrees?"

My traitorous tears betrayed me as they slid down my cheeks and dropped onto the earth at my feet. "You want to marry me?"

He nodded.

"Yes! Oh, yes! I thought you would leave me behind, only to return with a wife from some far-off land."

"No, Ganet. I love you." His arms were around me again, his hand rubbing my back. "May we visit with your papa?"

"My papa?" The words settled in me. "Yes! Although I believe you will need to visit with my mama, too. She would never forgive papa if he answered without consulting her."

Seth kissed me, not deep and long like the day before, but in a hurry.

"Where are they? I must speak with them today, now."

"Now, Seth?"

"Yes. Now. Jehovah will not give us much time before we will be required to depart on our journey."

"Oh. Well, then, Papa is usually in the barn this time of day, feeding the animals."

He clasped my hand in his and turned toward our barn. We walked together in silence. I feared to waken and discover this dream. Seth mumbled, perhaps rehearsing the words to speak to my papa.

We entered the barn, pausing inside the door for our eyes to adjust to the dimness after the bright sunshine. I saw Papa first, pouring a bucket of grain into the trough for the cows, and pointed. Seth tucked my hand into the crook of his elbow and led me to papa. We waited, silently, until Papa noticed us.

Seth straightened his back and threw back his shoulders. "Papa Hadar, I am to take a bride and travel throughout the land, teaching of Jehovah's love. I love Ganet. Will you allow her to marry me?"

Papa set the bucket in the barrel of grain and stared at Seth, then at me. "Do you love him?"

"Yes, Papa, I do. I have loved Seth for many years."

Papa turned to stare at Seth. "Jehovah commanded you to take a wife? Is that the only reason you ask for her now?"

"No. I desired her as my wife for many months. But, I am a goat herder, in the service of my papa. I did not expect you to allow Ganet to marry me. Now, …, now, I have a different occupation. I am to teach. Will you give us your blessing?"

"Seth. You are Adam's son. My daughter could do no better, especially now that Jehovah has favored you. However—"

"However? What must I do to convince you?"

"You must convince Ganet's mama. She adores her youngest daughter, and will not easily give her up to journey so far from home. Even if I give my consent, it is nothing without the consent of Bethel."

I threw my arms around papa. "Thank you, Papa. Thank you."

~

"No thanks to me, yet, Ganet. We must speak with your mama."

Mama withheld her permission for three days. Then, she enlisted my sisters and Grandmama Eve in planning a wonderful wedding dinner.

My head spun with all the preparations. I did not care if I had a new dress. I was marrying Seth! Mama insisted. I bowed to her wishes and participated in stitching it. I did not make it fancy, to her chagrin. I required travel clothing, dresses and robes to wear while riding across the land.

To my surprise, Mama added three pairs of wide-leg pantaloons, similar to those worn by my brothers—sturdy, but softer. "You will be riding Listella. Your clothing needs to be comfortable and durable." Overdresses and robes completed my wardrobe.

My sisters, and the women of Home Valley, presented me with pans, dishes, sleeping mats and blankets, and all the other necessities of life to be lived in a camp rather than a home. Susanna wept as she stitched the hem of my dress.

"Ganet, I will never see my little sister again."

"You are silly," I said. "Seth will be required to report to Papa Adam. We will return."

She wiped her eyes with the hem of her dress. "You will?"

I nodded.

"Oh, then. I am happy for you." She flung her arms around my neck and kissed my nose.

Only two weeks after Seth asked me to be his wife, we knelt before Papa Adam as he blessed us in a simple rite, joining us as husband and wife. We stared into the eyes of the other, unable to break away to respond to Papa Adam's questions. I was Seth's wife.

We sat with our families, as all of Home Valley celebrated. Everyone enjoyed a celebration and they eagerly participated in our joy. Seth and I sat across from Mama Eve and Papa Adam. My eyes opened wide when he kissed her, then she whispered, "Do you remember the day of ours, so long ago in Eden? Father used those same beautiful words."

"Of course, I remember that day. How do you think I remembered the words?" He grinned at Mama Eve and kissed her.

"Your marriage used the same words you used today?" Seth asked.

"Yes, son." Adam turned to him with a smile.

"They are beautiful. A perfect pattern." Seth kissed the knuckles on my hand.

"In this and all things, Father gives a perfect pattern. Sad others do not know the joy of obedience." Papa Adam kissed Mama Eve between the eyes.

Seth nodded solemnly. "I eagerly anticipate sharing with those who have lost it."

We left the calm and quiet of Home Valley the next day.

Chapter Two

Race

I glanced behind me one more time to see our mamas and papas waving good-bye to us. Seth's parents, Eve and Adam, are also my grandmama and grandpapa. We rode over the low hill and out of the sight of our little community, known as Home Valley.

Excitement filled me, battling with the sadness of leaving my life-long home. I welcomed this new venture into the rest of the world. Newly married, Seth and I were excited to travel around our world and teach the gospel of Jehovah to the other grandchildren of Eve and Adam. We were at the beginning of a dream come true for both of us.

Seth, my beautiful friend, and now my husband.

"What are you thinking?" Seth asked.

"How handsome you are, goat herder."

"Goat herder? Yes, but now I am more. I am your husband and a missionary in the service of Jehovah with you by my side. How did I manage this great blessing?" His tender smile melted my heart.

"To be a missionary? That is easy. You are an obedient son of Adam and Eve." I grinned at him and urged my gray mare, Listella, forward in a cantor. "Catch me!"

As Listella and I rushed ahead, I enjoyed the wind in my face. We moved in a comfortable rhythm, no matter what her pace. I loved her almost as much as I loved Seth.

Blaze barked joyously as he raced at our heels. The dog went everywhere with Seth. He became as much a part of my life as Listella. The clatter of Seth's horse, Pacer Too, his great white stallion, reached me, along with the banging of pots and rattling of our necessary supplies on the pack horse following behind Pacer Too. I pulled Listella to a walk and waited for Seth. My face burned hot from the frenzy of the ride.

"I may be a goat herder," Seth said as he caught up to me, "but I remember the safety of my animals. Hester is laden with food and supplies. It is not good for him to dash across the hills like this. He could step into a gopher hole and damaged his leg."

All around me low sage brushes near the ground were surrounded by gopher holes. I inspected them for a long moment before raising my eyes to his.

"You are right, Seth. Any one of the horses could step into a hole and be seriously hurt. I will not run ahead again, unless we are racing. It feels so wonderful to be on the road, riding in the wind. I forgot about Hester." I turned to the pack horse and spoke formally. "I am sorry for the injury I may have caused you, Hester. I will not bolt away from everyone again."

Hester snorted and bounced his head.

Seth laughed and brought Pacer Too up to stand abreast of Listella. "Just learn from this, Ganet, my beautiful wild woman." He reached over and grabbed my hand. "But you must remember, as well, we will soon be in a dangerous place. I cannot keep you safe when you run off like that."

He kissed my fingertips. Warmth ran from his kiss up my arms and through my body. He loved me and I loved him. How did I ever manage to be his?

"No more racing. I am sorry."

"Unless we are racing," he agreed.

"I can still beat a goat herder in a race." I leaned forward, ready to dash away once again, then sat up.

"You will learn about goat herders, later." His eyes twinkled and his mouth twitched into a grin. "But, for now, we need to travel safely."

He dropped my hand and urged Pacer Too forward. Chastened, I nudged Listella forward with my knees, riding beside Seth, allowing Pacer Too to take a slight lead. My heart continued to beat wildly from the run. As I gave myself permission to admit it, much of my excitement came from riding away into the unknown, not knowing when we would return.

We visited and watched the trail, careful to avoid the gopher holes and other dangers. Filled with the wonder of being alone together, I relished time without others watching us, an opportunity to be alone, away from the loving view of family and friends in Home Valley came rarely.

"Where are we going first?" I waved my hand in front of us. "Do you have any idea?"

"West. Is that not enough to know?"

I drew my eyebrows in and poked my tongue out at Seth. He laughed at me.

"We are traveling west, are we not?" He waited until I nodded. "Grandpapa Adam directed us to travel west. We will encounter people who are ready to listen to the words of Jehovah."

"That is all you know?" My voice rose in pitch and I breathed deeply to control it. "Nothing else?"

Seth laughed shortly, once. "You would think we would receive better instructions. Grandpapa suggested we are required to trust Jehovah and have faith."

"I have faith, and I trust Jehovah. But could we not have received better directions?"

Seth shrugged. "I suppose it is not for us to know, just yet. I do know Geber is along our path."

We rode in silence a few long moments, before returning to other topics.

The smooth track narrowed and dwindled to nothing. The trail led up through boulders interspersed among the sage and trees. We faced a rough, uphill climb. I followed behind Seth and Hester between thickening pines, standing straight and tall. This new environment invited me to strain my neck to look up at all the tall trees.

We stopped in a little glade near mid-day. I slipped off Listella and stood a moment, letting my legs to regain their strength. Though I rode regularly before now, traveling this long strained my legs and spine. Hunger rumbled my stomach, drawing me toward the pack on Hester's back. Dried meat and fruit sat on the top where I put it earlier that morning, waiting to provide us with a filling lunch.

I resisted the pull of lunch and first helped hobble the horses giving them a break to rest and graze in the tall, green grass and refresh themselves for the travels of the afternoon. Seth tossed a bit of dried meat to Blaze. He gulped it down and looked to him for more.

"Silly dog." Seth shook his head.

Blaze lay next to him, his dark brown eyes staring into his. I scooted close to them and leaned my head on Seth's shoulder. Drawing me close, we sat close, enjoying the midday sun.

Unaccustomed to riding so long, weariness rose from my seat up my spine and down my legs—aching from sitting on Listella's broad back. An afternoon of riding rose up to taunt me. This ride already extended longer than any other. With many new villages to visit and many days to ride to share the gospel, I knew I must strengthen my body, and soon.

Seth's call to teach included no completion date. When the time arrived, Jehovah would let Seth know. Until then, we journeyed across the country side, prepared to teach and share. I took a deep breath, let it out in a sigh, and mounted Listella.

Chapter Three

Flood

P acer Too stepped over an edge, drawing me from my thoughts. I exhaled. Seth heard me and turned. "We must cross this ravine. The horses can cross safely. You will be safe if you trail behind me."

"I am not frightened. Can I—?"

"No!" His strident voice surprised me. "Now is not a time to be a wild woman. Please, just follow me."

How did he know I wanted to rush down the ravine? He knew me so well already. "I can do that."

Shuddering, I imagined the horses stumbling and falling down the extreme slope. I trusted Seth to keep us safe on our strong horses, with their sure footing. Hester stepped down, his pack rocking gently in Pacer Too's steps, trusting Seth and Pacer Too. Blaze skittered down next to them, sending rocks rolling.

My time came. I looked for a different place to cross, grumbling under my breath that Seth did not know everything. But as I stared up and down the ravine, I realized no other safe crossing presented itself. Only this path could be used without a long ride up or down the ravine. I pressed Listella ahead and we followed the others down the ravine, leaning back across her broad hindquarters to help her.

Seth took us down in a safe angle, moving the opposite direction several times. A direct line down would be more exciting. I wanted to cut off and go straight down, until I considered Listella. Riding down that way would endanger her. I sighed and obeyed Seth, goat herder that he is.

At the bottom, I urged Listella up to walk near Seth and Pacer Too along the broad, flat, base of the ravine. He reached behind him for his water skin and offered it to me. I washed dryness from my throat and handed the skin back to him. He took a long pull from the skin before tucking it once more away.

"How are you doing?" He reached out to grab my hand. "I felt your desire to rush down, but you kept your wild woman under control. Good for you."

"I did want to race directly down the ascent, until I thought of Listella. I do not want Listella to be hurt, so I restrained myself. I can maintain control, though it is difficult."

"Yes, well—" Seth gazed toward the other slope of the ravine.

I followed his eyes and found my eyebrows climbing as my head tilted back. The precipitous opposite bank rose steeper than the one we descended. I felt a sharp intake of air and glanced up into Seth's face.

"Can I lead?"

"You want to?" He paused to look up the abrupt incline. "Of course, you do, but no. I think I will. We need to travel a distance down the ravine to where the slope is not as sharp before we can scramble out."

We rode beside each other, enjoying the togetherness.

"How many children would you like to have?" Seth asked.

I glanced at him. "How do I know? Mama has fifteen. Grandmama Eve had thirty-six. I hope to have more than mama and less than Grandmama."

"That many?"

"How can I tell how many Jehovah will send to us?"

"How, indeed?" He smiled and glanced at the sky before returning his gaze to me. "You will be a good mama."

"I hope to be. What makes you think I will? I am the youngest."

"I watched you with children around Home Valley. You were always patient with the little boys."

"Those little boys who found pleasure making my life miserable?"

Seth laughed. "Yes, those. They reminded me of myself. Your patience impressed me."

Seth stared up at the sky, again. The bright sun dimmed as dark clouds drifted across it.

"Are the clouds a problem?"

Dark clouds far up the ravine sparkled with lightning, too far in the away to hear the thunder. Gray lines of rain fell, barely visible at this far away. A gentle breeze stirred the grass along the bottom of the ravine.

Seth briefly looked up and encouraged Pacer Too up the incline, though it did not appear any easier. "We must hurry to the top. Now. If there is a flood, we will be in trouble. Take Hester's reins. There is no time to delay."

"We can do it."

He handed me the reins and urged Pacer Too on. Listella followed close after. Hester felt our tension and trailed us without any argument. Even as we rushed up, we switched back and forth up the slope to manage the precipitous ascent, bent low over our horse's heads.

I glanced up, frequently, toward the distant clouds until they drifted out of my vision. I began to relax, thinking trouble lay behind us. Seth pushed Pacer Too up the ravine at a blistering pace, urging me to keep up. Listella panted from the efforts. I wanted to let her rest, but knew better and exhorted her onward, but I needed to stay near to Seth. Hester huffed and complained, but he kept up with us.

"Are we almost there?" I called. "Hester is complaining."

"He does that, but we must go faster. Look up the ravine."

I bent to look down to the bottom and up the ravine. A small stream of water swelled around the bend. I pressed Listella upward. When we turned to travel the other way up the ascent, I looked down, horrified to see dirty brown water, filled with trees, rocks, bushes, and animals churning toward us. The water rose fast and we were not high enough.

Listella whinnied, as in answer to a command and surged forward. Hester screamed and charged up beyond me. Listella and Pacer Too joined him, facing straight up the incline. I dropped Hester's reins and gave Listella her head. They knew how to scale the ravine better than me. I bent low and held on. Blaze barked once, and then raced up the slope.

The racing water rose at a fast pace, a broken tree spun nearby. I screamed as the leaves brushed my face. Listella bunched her rear feet together and lunged ahead over the lip of the ravine. The impetus of horses carried us on past the edge of the ravine.

Listella slowed to a stop, her head drooped, breathing hard. I slid from her back and threw my arms around her neck, tears soaked into her mane while my breathing eased. Pacer Too stopped a short span ahead of us. Hester slowed and came to a stop beyond him, our pans and packs banging and rattling. Blaze barked once and flopped beside us.

A roar below us caught my attention. I turned in time to see the edge of the ravine crumble into the rushing water. A bison struggled to keep its head above the surging torrent. A huge uprooted tree spun in the raging flood, battering into the bison. Seth slipped his hand into mine and we stood together, watching the flood carry debris of all shapes and sizes.

"Without Listella's strength, I would be part of the debris." My whole body quivered in fear.

We fell to our knees and Seth voiced our prayer of gratitude to Jehovah. Seth took me in his arms and we shivered. Then with a snorting and shaking of manes, the horses called to us. We pulled the saddles and packs off them, found the grooming brushes, and brushed away their sweat and dirt. Blaze shoved his nose into my hand, begging for some love. I dropped to my knees and hugged her. Seth joined us, petting his dog, with an arm encircling me.

~

As the sun set, Seth hobbled the horses and set them off to feed and rest. We gathered stones to make a ring and gathered wood to burn. Seth started a campfire as I searched through a pack for food. We needed to recuperate as much as the horses

I started a grain stew and broke some dried venison into it, along with a sprinkling of salt. I walked from camp to hunt for savory vegetables and herbs to add to the soup.

"Stay close," Seth called.

I nodded. The setting sun dropped behind the hill. My plans did not include straying far from the light. I dug carrots, onions, potatoes, garlic and parsley to flavor the soup. I cleaned the vegetables and added them to the pot, then chopped the herbs and dropped them in. I mixed up a flat bread and slid it into the blaze. The fragrance of the cooking mixture filled the tiny clearing. I hunted into the pack one more time, searching for bowls and spoons.

While I prepared dinner, Seth retrieved our blankets and laid it near the heat of the flames. We sat next to each other to eat, enjoying the setting sun and listening to the roar of the surging water.

"I thought the torrent would be beyond us by now." Seth pointed to the ravine with his chin.

"It must have been a huge storm to produce so much."

Water flowed over the banks, trickling toward our camp.

"A great flood, to brook the banks of that deep ravine. It should be past us soon." Seth eyed the raging torrent.

"I hope it will be. The roar is exciting, but I yearn for silence."

A bull mammoth, caught in the mess, bellowed. Blaze raised his nose and shook his fur. Seth's warmth and manly odor mingled with his perspiration comforted me. He drew me near, regardless of the fact I, too, smelled of dirt and sweat from our ride and the excitement of our escape from the roaring torrent.

A trickle of cold touched my toes. I jumped and pulled them back, grabbing to drag our bedding up. We watched a small runnel of water ooze past. It stopped, almost as suddenly as it began. Still, we moved the blankets to the other side. Blaze tiptoed around the stream. Funny dog did not want his feet wet.

I cleaned up the dishes, leaving the pot of stew in the edge of the banked fire, ready for breakfast, and then sat by Seth, who waited for me on our bedding. He lay back and pulled me down beside him. Our kisses were no longer chaste and gentle as in our days of courtship. I returned his hungry kissing, happy to agree to all the kisses proposed.

~

Rays of early sunlight warmed me the following morning. I shut my eyes against the brightness, breathed in the scent of Seth, and reached out to touch him. My hands met with only the warmth of body in the empty space. I sighed and opened my eyes. With much to do, he vacated our bed already. My hopes for another snuggle before we climbed on the horses slipped away.

I removed the length of woolen ribbon and brushed out the nighttime snarls. As I re-braided my hair I saw Seth searching in the mud near the rim. Occasionally, he kicked a rock into its depths. He bent to retrieve something, lifted it to his face, and hurled it to join the rock in the ravine. I wondered if he lost something, though he had not said he had. I tied the braid with my woolen ribbon, wound it around my head, and pinned it up, out of my way. The heat of the day caused sweat to pour down my neck if I allowed my hair to hang free.

Blaze ran along the lip of the ravine barking and sending scavenger birds leaping into the air. He ran farther down the ravine and they resettled onto the carrion. Seth bent again and dug through the muck. He stood with a larger object in his hands. Again, he brought it to his face. This one he did not fling it into the open space above the ravine. He turned and strode toward me, his discovery dangling from the ends of his fingers. I met him between the fire and the edge of the muck left from the receding waters.

"I thought there would be something worth eating left in the remnants of the flood. Many fish have rotted already. I discovered a reward better than fish." He held up a muddy rabbit.

"He will make a nice lunch."

"And the fur will keep you warm."

"That little fur? How will it keep me warm?"

"I will catch many more and you can sew them together." Seth stooped to clean the innards from the animal near a bush. "Too bad one of mama's cats are not here. They would love this mess."

I breathed through my mouth to block the stench. "What will you do with it?"

"Oh, it will not be wasted. Look, slowly, over to your right, under the bushes."

I let my head fall to the left and let my eyes move in a slow arc toward the bushes he indicated. A yellow and black spotted lynx stared at us from the shadows.

"Will it hurt us?"

"No. I will leave this for her. She needs the food for herself and her kits."

"Kittens? How do you …? Oh. I see." I glimpsed swollen teats and the tiny ears of kittens behind the lynx.

We left the putrid mess and returned to our campfire. I stirred the embers to life and heated the last of our stew. Seth skinned the rabbit, hung the carcass from a tree limb over the flames, and stretched the pelt along another branch. Together, we gathered up our blankets and repacked our packs, ready to be slung across Hester's back after we ate.

"Can you ride today?" Seth squatted beside me to eat. "I saw you limping earlier today."

My cheeks warmed. "I can manage, though it may help if I walked part of the day. Are we in a hurry to reach Geber?"

"We must not dawdle, for Jehovah expects me to teach my brothers and sisters. We can walk some today and tomorrow, while your body becomes more accustomed to traveling all day."

I grimaced and tossed Blaze a bite of food.

We spent the next days riding and walking, riding and walking. Each day found me able to stay in the saddle for longer periods of time. By the third day, my ability to ride all day without needing to walk improved. I did not limp any more, either.

Seth proved his skills with a slingshot, killing a rabbit most days, feeding us and adding to his stash of fur to "keep me warm." In the heat, I had no idea when a need might arise causing me to prefer to stay warm, especially in the hot morning sun.

As we traveled, we discussed Seth's plans for teaching the people at Geber.

"Jehovah's charge included you. Papa instructed me to choose a partner or a mate to help me. You are both." Seth leaned in, his startling blue eyes searched mine, and then kissed my lips.

A flock of yellow love birds flew past, fanning our faces. Seth followed them with his eyes, then turned back, staring into mine.

"What will be my purpose?" I asked. "How shall I help?"

"I am not even certain how I will manage to serve. We will work it out as we go."

Chapter Four

Geber

Near midday in our eighth day from home, we spotted a village. In his excitement, Seth led us toward it without stopping to pray. We were certain these people waited to receive the words of Jehovah. We hurried to share.

Surprise filled me at the size of Geber. I expected it to be bigger, similar to Home Valley. Instead, a small hamlet, with only a few small, dismal houses stood haphazardly around a village square. They seemed to be in good order, though a sense of imminent collapse tickled my senses. I could see no reason for the feel, it felt … wrong. A redolence of decay seeped through the aroma of warm soil and cooking food.

Voices dropped into nothingness as we rode into the hamlet and all eyes turned us. Even the children stopped their play and stared toward us. I glanced at Seth, who warned me into silence with a small shake of his head. Blaze considered the faces of the crowd, a growl hesitated in his throat, and his fur stood on end.

We pulled the horses to a stop and Seth raised his hand in greeting. "I am Seth. This is my wife, Ganet. We came to visit you."

A burly, dark man stepped away from the group of men—obviously, the leader. I saw no friendliness in his black eyes.

"Adam's spawn. You are not welcome here."

"Not welcome?" Seth turned to the others, his eyes weighing each man. "Do you others think the same thing?"

Men shuffled their feet as they stared at the ground. Someone coughed in the back, but no one stepped forward to suggest we might be welcome.

"No one bids you welcome. Go," the dark man ordered.

Blaze growled softly. Seth signaled him to silence. His eyes focused on each man in the group, seeming to bore into each mind. Some stubbornly stared back; others looked away.

The crowd shuffled back, until the dark faced leader shouted, "Do not be afraid. This man is not welcome. He wants to force us to worship Jehovah, offer all our flocks as sacrifice, and bow down to him. Seth wants power over us. He will expect us to listen to our women—our women." He spat into the ground near Pacer Too's feet and the crowd took a tentative step forward.

"How could that be so bad?" I wondered. "Women have things to say and you should listen. Your little village would be healthier if you listened." I rolled my lips inward, preventing the words from slipping out.

"Yes. I have been sent to teach you of Jehovah." Seth's voice rang through the square. "Yes. It does include a desire for you to worship Jehovah. And, yes. You would be happier and more prosperous if you obey His laws."

"How can we prosper if we sacrifice our flocks?" a man's voice called.

I glanced around, trying to see who spoke. Seth turned slightly, he knew.

"It does seem strange, a herd growing by giving away your best. However, I assure you, it happens. I have seen it many times. Jehovah blesses you with more flocks and herds than you have now. When you offer one, not all, more will be born. Your fields will increase and your children will be healthier."

"Our children will be healthy?" a woman's voice spoke barely above a whisper.

I recognized it coming from a woman near me. I turned slightly to see a group of women bunched near me, yet carefully separate. I smiled, but there was no response, not even a twitch of lips in recognition.

I turned back as the big man growled, "Do not listen to him. He wants us to bow down and worship him, because he is the son of Adam."

"I do not desire you to bow before me." Seth raised a hand. "We are all sons of Adam. He is my papa, but he is also your grandpapa. It is Jehovah who expects your honor and obeisance. I join Adam in his desire that you find joy and prosperity that comes only from reverence to Him and His commands. I have been—"

The arrogant leader interrupted Seth with a snort. "Only our honor and obeisance? And then, you will want us to follow you. Not going to happen. Not here. Not ever."

Blaze bared his teeth.

Seth lifted one shoulder. "I will not argue with you. Know this: You are not happy in your disobedience. It is my duty to call you to repentance, for if you do not, the Lord will cause that you will be overcome by drought. You will lose all you have now. You will plant, but the rains will not come. Your fields will wither and dry. Your children will starve and shrink until they are near death. This will happen if you do not repent and obey the commands of Jehovah."

Though his voice had not risen, his words penetrated the crowd with authority, stopping all murmuring. Everyone stood rigid, staring at Seth.

He dropped his voice to a whisper. "Come Ganet, Blaze. We will leave. If they change their minds, they can find us camped in the trees east of town." He looked to the knot of men and raised his voice. "But do not think of coming to harm us, for our God is with us and will not allow it."

Seth nudged Pacer Too forward, signaling for me to stay close. Hester's nose brushed against my leg while Blaze paced close beside Pacer Too, as we pushed through the crowd until it opened for us to pass. My knees touched Seth's as we passed through the few houses, separating only when we rode through the open fields toward a copse of trees.

At last, I breathed deeply and allowed my rumbling anger to be expelled in a murmur. We were too close to express my rage. Even I could feel the need for silence. The horses seemed to understand the situation and crossed the fields in a silent canter.

When we slowed to a stop, the horses blew softly as they regained their breath. Blaze paced around us, his fur still standing up. The horses moved restlessly as we brushed them down. The tension I felt had passed to them. Seth spoke soft, calming words to them, until they settled. He hobbled them and allowed them to graze on the grass within the small glen inside the trees. He reached down to pet Blaze, calming the dog with his touch.

"The audacity of that man!" I said, finally feeling safe enough to speak. "What makes him think you would have him worship you? I have never heard of people who refuse to give shelter to visitors." I looked around the copse. "Will we be safe here?"

"We are safe." Seth spoke in his normal, confident voice. "Jehovah will protect us. Is there any bread left from this morning? I am hungry."

"Yes. I will get some food for us."

I grumbled as I opened the pack and retrieved bread, cheese, and an orange while Seth started a small fire. I brought the food to the fire and sat near him, swallowed my frustrations, and offered him a share. He took it, thanked Jehovah for the food, and asked for protection before slowly eating.

"Ganet, my love," he whispered into my ear as he held me close, later, "Jehovah did not send us to be harmed in the first village we enter. This is a test of our faith."

A test? Through a crabby man who refuses to listen to the word of God? I stared into Seth's earnest face. Perhaps. Jehovah works in strange ways.

The sun set in a glorious show of pinks, purples, and oranges against the backdrop of dark, jagged mountains. Their beauty helped calm me in this rough place with tough, grumpy men.

We sat near the fire watching the sliver of moon rise above the mountains to our east, soon joined by bright stars in the black night.

~

I loosened my braid and sat on a wide rock beside Seth in the warm night air. My brown hair splayed across Seth's shoulder as I leaned against him, relaxing after a long day.

"I cannot understand the attitudes of the people in Geber. Why would they prefer to be sad and sorrowful, Seth? Why are they insistent on being unhappy?"

"I do not know, Ganet. Perhaps it is because they have been angry for so long. They do not know how to feel any other way."

I wondered if I had been angry too often. Possibly. Was Seth teaching me something? My nature tended toward cheerfulness more than animosity. My indignation toward the residents of Geber troubled me. I sat a long time, considering my uncharacteristic mood. I needed to control it better. I did not want to be irate all the time like the men of Geber.

"I heard a woman there who wanted a better life for her children." I tucked a stray strand of hair behind my ear, away from my face. "Maybe we can reach people through the women and children."

"That may work," Seth said softly, "but how do we get past the men?"

We sat together in silence, trying to think of a means to share the Lord's love to those living in Geber.

A branch snapped, ringing through the night air. Blaze leaped from his place beside our feet, his eyes focused on the noise, his tail wagging. We, too, turned toward the noise.

The woman who spoke out in Geber stood just outside the light of our fire, grasping the hand of a small child. Another stood right behind them, grasping her robe.

"Hello." I stood and walked toward them, followed by Blaze. "It is good to see you. How can we help you?"

"Ya said our children be healthy," she raised her hand to point at Seth. "Is it true? Or were ya tellin' lies, like Gemin said?"

"I did not lie." Seth came to stand beside me. "Your children will be healthy when you obey the commandments of Jehovah."

I bent low to speak with the children. "Hello there. What is your name?" I smiled.

The little boy moved forward. "Ayab. My sister is Elpis."

"It is nice to meet you, Ayab and Elpis." I touched them on the shoulder. Ayab gave me a little nod. Elpis twitched as though she wanted to jump and run, staring at the dog.

"Girl canna hear you," the woman said. "I be Rivka." Her chin lifted.

I gazed into Rivka's eyes and saw pain. "Oh, I am sorry, Rivka. Is this what you want for your children?"

"My little 'uns are important. I want them to be healthy. Would you not?" she growled.

A retort sat on my tongue, but I kept it to myself as I scrutinized her children. They were dirty and unkempt, wearing rags in the shape of robes, barely covering their skinny little bodies.

"Yes, when I have children, I want them to be healthy." I took Elpis's hand and stroked the dog's thick fur with it. "Blaze will not hurt you. He loves children."

The look on her face changed from fear to awe. Soon Elpis and Ayab played with Blaze, chased him, and crawled all over him.

"How old are our children?" I looked away from the children romping with the dog toward Rivka.

"Five."

"Five? Both of them?"

"Yea. Is a problem?" Rivka stared at me.

"No. I have never seen two born at the same time, though I have heard of it." I broke the stare and glanced at the children. "When did Elpis lose her hearing?"

Rivka responded in a low voice, "Could hear 'til a few months ago—do not know why."

"What can we do for you, Rivka?" Seth asked. He leaned down to touch each child, now sprawled next to the dog, on the head.

"My children ta be healthy, Elpis ta hear like others, them ta laugh and play—not shrink from the eyes of others."

"Those are important things to desire for your children. You must be a good mama." Seth sat beside to me and leaned his elbows on his knees.

"Not, but I wanna be. No man ta help."

Seth's eyebrows jumped up at this. "No man? Did their papa die?"

"Naw. Never married their papa. He is mean man. Beat me and took me. Then walked away. Gave me these, both at the same time."

Conflicting emotions swirled through me. How could a man be so cruel to take a woman against her will? Would not happen in Home Valley.

"Do the children see their papa?" Seth asked.

"He comes ta Geber a'times, but I never told him about the little 'uns. Didna' want him ta hurt these 'uns. He a mean 'un, you know. Don' want him ta claim them. He would sell 'em."

I gasped. "Sell his children? He would not. Would he?"

Rivka nodded.

"Then, you are a better mama than you think." Seth sat up. "It must be difficult to care for two children without a man."

"Is. We 'as starving the first year. I could not work in the fields, or any place, while they 'uz tiny. Mama took us in, but papa didna' like it. We all struggled, near ta starving."

The fire settled, sending sparks flying. Seth moved to put another piece of wood on it. The children crawled up onto the log their mama sat on and snuggled up next to her.

"How do you stay alive?" I asked. "It cannot be easy."

"Not easy. Men willna' let me in the fields and the women push us 'way. I try sellen' baskets, but few will buy. Women in Geber make their own. Clay there isna good for pots. Crumble. No one will take me as a servant, not wi' these," her head nodded toward the children. "Had ta sell my body. Men give me a bit of food ta use me. Do not like it," she shrugged, "but, what choice do I have in Geber?"

I felt cold fingers tickle my core and glanced at Seth who shrugged slightly. "Your life is difficult, but what do you want from us?"

"Teach me. I want healthy children." Passion glinted in her eyes.

"We can teach you some tonight, but there is not enough time to share you all you need to know. If we are not welcome in Geber, we will travel on tomorrow."

"And my children be healthy?"

"Their problems take time. If you do your best to obey, they will be healthier. Perhaps, Elpis will hear again."

"One thing I know, a bath will bring your children greater health," I stood. "Mama told me children and adults fare better when they are clean. While I finish preparing dinner, why not go wash yourself and your children in the stream over there?"

I rummaged through my pack and found soap and a cloth for washing, a cloth for drying, and a spare robe. I gave them to Rivka and sent them to the stream to wash.

"What can you do about Elpis's hearing, Seth? Cleanliness will help keep her from sicknesses, but it will not restore her hearing."

"I cannot promise she will hear, but we must try to teach Rivka the plan of happiness given to us by Jehovah. I will teach her all I can, but I wonder at her honesty. She made no mention of a desire to follow Jehovah. Perhaps, tomorrow we can return to Geber. Maybe they will then have more sense."

I returned to our packs to find the makings for flat bread and knelt next to the fire to mix it together.

"Tell me uv Jehovah's commands," Rivka demanded as I spooned stew into a bowl for her and her children.

"He expects his sons and daughters to love him. He gave us this wonderful earth and asked that we listen to him and try to make it a beautiful place. Is this not an amazing earth?"

"Land's beautiful, but people are not. Folks in Geber ugly. Want ta take all they can. No beauty or kindness in them, only greed. Is that what Jehovah wants from his children?"

"No, Rivka. Jehovah sent me to teach the people of Geber to become better." Seth said.

He taught her as we ate and long into the night. While he taught, I cut a blanket in half and formed robes for the children. Their eyes danced when I pulled the robes over their heads. I pulled another blanket from our pack and helped them lie down, with the blanket forming a pocket for them to sleep in, one side against the ground to keep them clean, the other over them, to keep them warm. Blaze crawled on top of the blanket between them. Elpis and Ayab slept with their fingers entwined in Blaze's long hair. Long after the moon climbed high into the night sky, we finally stopped talking and found our own beds.

"Will we return to Geber tomorrow?" I asked as we snuggled together.

"We will escort Rivka home, if she wants. Geber is not a place for her or her children. Where will she go, if not back to Geber?"

Chapter Five

Rivka

"The people of Geber are pigs," Rivka declared as we broke our fast the next morning. "Don' want to live there."

I was startled by the force in her words and glanced across at her, my eyes sliding to her children. "Is there nothing there for you? Nothing you would miss? Nothing to retrieve?"

"Elpis misses her doll," Ayab whispered, "and I want my spear."

"You would, Ayab." Rivka stared about her, lost in thought. "No, Ayab." She shook her head in the direction of Elpis. "We can make a new doll and spear. Not safe in Geber." She swung her head to stare at Seth. "Are you returning ta that pit of vipers?"

"No. I think not today. Perhaps at another time. We need to find a safe place for you, Elpis, and Ayab." Seth turned to me. "How long before you can be prepared to leave?"

"Not long. I have to clean up our dishes and finish packing up the food and bedding." I rinsed the dishes and stacked them together.

"Good. I will saddle the horses and bring Hester. We need to be packed and on the trail as soon as we can. It no longer feels safe here."

He hurried to the horses and prepared them to travel, Blaze dashing back and forth between Seth and the children. Rivka helped me wash up the dishes while Ayab helped Elpis roll the bedding and gather the supplies. We were ready to push things into the packs when Seth brought Hester to me.

"What is the rush, Seth?" I asked while Rivka took the little ones and the dog to the stream for a last drink and to fill our water skins. "You do not hurry like this."

"Company from Geber is coming. They are angry. It is time to leave, now."

I looked around, seeing no sign of men riding toward us. I shrugged. Seth knew. "How will we leave quickly and take three more people? We have only our two horses and Hester."

"That is a problem I have been attempting to solve. Can Listella carry you and the two children? They are small."

I nodded. "What about—?"

"Rivka can ride on Hester. I will lead him as always. I do not trust her completely." I raised one eyebrow, but he continued, "I do not want her behind me on Pacer Too. If I need to confront those men, it will not be good to have her there."

Both of my eyebrows rose. "I do not want a woman of her virtue riding behind you either. My concern is our supplies. Do you trust her with those?"

"Not really. We have no other choice. Jehovah will not allow us to leave her alone and she has expressed her dislike of the people of Geber."

"Rather forcefully, I would say. But—"

"I will lead Hester, as always. He has been with me many years. I do not think he will leave us without a fight."

"Rivka returned with the water. "Fight? What fight?"

"The men of Geber will be upon us if we do not leave now." Seth took the water skins from her with a nod of thanks and tied one behind his saddle, one behind my saddle, and two with Hester's packs. "We must leave now. You may leave with us or stay here. It is your choice. You need to know that if you go with us, we will be traveling as fast as overloaded horses can move."

The riders stirred up a cloud of dust, rapidly coming into sight. Rivka darted a look at the men of Geber and back at the animals.

"Ayab and Elpis will ride with Ganet," Seth said in answer to the question in her eyes. "I am sorry, but you will need to ride in front of the packs on Hester." Seth shrugged.

Rivka lifted a shoulder. "I heard you plan to lead the pack animal with me on it."

Seth nodded. "If you choose to join us. Choose now, stay or go. You should know a large group of angry men from Geber is racing toward us. They hope to catch us sleeping. Their anger is strong, more than their desire to take us as servants or slaves. It is your choice. You know them better than we do."

All color drained from Rivka's face. "They will kill me if I return to Geber," she whispered, "and they will kill me if I do not. I am a dead woman and my children are lost."

"No," Seth said. "You need not die. I will protect you if you are with us. You have to give me your word of honor that you will not try to harm us. However, you must decide now." He stared into Rivka's eyes. Without looking at me, he added, "Ganet, get ready to leave."

I climbed on Listella and looked at Rivka. "Will you go or stay?"

"I ...I cannot. Gemin believes you have wealth. He will try to kill you. I will stay, slow them down, maybe change their minds."

"Jehovah will protect us," Seth moved to his horse. "You do not need to stay."

Rivka shook her head, great tears falling across her clean robe. "No. I will stay."

"I am sorry, Rivka." Seth mounted Pacer Too and took Hester's lead from me. "We must leave now."

We touched the horses with our heels and they began to move. Rivka called, "Take the children, please." She threw

Elpis in front of me as Seth reached down and grabbed Ayab around the waist, pulling him up behind him.

Fear contorted Rivka's face. Something about those men frightened her. They frightened me, as well. She touched Elpis's foot and smiled up at her.

"You have no time. Go!" She shooed us away and turned toward the oncoming men.

She was right. We had no time to discuss the situation. We touched the horses' sides again, leaned forward to urge them into a gallop, and raced away. Blaze ran ahead of us. I glanced behind me to see riders galloping into what had been our camp. Rivka stood with her arms up, slowing them to a stop. I faced forward, tightened my grip on Elpis, and chased behind Seth through a stand of trees and out into an open field.

I searched ahead for gopher holes in the field as we ran past, a futile search at the speed with which we moved. I could only hope no gophers lived in this field, or the horses would somehow miss their homes in their headlong rush.

We ran past stands of brush and leaped over rocks. I clasped the little girl's waist and bent lower over Listella's neck, gripping the horse between my knees behind Pacer Too. Seth knew where to go.

I heard a whoop and glanced back. Some of the men stopped to talk with Rivka. Most chased behind us.

Listella gathered her feet beneath her and leaped over a stream and ran faster. Seth led us into a thick glade of trees. He slowed to duck under heavy hanging vines. I followed behind, fearful those men would see our hiding place behind the large red blooms covering the green and hanging almost to the ground. Blaze sat between the horses, whose heads hung low as they struggled to breathe after their run. Blaze sat still, breathing hard. Would the sound of their breathing give us away?

~

Seth motioned for silence, and covered Ayab's mouth. I placed my hand lightly across Elpis's mouth in a signal to be quiet. She pulled my hand away nodded her head.

We stood near a flat, rocky mountain face, covered with vines. I heard men charging past, cursing threats at Seth. The last horse clattered beyond our hiding place and I relaxed my shoulders with a soft sigh. Elpis allowed her shoulders to droop.

Seth motioned to me and brought his finger to his lips, though he, too, removed his hand from Ayab's mouth. I listened for noise from the men from Geber, in an attempt to sense where the men went. They shouted some profanity in the distance.

Seth rolled his lips together in warning. The sound of rattling hooves and noisy, shouting men returned, until they stopped on the other side of the hanging vines separating us from them, arguing.

"Where did they go?"

"You should know. Why did you not watch them closer?"

"It is your fault."

"Why did you let them get away?"

"I did nothing."

"I watched. They disappeared!"

Ayab's eyes opened wide and Elpis quivered against me as they sat still. A crash and rattle sounded. Two deer broke through the hanging leaves and dashed away. With a cursing shout, the men chased after them. I let out my breath in a soft huff.

We stood in hushed silence, listening for them to remove. Seth climbed off Pacer Too and led us along, behind the screen of vines. Elpis shuddered when a low branch swept across her arm. Ayab gripped the front of the saddle, twitching away from the leaves.

Seth reached up and lifted the children down from the horses. I slid from Listella and stretched my back. The sound of a waterfall crashing into a pool soothed my nerves. I knelt to scoop some into my hand, but Seth touched my shoulder.

"Not yet. Something is wrong here. It is too quiet."

I had thought it came from our need to be still, until I listened. No birds sang. No small animals rustled in the brush nearby. Was the silence caused by the men who chased us? Or could it be something else?

Seth leaned out, stared into the water, and searched the banks of the pool. He peeked past the cattails growing along the edge.

"Ugh!" he grunted. "It is not good. Come look."

I strode to his side and stared into the pool. A mongoose and rattlesnake lay, entangled together, drowned under the waterfall.

"It is poison." Seth raised his voice so Ayab could hear. "Do not drink from this pool."

Ayab dragged Elpis back from the bank and shook his head so she would see. "No water." He spoke so she could read his lips. "Poison."

Her little face shifted from anger to fear and relief in a moment. I pulled my water bag from behind my saddle and held it out to the children. They ran to me and reached up for it. Ayab grabbed it and handed it to his sister, who took a long drink before returning it to her brother. He drank deeply and returned the bag to me.

I took a sip and noticed with surprise it cooled my throat. Of course, the sun had not moved very high above the western hills. It had been dipped from a stream only a short time earlier.

Seth retrieved his water skin and took a sip of the cool liquid. "They will be back. We need to leave."

"What about my mama?" Ayab's voice became shrill.

Seth cast a glance in my direction. Danger awaited us in Geber. However, Elpis and Ayab needed their mama. Rivka had delayed the mob briefly.

I shrugged. "Why do they chase us? What can a man, a woman, and two small children do against a throng of enraged men. You must decide."

"Jehovah is our protector. If we listen to Him and follow His direction, we will be safe. It is, however, much too risky for the little ones to return to Geber. It would not help Rivka if they were taken captive. We will locate a place for you to hide in safety with Ayab and Elpis. Then, I will go see if I can free Rivka."

"I go!" Ayab yelled and ran toward Seth, echoing my thoughts.

Seth caught him and lifted him into the air allowing his small feet and hands to kick and flail at the air in frustration. "Of course, you want to go, Ayab. Any good son would want to liberate his mama. But, you are small and those men are big. They will laugh and throw you out of the way. It will be difficult for me to recover your mama. If I must constantly watch out for you and fear for your safety, it will be almost impossible."

"Can fight," the little boy shouted, still trying to kick or hit Seth.

"I see you can. You have done well to protect your sister and mama so far. This is different. The fury in those men presents a different type of hazard than you have faced. They will be watching for a rescue."

The boy continued to battle Seth.

"I will make an agreement with you. I will sneak into Geber and see if I can find your mama. If there is a way for you to help, I will return for you. You do have a right to help, as man of your family, if there is a way you can."

The kicking and punching slowed as Ayab thought about this. At last, he relaxed. "You promise?"

"I promise. Until then, there must be a place for Elpis, Ganet, and you to wait, a place close enough for me to come get you, yet somewhere where the women will be safe. Do you know of a place like that?" Seth set Ayab on the ground.

The small boy's hands found Blaze's thick fur. "Do."

"Close? Can you find it from here?"

The boy stood thinking. His sister sidled close and tucked her small hand into the fur beside his.

"Um, yes. Can find it. Show you." He smiled at his sister.

We hid again behind the screen of vines, waiting to be certain our pursuers would not return until the sun shone well past its zenith. No one came back.

Seth lifted the children onto the horses and we mounted behind them. We slowly rode toward our camp of the night before and Geber, searching each shadow and recoiling from any sounds. Blaze walked beside us, ears up and alert.

The return trek to the woods near the campsite took longer to reach than I expected, our race to safety extended the distance of our travel. I climbed from Listella near the stream. She and the others lapped from the stream while I refilled our water skins. My fear caused my innards to jiggle like mama's crab apple jelly.

Ayab directed us to follow the stream closer to Geber until we came to a low hill. We followed its rise a short way until Ayab slid from Pacer Too and poked around among the rocks.

He reappeared, dust and spider webs decorating his robe. "Here it is."

He led us into a low cavern, barely tall enough for the horses to stand. Blaze ran in and inspected it. He returned with a yip.

Seth helped build a cold camp. "No fire. The odor of smoke will draw the Gebers to you like mosquitoes to warm bodies. You have food to eat and warm blankets to protect you from cold. You do not need a fire."

I wanted to go with Seth, but stayed, knowing Ayab and Elpis could not. They needed me to stay with them to keep them safe for their mama.

"Blaze stay with us?" Ayab's eyes followed the dog.

"He will help me discover your mama with his superb nose."

"And what will protect us from wild animals?" I whispered to Seth before he left.

"Your prayers to Jehovah."

We knelt together, praying for Jehovah's help in detecting Rivka's location and bringing her back to her children. Then, Seth and Blaze disappeared into the trees.

Chapter Six

Waiting

M y courage wobbled as I sat to watch Ayab and Elpis play quietly. I feared wild animals. Worse, I feared the Gebers would discover us. I reminded myself this adventure never would have happened in Home Valley. Protection from Jehovah came to the obedient, and I obeyed. Jehovah had not asked me to accompany Seth on this journey to allow our death so soon.

I checked on the hobbled horses in the back of the cavern and gave them oats from a bag Hester had carried and poured water into a natural cavity on the floor. Seth and I had brushed the sweat from them before he left, so I patted each on the nose and walked to the front where I sat on a log.

It did not take long for Elpis and Ayab to sit beside me, one on either side.

"Tell us a story," Ayab begged.

I gathered them close and shared stories Mama Eve told me and the other children in Home Valley when I was small. Ayab moved to sit near Elpis so she could see my face and lips to better understand the stories.

She twitched, startled, when I described the serpent that talked to Mama Eve and convinced her to eat the forbidden fruit. Ayab brightened when I told of the wolf pup, Bark, that became the family pet. Tears rolled across all our faces during the telling of faithful Pasha's death.

Day passed into twilight. The little ones slumped in exhaustion against me. I slid out from under them, gently setting their heads on the log.

I wandered around the tiny space working out the sharp pains of sitting with heavy weights on my legs. When my legs felt strong enough they no longer threatened to buckle beneath me, I retrieved blankets from the pack and lay one out on the cold floor. Cradling each head, I moved them to lie side by side and covered them.

With no one to occupy and nothing to do, I stood restlessly at the opening of the cave. Fear bubbled to the surface of my thoughts. *How long had Seth been gone? Had he rescued Rivka? Or been captured by the men of Geber? Were wild animals waiting in the woods for me? Would Rivka return for her Ayab and Elpis?*

I paced within the tiny enclosure. The horses lifted their heads and snorted. I stared about me, fearful they sensed something. I forced myself to stand still and listen to the quiet.

Listella pushed her nose into my hand, calming me. I stood, petting her nose until I managed to force the fears away.

I peeked past the rock standing near the entrance. The sun sat above the tops of the trees, ready to drop out of sight. All was safe, for now.

I sat on my log and watched the little ones sleep. I thought of Elpis and her hearing difficulty. Could Mama help her? Mama Eve might be able to. She knew how to aid in healing. It depended on the cause of the loss. More questions. More fears. Why did I not learn about healing? I should have known I needed the knowledge. Papa Adam could surely heal Elpis with his Priesthood, if Jehovah willed it. Could Seth?

Perhaps a healer in the next village knew what to do. Certainly, we would travel as soon as Seth and Rivka came back. Geber's lack of hospitality prevented staying anywhere nearby. I determined to tell Seth of this conclusions, when he returned.

Seth warned me earlier that his rescue of Rivka may not be short nor easy. "If she wants to be rescued," he had whispered in my ear. Time extended into eternity while I waited.

I strode to the packs on the floor and loosened Seth's cudgel from its place behind his saddle. Seth had not taken it, preferring to use stealth and Blaze to free Rivka. I planned to have some means to protect myself, besides my little belt knife, if we were attacked. My smaller size, compared to most men, meant nothing as I prepared to protect the children. I decided to be as dangerous as any mama bear.

I prayed for Rivka's return with Seth. I enjoyed her off-spring and they were not too much trouble; but I really did not yet desire the responsibility of them, especially this early in our marriage. I preferred the responsibility of our own, not those brought into this world by another woman.

Ayab sat up, rubbing his eyes. "Where is Mama?"

"They are not here, yet. It will not be long."

Elpis stretched and sat up. Her little face wrinkled in fear until Ayab clutched her hand. They walked to the corner to relieve themselves and returned to drink from a water skin. I checked on the horses and gave them more water.

"Hungry," Elpis said. Ayab nodded.

I rummaged through our packs and brought out apples, dried elk meat, and a chunk of cheese for us to share. Elpis and Ayab snatched their share and sat together to eat. All the comfortableness between us during my storytelling seemed forgotten.

I took my food, and the weapon, to the entrance and gazed into the heavens. Brilliant oranges and purples streaked the thin clouds. Birds flapped home to their nest, calling out to others. Soon their songs settled into sporadic chirps. Above me, a small family of bats flew out the opening in their search for insects. I set the club against the wall, to eat.

I nearly jumped when a tiny hand brushed softly across my thigh. I glanced down to see Elpis standing beside me, eyes on the darkening sky, her mouth open.

I stooped to allow her to see my lips move. "A beautiful evening."

Her blond curls bounced as she bobbed her head.

"Jehovah created a wondrous earth for us." Her hair tickled my face as she nodded again.

Ayab slipped his hand into mine. "Does it burn?"

"Though it looks to be on fire, it is the glory of the sun, reminding us it will arrive once again in the morning."

The children stared upward, their mouths in identical round "O's", their eyes on the darkening firmament. We observed the colors fade and the pinpoints of light appear.

"We can watch the stars come out for a while, then we must return to the safety of the cave."

We leaned close against the edge of the cave entrance as the stars popped out against the blackening sky. The bat family fluttered amongst the trees and swooped almost to our ears. Ayab shivered.

"Bats will not hurt you. They scoop up the mosquitoes and midges that want to taste you. Their meal saves you from their bites." I saw both of their eyes widen as they followed the bats dance through the night air.

"Have you never been outside in the darkness? Never enjoyed a sunset or watched the stars?"

"Mama kept us in, mostly." Ayab's matter of fact voice surprised me. "She always afraid. Doesna want us seen. Sometimes, I sneak out. 'S how I found this." He waved toward the empty space behind us.

The bats soared across the huge, golden moon that lifted over the trees and stood above the clearing where we slept the night before. It lit the world in grays. Only Seth's absence, and Rivka's, prevented the peace of the evening to settle around me. I shooed Elpis and Ayab in and carried the club in with me. I wanted it nearby.

The cool air chilled us. Elpis and Ayab scooted together for body heat. I draped a blanket over them and wrapped another around my shoulders. In the dark of the cavern, lit by the reflection of the moon, we had nothing to say.

The little ones lay close to each other and soft sounds indicated they shared secrets, until those, too, quieted. Crickets chirped, breaking the stillness. My eyes drooped. The day had been long and Seth had not come back.

"Please keep him safe," I prayed.

I must have dozed, for I did not hear movement in the trees toward us or enter our cave. My eyes popped open and I jerked upright when something touched my arm. My fingers wrapped around the cudgel, ready to defend us. A finger touched my mouth. I trembled momentarily, until I recognized Seth's touch, warning me into silence. A shaft of moonbeam broke the darkness. I stared about me, searching for danger. My heart pounded in my ears so loudly I no longer heard the crickets chirp.

Whatever the danger Seth warned against, I would be safe. He was with me once more. I breathed slowly to help my heart calm. Seth was back, and safe!

~

Rivka stooped and ran her fingers through Elpis's hair, her body a dark shadow in the dark. "Mama," the girl muttered in her sleep. Ayab turned and put his arm protectively across her little body.

"We must leave here now," Seth whispered in my ear. "Gemin and his men are in a drunken stupor, but will not be forever. We must be far from here when they waken."

I nodded and stood. I shuffled to the back of the cavern and our packs and located the food I saved for them. I passed Seth and Rivka each a chunk of cheese. As they ate, I gathered the remains of our dinner and stuffed it into the bag.

Seth saddled Listella and quietly hoisted the packs onto Hester, tying them on. I tucked my blanket once again around the hanging pots to muffle their banging.

"What about Rivka and her children?" I whispered as Seth helped tie it down.

"She claimed a sturdy mare from Gemin as payment for his use of her."

I shivered. "Will Gemin like that?"

"No, not much. The mare she claimed is his favorite. We chased the others off to give us more time. They will be forced to search for their animals on foot before they can follow us. When they wake, they will be angrier than they were yesterday. We do not want to be here when they do."

Rivka handed me a water skin, freshly filled with cool water. Her eye was bruised, her lip split, and she touched her stomach as though it hurt. I raised an eyebrow in question: What happened? She shook her head.

I tied my water skin behind my saddle and walked Listella out. Seth assisted me to climb up where I sat waiting. The children mumbled, more asleep than awake. Rivka got on her mare and reached for Elpis. Seth helped set her in front of Rivka, then lifted Ayab behind her. He folded and wrapped their blanket around the three of them and tied it together to prevent either child from falling off the horse as they slumbered. Rivka let her palm rest a moment on Seth's arm before turning to urge her mare forward.

Thoughts rushed through my mind, wondering why she would do that. *Seth is my husband.* Recognition of my negative feelings toward her startled me. I brushed them away.

With a last glance to ensure nothing remained, Seth mounted Pacer Too, took Hester's lead rope, and nudged his tall, white stallion into a slow pace. I followed Hester out of the small glade. Rivka followed me.

I looked for Blaze. He stepped from between the trees, limping a bit. I opened my mouth to ask, but Seth held up a hand. I would have to ask later. The moon set low behind the mountains at our backs. The outline of them becoming distinct as the darkness lifted.

Once away from the cave, Seth led us into the stream, traveling many hundred paces before directing Pacer Too up the side and across a shelf of rock.

"Stay in a single line," he called softly to us. "It will make it difficult to follow."

He pushed Pacer Too to canter. The others joined him, eating up the distance as mountains changed from black to gray, then purple and green. We cantered a distance, and then slowed the horses to a walk, allowing them to breathe and rest. They tore grass with their big teeth as they passed through a meadow. We stopped briefly to let them drink when we waded through a shallow river. I leaned across to Hester and pulled dried elk from the pack. This I passed silently to Seth and Rivka to munch on as we traveled.

The children's voices rose occasionally during the long ride, voicing their complaints in low tones. They looked about them, quietly chirping to each other about things they saw. Sometimes they slept. We adults could not slumber, and exhaustion overwhelmed us. I wondered how Seth managed to continue forward, having had no sleep. Asking was not possible now. Later. Hanging on to the saddle and staying upright required all my effort.

We rode until the sun dipped almost below the distant mountain and the heat of the day began to cool. I urged Listella to move up beside Pacer Too and put my hand on Seth's arm.

"You cannot continue on like this. You need rest. Is there a place we can stop safely so you can sleep?"

His body quivered, much as Blaze did in his dreams. He shook himself and stared around.

"There." He pointed toward a hill not far from us. "I believe there is a cave there. Stay here. I will check to be certain it is safe."

Before I could object, he passed me Hester's lead rope and cantered toward it. As always, Blaze followed at his heels.

Rivka rode up next to me. "Your man leavin' us?"

"No. He searches for a safe place to rest." I held my eyes on his form. "He thinks there is a cave over there."

"Where? I don' see nothin'."

"Good. If you do not see it, our pursuers will not. I do not know if you slept yesterday or last night. Seth did not. He needs sleep."

Rivka nodded. The children sat in the stillness, waiting for Seth to come cantering toward us. I smiled, glad to watch the grace of his ride. As he drew closer, I recognized the slump of his fatigue. Blaze followed, his limp pronounced.

Rivka's mare snorted and I glanced her way to see her face brighten. My lips dipped down on one side, thinking, 'He is my man.' I tossed my braid over my shoulder and toed Listella into a walk in Seth's direction.

He smiled a slow, exhausted smile. "It is empty. The animal that used it before is gone, though its smell lingers. We can sleep here." He raised his voice to call, "Come, Rivka."

We followed his slower pace over rough, rocky ground, hiding our path from hunters until we reached the mouth, which was screened by tall trees. Seth almost fell off Pacer Too before leading him inside. I slid from Listella and led her through the narrow entrance.

The cave opened in the rear, rose to a high ceiling, and provided enough room for the horses and all the people. Listella tossed her head and snorted. An unmistakable odor of a wild animal disturbed her.

Rivka bent over her mare's ears, pushing Elpis low before her, and urged the mare in. Ayab ducked close to his mama's seat as the opening narrowed in front of him, avoiding a bump on the forehead.

Seth assisted Rivka to untie the restraint. I dropped Listella's reins and stepped around her in time to catch Elpis while Ayab fell into Seth's arms. I set her down and turned to observe Rivka's hand lingering on Seth's chest. I clenched my jaw as bile rose in my stomach.

Rivka put their blanket by the wall in the back of the cavern, though apart from the animals. I directed Elpis to it. Seth lay Ayab next to her. They scrambled to sit, staring with round eyes after their mama. I brought bread and cheese from the pack and passed it to them. They slumped together as they ate, exhaustion filling their little bodies. Rivka pulled the edge of the cover up over them and sat on a rock nearby. I gave her food, as well.

I helped Seth care for the horses, even Rivka's. She sat staring at the wall in front of her, her food hung loosely in her hands. Seth discovered dry wood and started a small fire just inside the mouth. I drug our luggage near the flames and sat beside to him.

"Will this not show our followers where we are?"

He glanced toward the entrance. "No. It is far enough away. It will not show from the outside. The trees screen the smoke and the sky is bright. We need fire to keep wild animals at a distance."

I shuddered. Then I pulled bedding from the pack and put it next to the blaze. Rivka nestled beside Elpis and Ayab with an arm curled around them. I put our bedding on the opposite side of the flames and pulled Seth down by me. His strength for arguments was long gone. He fell into my arms slept immediately. I watched him relax in sleep. I followed his deep breaths and gently traced the shape of his face. Gratitude for this man and his love saturated my soul.

Chapter Seven

"Thing"

I woke with a start to a dark cave. The fire had burned low, only bright embers remained. I reached out with my senses to discover what woke me so suddenly. I heard only the sound of scratching outside the cavern.

I lifted Seth's arm from across my hip and inched my way from the bedding until I could stand. I stepped silently around the embers to the cave opening and peeked out from beside the rocky lip. Rain fell. Wind blew the tree near the entrance, brushing a branch against the rock wall.

I released the breath I held. Only rain. Why would a storm waken me?

A horse nickered outside. We were not alone. I glanced at the wall to see if I could see the embers. No. It burned low with no glow lighting the mouth. *How did they find us?* Better wake Seth.

Turning to wake him, something touched on my spine. I jumped, holding in a screech until I recognized Seth's touch.

"Rivka is gone," he whispered.

I scanned the wall where she and the children slept. Blaze lay beside Elpis and Ayab. Rivka no longer there with them. A glance toward the horses proved Seth right. Rivka's mare was missing. Seth looked back at the entryway. I nodded.

We crept the few paces to the mouth. Seth signaled for me to stay hidden and stepped past the cave mouth.

"Rivka. Where are you going?"

I heard her suck in her breath and step close. She leaned in near to Seth. "I am leavin'. She can have the young 'uns. Come with me. I can make you happier than her. If we go in the rain, she will na' be able ta follow."

My heart stopped beating. *Would Seth go with her? Would he leave the children and me alone? Surely not.*

"No, Rivka. You are responsible for your children. Do you not want them to be healthy? They will be healthy if you care for them and obey Jehovah's laws." I imagined a small nod. "I will not abandon Ganet for you or any other woman. She is my wife, covenanted to be mine for eternity. Ganet makes me happy." He turned to pull me under his arm.

"What about me? Where will I go?" A whine filled her voice.

"You have choices. You can return to Geber and your life there. You can journey with us until we arrive in another community. Or you can travel on your own to a place of your choosing. Whatever your choice, you must take Elpis and

Ayab. They are yours. They would miss you and you would miss them."

A deep growl sounded in her throat. "They are naught but a chain aroun' my neck. I canna' care for them, or myself. I have no way ta feed or clothe them. You heal Elpis. They drag me down. You keep them. You feed and clothe them. I am done with them."

I heard a light shuffle of steps behind me and Ayab pushed past us. Elpis trailed after him. "Mama? Where are you going?"

Each child tucked a hand into hers. Blaze limped to the small family.

Rivka stood still, looking neither at the children nor us, staring across the back of the mare. I saw her jaw clench and unclench over and over. Her head shook, barely noticeable. She raised her left foot into the stirrup and began to lift herself into the saddle.

"Mama! Don' go wi'out us! Mama, we willna be trouble. Please!" Ayab cried.

Rivka stood in the stirrup a long moment, staring into the downpour. At last she stepped from the stirrup. "No, lovees. I willna go withou' you. I was checkin' the path. We go after we eat." She handed her reins to Seth and gathered her small ones in her arms and shoved past me into the cave.

"Well? Where is our breakfast?" Rivka demanded.

I stared at her, wanting to tell her what I really thought. *Since when had I become her slave and cook? At this time of night, why would breakfast be ready?* I shook away my frustration and located dried mutton and a wheel of cheese. I dug deeper for apples. I found five, reducing our dwindling supply of fruit. We needed to find a friendly community and get more. I tried to shove down the growing burning in my stomach.

I glanced up at her through my lashes. Rivka rubbed her body against Seth. A growl rose, though I squashed it and planted a smile on my face as I stood with the food and passed an apple to each child before carrying the rest to sit on our bedding.

Rivka stepped forward to take her apple and another, which she passed to Seth. I grimaced momentarily at her familiarity with my husband. I cut cheese and meat with my belt knife. She accepted her share, plus some for Elpis and Ayab, and turned away. I quivered inside.

Seth sat beside me and accepted his share of the food I offered. He pulled out his knife and sliced the apple, cheese, and meat, stacked them together, and ate a bite. Blaze lay with them, at her feet, waiting. Seth tossed him a chunk of meat. He gulped it at once.

Rivka sat with her children, sharing her food with them. Elpis leaned against her, gazing into her mama's eyes as she nibbled on her food. Ayab sat squashed tight against her, trying to be as close to her as possible.

She stood to reach for her water skin and both children stood with her, touching her. I saw her jaw clench and her eyes furrow a moment before she relaxed and pulled them closer to her. Ayab relaxed a bit, but Elpis pressed tight into her mama.

"What happened? Why are those men following us? Do you know?" I asked.

Seth looked at Rivka. She shrugged. We waited, staring at her.

At last, she spoke. "I take somethin' belongin' ta Gemin's and hid it in your bag. He a mean man, wants things his way. Thought I da make him worry."

I raised an eyebrow. "Make him worry?"

"Well, he wants nothing ta do w' me or the children. Thought he' da be interested if I take somethin' of his, get his interest."

"Why put it in our packs? Why involve us?" Seth asked.

Rivka stared at her feet some time. "You offered hope. I could use some."

"By placing us in danger?" My voice raised an octave or two.

"No danger expected. Th's why I stayed behind, ta talk w' Gemin. But he have nothin' of it. He wants … his thing back."

"Just what is this "thing"?" Seth's voice hardened.

Rivka stared ahead, unwilling to answer. Blaze growled. Seth strode to pick up a pack, searching through it, while I hurried to his side and unfastened another and searched it. We carefully withdrew each item, opening or shaking it, hoping to discover the "thing" Rivka hid. She sat still, her children plastered against her, staring at the wall.

Near the bottom, a hard, round object fell from a blanket Seth searched. It rolled toward the glowing embers before he gathered it into his hands. I dropped my pack I and twisted around to see it.

"What is this, Rivka?" Seth's voice hardened.

I removed it from Seth's slack fingers to see it better. Round, brown, and hard, made from a hardwood, perhaps cedar, an image of a woman's face and swollen belly, almost like a pregnant woman, stared at me from the scratched surface. I stared at Rivka.

Her eyes twitched from Seth's eyes to the wall. "She his goddess. He pray her night and morning. Think she give him power over men. I stole his power. He angry."

I dropped Gemin's goddess image and watched it roll, as if enticed by the remains of the fire. Horror filled me. I knew Jehovah commanded we have no other gods. We had been carrying this image with us for two days. How could we receive His protection with this "thing" in our possession?

Ayab left his mama's side and scurried to pick up the idol and carry it to Rivka. She wrapped it in a corner of her robe, cradling it with care. I swallowed the bile rising in my throat.

"Now what?" I asked. "What will you do now, Rivka? Will you throw the thing in the fire or leave it here, to travel with us to the next village? Or do you plan to take it and return to Geber and Gemin?"

Rivka shrugged in defiance.

Seth stooped and folded blankets and repacked the packs. I bent to repack the one I had emptied and reorganized it, allowing the hurt and anger to flow from my fingertips. I felt Seth breathe beside me, yet neither of us spoke.

I worried for him. He had not slept nearly enough and now this. He leaned close and brushed his lips against mine, and then hoisted the packs onto Hester's broad back. I boosted my saddle onto Listella and tightened the straps. I found our water skins and tied them onto the horses while Seth saddled Pacer Too and prepared to depart. He tossed a water skin toward Rivka before taking Hester's and Pacer Too's reins in one hand, my hand in the other, and walked out into the storm.

We mounted the horses in the minimal protection of the tall pine outside. I half expected Rivka to run out, begging us to take her with us. We rode away, listening only to the sound of raindrops pounding against our drawn cloak hoods.

~

We rode in the rain, miserable and wet. When it ended, Seth twisted in his saddle, searching for Gemin and his mob of angry men. We continued during the day, stopping only to let the horses rest and eat. Seth pushed us onward, as he did the day before when he was certain we were followed. We were not, and still, Seth pushed us on.

As the sun dropped behind the purple mountains we traveled toward, Seth slowed to a stop. A gurgling stream ran through the welcoming stand of tall aspens, maples and sequoias. He climbed painfully off Pacer Too and dragged the packs off Hester in silence. I scraped leaf litter into a pile beneath a sequoia, careful to leave a wide space of open dirt between my pile, the rest of the dry leaves, and high branches above us. After all that happened in the past few days, we did not need an out of control blaze.

I retrieved my knife and flint from the bag tied around my waist and soon had a fire burning. I stood to get food from the pack, but Seth's warm arms around me prevented movement.

"What am I to do, Ganet? I carried the image among our things. I am guilty of having an idol. Will God end my mission before I even begin? Am I worthy to be Adam's son?" He buried his head in my shoulder, clinging to me.

I held him tight, murmuring soothing words, as I did for a small child, until he lowered his arms and shook his head.

"I am not a child. I am a representative of Jehovah. He will answer my questions. I will not return until I have an answer." He strode into the trees.

Blaze tagged behind him to the edge of the clearing, whined once, and limped to my side. I stared at Seth's retreating back until he disappeared behind a tall maple. I stooped in front of Blaze.

"What is the matter, boy? How did you get hurt? Let me feel." I ran my hands over his legs.

He had no broken bones, but dried blood stained the fur on his rear flank and down his lets. I filled a bowl with water from the stream. While the water heated, I found tall, hairy, white daisies blooming under the elms. I picked a few, chopped the stems, and dropped stems and blooms into the water when it heated

While the daisies stewed, I dug out the brush from a pocket in my pack and began to brush the horses, talking to them, as if they had my answers, then. I washed the blood from Blaze's fur.

"What do I do now? Seth is a good man, Jehovah knows. He will understand Seth will never willingly carry an idol or keep one in his possession. How long do you think it will take for him to understand?"

Listella shook her head. Pacer Too shoved his head under my arm. Hester waited placidly for his turn. I finished brushing Hester and stood a long time with my arms encircling Listella's neck.

At last I moved to my little fire. A breeze blew ashes in my eyes, all that was left of the flames. The daisies permeated the water with a clean fragrance. I called Blaze to lie next to me, dipped the cloth in it, and washed Blaze's legs with it, and then made a poultice I tied to his leg.

I stared at the ashes of my fire, sighed and carried more dry leaves and needles from the surrounding trees to my fire space. I gathered twigs, sticks, and larger logs to add as the blaze grew, before I restarted it. I dug a trench around the space to ensure its safety.

I retrieved bedding and food and sat to wait for Seth, rubbing between Blaze's ears. I decided to delay until he came back, ready to break his fast. He would be hungry, too. I nibbled at some cheese and an apple and shared dried elk with Blaze, while waiting, and added my prayers to those I knew he offered.

The stars sparkled in the darkening sky above the trees. I propped myself on my elbows to stare at them. The moon hung low in the sky, its fullness beginning to shrink like my apple with a bite taken from it. I looked for the star patterns mama identified for me long ago. The bear, the fish, and all the others twinkled in the night sky, cheering and comforting me.

The efforts of the past few days caught up with me. I reclined onto the bedding and allowed my eyes to close. I roused enough to add another log to the blaze and wonder when Seth would return, before relaxing into a deep sleep. Blaze whined and snuggled close.

Morning sun shone in my eyes, waking me. I turned, hoping Seth slept next to me. Disappointment swelled within me. The blanket lay cold and unwrinkled. No one slept there. He continued to entreat Jehovah. I could be patient.

As I waited, I busied myself preparing fresh bread and a stew.

The sun moved well beyond its zenith before Seth returned. A small smile painted his haggard face. He found success.

I ran to him, thinking to throw my arms around him. Instead, I felt a tingling as I drew near and stopped without touching him.

"You are forgiven?"

Seth smiled. "Yes. Jehovah understands my desire to serve him. He knows my heart is tender, understands I sought only to help the woman and her children. I am forgiven, though I, we, must be more prayerful, depend on Him for guidance."

"We have not prayed much these three days. We spent too much time running from an enemy."

"No, we have not. I spent the night in prayer, and now we should bow before our God."

I collapsed onto my knees beside Seth. He slipped his arm through mine, and offered a powerful prayer of gratitude, begged forgiveness, and sought guidance for our direction of travel. We knelt there a long time. The sun moved half of the distance to the trees before we kissed, with a tingle, and rose to our feet.

"Can you break your fast? I have stew and fresh bread for you."

He kissed me again, suggesting a need for a different fast we needed to break. I returned his kiss. Food would continue be delayed.

We spent the rest of the day and night together, talking of Jehovah's goodness and enjoying time alone.

We journeyed in no rush, riding slow enough for Blaze to keep up with us. He limped less, helped by the poultice I applied.

I nudged Listella to trot next to Pacer Too. "Seth," I said. "You never told me what happened in Geber. What caused Blaze's injury? What happened?"

"I would rather not relive that night, Ganet." Seth stared ahead, guiding Pacer Too down the path in silence.

I directed Listella past a low hanging tree limb. "Just tell me what happened to Blaze, then."

Seth guided Pacer Too around a stump, lost in the memory.

At last, he spoke. "We went to claim Gemin's prize mare for Rivka and chase the other horses away. After she got her mare, I sent Blaze to drive all the rest from the corral and out of Geber. Some refused to leave until Blaze barked and nipped them in the heels. He dodged most of their vicious kicks. One stallion aimed better. Blaze did not avoid his kick to the legs. He narrowly avoiding a kick in the head. He growled and snapped at the stallion's face. The stallion raced from the corral and away from the village, followed by all the others in the corral. They ran from Geber and us."

"Poor Blaze."

"He did his job." Seth leaned out to avoid a low hanging branch.

The sun rose on our backs as we traveled onward in a north-westerly direction. We traveled into the hills toward the mountains. Colorful blooms and greenery crowded the land. Many were unknown to me. Pines towered above us, their tall trunks empty of branches and greenery until high over our heads. The sequoia grew taller still, and so big around Seth and I could not touch the other's hands around the span of the trunk.

Rhododendron bushes rose taller than the willows that flourished near my home in Home Valley. Azaleas of multiple colors of reds and pinks joined the yellow arnica and late blooming hyacinths of every color. Their fragrance, and that of laurel, scented the air. As we rode higher into the mountains, we saw many other unknown plants, trees, and flowers different from those growing in Home Valley. An air of constant awe filled me. We halted amongst this wilderness to celebrate the Sabbath.

Chapter Eight

Rivka's Parents

Three days later, we stopped at a rocky point. The thick pines and aspen separated allowing us an open view of the valley below. Outcroppings of bright red and orange rock stretched in contrast against the greenery of the trees.

"Have you ever seen such beauty, Seth?" We stood together, arm in arm, gazing across the valley.

"Never. Jehovah created a magnificent world for the people of this earth."

A tingling spread across my back and down my arms and legs.

"Look, Ganet," Seth pointed to the valley, "there is our next place to teach. Jehovah promised me we shall achieve success there." He tugged me to my knees to offer a prayer of thanks and a plea for direction and success.

Riding there took more than another day. As we drew near, my excitement rose.

Axleston was a small village, but larger than Geber and much friendlier. No visitors had arrived in their mountain home in many months. Children gathered around us in the square, questioning our objectives and identity. Why had we traveled so far out of our way?

The oldest girl, apparently responsible for the mob, called to a younger boy and whispered in his ear. He nodded and darted away, into the hills. I glanced at Seth who barely lifted a shoulder in a shrug and turned back.

We sat on comfortable seats on a large log that looked to have been placed on the edge of the green for sitting on. Young children gathered around us, crowding close, touching our robes, and sitting at our feet.

"What did you want to know?" Seth laughed at the perplexed look on a tiny girl's face.

"Who are you?"

We sat side by side, sharing names and stories. I retrieved a bag of dried plums to distribute to the young people. A little girl climbed into my lap and threw her arms about my neck. I kissed her dirty cheek. The children begged for a story. I shared my favorite, the story of Eve tasting the fruit that made her and Adam mortal.

Adults and older boys and girls worked in the fields, planting in the few days available. Chadad and Nita hurried from there to rescue us from the little ones, their task as village leader and his wife. Their warm welcome included concern for their citizens. Chadad questioned our purpose so far in the hills.

"Jehovah sent us to teach our brothers and sisters of His love and commands. We are here to offer the blessings of his covenants." Seth touched Chadad's shoulder.

Chadad nodded. "You are welcome to try, though not all will listen."

"That is their right."

Nita led Seth and I to a small guest house, hurriedly cleaned and filled with food and bedding. It was cozy and warm, big enough for the two of us.

"We will not spend a lot of time here," Seth told me as we unpacked. "This is a place to leave our possessions and to sleep in at night."

"And eat meals. We cannot expect to be fed every meal. We need not be a great burden on our hosts. We should not expect to be always fed by others."

"No, we cannot. We cannot ask them to feed us every meal. I love the food you cook."

"I do hope we can restock our supplies. Our fresh fruit is gone." I moved our meager supplies from our pack to the shelves.

We knelt in prayer before meeting with Chadad and Nita for dinner. Seth begged Father for understanding and a willingness to hear and understand from these people, unlike the reception we received in Geber. He stood with a smile I had not seen for many days.

We had a pleasant dinner with Chadad and Nita in their home, where we learned about them and Axelston. After eating, we joined with the other residents of Axelston in the central square where we met earlier with their children. They welcomed us in search of news and gossip from the world outside their village. We freely distributed what news we had, though old, coming from the time we left Home Valley, but this did not matter to them. Old news was better than none at all. They asked us about others, hoping to hear of family left behind in other hamlets and villages. We shared the little information we knew.

Seth answered their questions and explained our purpose for traveling. The throng settled on the grass to listen. They listened, nodded, and murmured a soft "oh" now and then.

The warmth of their response directly opposed the coldness of the people from Geber. Seth mentioned this as he closed, thanking them for their attention. As the crowd broke up, men and women shook our hands. Most spoke kind words.

"Thank you for coming. I cannot understand a village providing you with so little hospitality."

"We are glad you left Geber and came to us."

"I am sorrowful you were treated badly there. Stay here and teach us."

A bent couple stood on the side, waiting for the crowd to thin. When everyone else had left and we walked to our guest house, they stepped out of the shadows.

"You were in Geber?" the man shuffled his feet in the dirt.

Seth turned toward them and answered, "Yes, briefly. They refused to hear anything I had to say. We did not stay more than a day."

"Did you meet a woman?" the woman lifted her head to stare at us. "One with two children, born on the same day? One a boy, the other a girl?"

I stared at the couple, wondering about their relationship to Rivka. "Yes, we met her."

"How do you know her?" Seth answered carefully.

"Rivka is our daughter. Gemin took her from our house and did not bring her back. Are they well?" The man shifted uneasily on his feet.

"She was well when we left them. She was with us for a short time, she and her children." Seth gripped my hand. "They are beautiful, when they are clean. Ayab protects his mama."

"And Rivka?" The woman stared into my eyes. "Is she well, too?"

Seth glanced at me. I saw he wondered how much to tell Rivka's parents. "She was well when we left her."

"When you left her?" Rivka's mama's spoke in a taut voice.

"Rivka traveled a night and a day from Gemin with us." I hoped to soften my words. "We were escaping Gemin. She took something from him, something he considered precious. He wanted it back."

"Something precious?" She folded her arms. "The children?"

"They were with us," Seth said, "but she insists they are not his."

"Not his?" Rivka's papa's eyebrows creased in question.

"She declared the papa left her. Since then, she claimed to have been used by a number of men in Geber. She told us the papa would sell them. She needed nothing from him." Seth frowned.

"I have heard that story. I do not believe it. If Gemin did not chase you for two days to return the children, what did she have he wanted?" Rivka's mama would not be drawn away.

Seth took a deep breath. "An icon Gemin prayed to each night and morning. He claimed it gave him power."

"An idol?" She pressed her lips in a tight line. "Why take that?"

"She did not tell us." Seth shuddered slightly. "I believe she wanted something from him. When I rescued her from Geber, her face shone as Gemin and his men shouted at her. Her face was red from being hit, her lip bloody, and she held her stomach like she had been punched. But she stood tall among them, smiling. I cannot identify her reason for taking the idol."

Her face crumpled with each description of her daughter's injuries.

"You rescued her. Where is she?" Her voice held a sharp edge.

"She chose to stay behind with her Ayab and Elpis, even after we discovered the icon." Seth stared steadily into her eyes. "I do not know if she will return to Gemin or make her way here."

"We gave her the option to come with us or choose a different place to live." I looked over her head at the trees. "She chose, instead, to stay. We left her in a cave to wait for the rain to end. She did not come with us."

Rivka's papa stood with his head bowed, tears freely falling down the front of his robe. He reached out and pulled his wife into his arms. She stood stiff there for a long moment, then slumped into the comfort he offered.

"Thank you for telling us." He wiped the tears from his face. "I understand you did not want to tell us everything. We needed to know. Thank you." They hobbled away, arm in arm.

We stared at their bent backs until they disappeared around a corner and were lost from our sight.

"She could have come home," I breathed.

Seth took my hand and led me to our bed in the tiny guest house. "Rivka made her choice. She must now live with the consequences of her choice."

I agreed. "Jehovah gave us the right to choose our actions. He must feel pain, watching His children suffer for their decisions. Rivka's parents certainly do."

Seth drew me closer to him. "Let us not give him a similar pain."

~

Many days were spent working beside the people of Axelston. Seth aided the men with the planting. Planting time in the mountains required them to work in a short time. Their fields warmed a month later than those in the valleys, and cold arrived a month sooner. Seeds had to be in the ground and growing as soon as the ground thawed.

I went time with the women to the banks of the small river running past Axelston. Merav tucked her skirts up and stood knee deep in the water's edge, digging orange mud from the river bank. Elaina handed her another basket and stretched down to lift it to the bank. I helped her drag the mud to the waiting hands and returned to help drag the next one. Merav stooped into the stream to rinse the mud from her arms and legs. I reached out to help her up the bank, nearly falling in the mud with her.

We laughed as we joined the others to form jars.

"This clay must make beautiful dishes." I brushed my hair out of my face.

"It dries a dark orange." Elaina gathered a glob of the wet mud onto the flat rock in front of her. "Is it different from what you use at home?"

"Ours dries a light tan. This orange is gorgeous."

We compared the features of the mud in Axelston and Home Valley. We worked together smoothing and shaping tall, fat jars and lids. They needed new containers to store their grains. Most of the baskets absorbed moisture during the last raining season, spoiling the precious wheat within. Some children sickened from eating bad wheat. For this reason, we worked.

Our conversation turned from mud to and Eve.

"Is she as kind as they say she is?" Merav asked.

"She is," I said. "There are times she is tough, when we do not listen and forget to be obedient. Even in correction, she shows great love. We all know she loves us."

"Do women work in the fields there, still?" Ana raised an eyebrow. "Our men tell us it is men's work and our responsibility is to care for our houses and children."

"Everyone helps, especially at harvest time. It takes many hands to gather and winnow the grains. After it is cut, even children join us. When everything is winnowed and stored, we join in singing and dancing in the moonlight." I smiled and accepted a portion of the orange clay, remembering the last celebration.

"What do you remember?" Elaina nudged me in the side. "You have a strange expression."

"The last harvest celebration and dancing with Seth. On the last day, Seth and I admitted we liked each other."

They squealed. "Tell us."

"We were children together. He is, as you know, the son of Eve and Adam. He has younger sisters, but he is their last son. All the other sons were disobedient or chose to do something else. None have chosen to follow Adam in his responsibility of teaching the gospel of Jehovah. When Seth determined to be obedient and follow in his papa's footsteps, learning the Priesthood of God, they increased their special care and watchfulness. Because of the sadness they felt after Cain murdered Abel, Eve and Adam feared no son would be eligible to receive the Priesthood. Seth's obedience relieved those fears.."

"Special care? You mean he is spoiled? How can you love a spoiled man?" Ana stared at me.

"Spoiled? Perhaps. If you consider him without understanding his character, you may consider him to be spoiled. For years, I did. I suppose I am spoiled, as well. I am the youngest, petted and coddled by my parents and family. I had only to ask and papa managed to get what I desired for me. Mama chided him, then gave me the tastiest tidbits of my favorite treats. She worried about me when I explored the hills alone, so she sent a brother to be with me." I shrugged. Their heads bent in understanding.

"I watched him smile to someone behind me and my heart ached. I thought he radiated for one of the beautiful girls who sought his attention. Then I learned he smiled for his mama. His thoughtfulness and tender care for her astonished me. Few men work as hard to ease their mama's trials."

"Eve has trials? The perfect, first woman?" I heard Mirav's sneer.

"You think she has an effortless life?" With surprise, I looked to see nods from the women around me. "Eve has not had a painless life. Father declared it would be difficult the day she ate the fruit of the forbidden tree. I listened to her stories as grew older. Nothing has been uncomplicated for her. Imagine giving birth with only your husband. Much of what we have today," I waved my hand toward the pots we were making, "comes from Eve's creativity and willingness to try new things."

"Who thought Eve had problems and sorrows?" Elaina looked at me. "Has she lost a child, as Merav has, early in the babe's life?"

"Oh, Merav. I am sorry. No. Eve did not lose a child before Abel, not as children. But she lost more than half to the Destroyer. We all have our own sorrows. Do others suffer from such a loss?" I gazed at them until they shook their heads. "Eve endures the sorrow at the loss of every one of us who chooses not to accept the love and joy of Jehovah in their lives."

"Jehovah? Is Jehovah not an angry god?"

I shrunk back as though I had been slapped. "Jehovah? Angry? No." I breathed deeply to relax. "He is full of love for us. Seth and I travel among the people away from Home Valley to share his love and commands."

Hands abandoned their work, dropping into their laps.

"You talk of Jehovah's love." Ana leaned toward me, as did the others. "How do you know He is real? Have you seen him?"

"I do not need to see Jehovah to know He is real. I feel it, here," I put my hand over my heart, "as I feel Seth's love. This earth is so beautiful, providing us with all we require. How can we deny his love?"

"I am awed when I look at the heavens at night," Merav whispered.

"As am I," several others murmured. The women shifted and worked on their pots again.

"Jehovah protected Seth and me as we journeyed here. His protection is another way I experience his love."

They bent in my direction, their work forgotten again, ready to hear my story. I told them of crossing the ravine, of the steep descent, and my relief at riding along the flat bottom. I shared our concern when we saw the far-off clouds and the danger of the steeper climb.

"Then, when we had clambered only part way up the incline, Seth pointed to the trickle seeping around the bend at the bottom. A deluge raced toward us, filling the narrow space beneath us. Seth turned the horses so they could move straight up the incline."

They stared at me, following my every word. "They demanded little urging, for they smelled the filthy water as it streamed below us, growing ever higher. I leaned flat over Listella's ears, encouraging her. It rushed ever closer. Trees and animals snared in it passed near our feet." I took a deep breath.

"What did you do? How did you get away?" Ana mirrored the wide eyes of the listening women.

"Listella whinnied, as in answer to a command, and with a final giant lunge, she carried us over the lip and onto the plain. Pacer Too and Hester slowed beside us. When we stopped panting, Seth and I slipped off our saddles and fell to our knees to offer a prayer of gratitude for our safety. The raging water and the screams of the animals captured in it filled our ears most of the night."

"Scary to be almost caught in the flood." Nita sat back on her heels. "But, how do you know you were protected? Could you not have arrived at the top because your horses feared the torrent and listened to you urging them up and out of danger?"

I stopped to remember. "Perhaps. I am certain they rushed upward as they heard the noise of the surging waters. The trees swirling near their feet certainly had an effect on them. However, Listella leaped ahead in answer to a command I did not give. She lunged harder than before, like someone pulled on her reins, helping her. No one was there but Seth and me. Who, but help from the unseen world sent by Jehovah, helped us?"

They sat in silence pondering my story. I lifted my pot and finished smoothing its edge, waiting for them. They, too, picked up their work and sat concentrating on it. A few shivered while others nodded.

"Jehovah is with you," Ana murmured. They agreed in quiet voices.

"He is and he can be with you, too." I lifted my head to gaze into each woman's eyes.

"How?"

"It is a simple thing to pray morning and night, and during the day when you desire extra help. Then, obey His commands, I am certain you obey already. Be kind. Help those in need. Be honest. Pray and fast. Listen tonight. Seth will teach you more. He brings the words of Jehovah. These words will bring you peace. When you know it is right, ask for baptism."

They began to speak quietly among themselves, questioning and wondering at my words. I scooped up a small blob of clay to form a lid.

Chapter Nine

Obedience

I met Seth that evening at a quiet pool that passed near the village to wash away the efforts of our day's work.

"How did your day go?" He splashed water up to his elbows.

"Interesting. The women questioned me about your mama. They were surprised her life is not filled with ease. They asked of Jehovah. I told them of our escape from the flood. They wanted to know what to do to invite Him to be with them. They will be listening to you tonight."

"Ah, good."

"And yours?" I scrubbed clay from my knuckles.

"The men were surprised and happy to have me join them in the fields. They do not always get enough rain here and they must coax water through the fields in ditches, much as we sometimes did in Home Valley. I joined them in getting muddy."

I laughed and pointed to some behind an ear he missed.

He wet his hand and scrubbed at the spot. "When we sat together for the midday meal, they asked of Papa Adam. They were willing to hear me speak of Jehovah. They, too, are waiting to hear me speak this evening."

We washed away the last of the clay, mud and dust before stepping from the pool.

"What did you tell them of Jehovah?" Seth dried and slipped into his robe.

I pulled my robe over my head and reached for my cloak while I shared with him the things we discussed. Seth plucked a blue periwinkle and tucked it behind my ear, and then kissed me.

"Your mama wears a bloom in her hair. Some older aunties in Home Valley follow her example. I never thought to wear one. Thank you. But why?"

"You are beautiful, Ganet. I want to add to your beauty with Jehovah's creations. As you said, Mama is known for the flower in her hair. You are like her. You need one in yours, as well. It will give you confidence as we teach tonight." He took my hand as we walked toward our guest house. "What is for dinner? I am starving."

"Baked yams, greens, and a fat fish I caught in the stream."

"Yes. Yum. Sounds good. But one? For the two of us?"

"Wait until you see it."

Surprise overcame him, showing in his wide open-eyes, when I pulled the fish from the fire, wrapped in sweet leaves, and set it on the table. I think he expected trout, but the huge fish fed us for dinner and two more.

"You are right. One is enough."

Chadad stopped by to escort us to the village square. We sat in seats of honor at the front of the crowd. I sat back to listen to Seth teach.

I sat on the side of the green watching Seth teach. The people of Axelston angled forward, absorbing the words he spoke. Some offered nods and short comments, even turning to a neighbor to share a brief thought.

"It is the will of Jehovah for each man to marry and be faithful and true," Seth said after sharing other commands. "Men should have but one wife and have no relationships with any except his wife. Women are to remain pure, waiting—as young men must also wait—for marriage before entering relations with her husband."

Rumbling rose from the audience as they cried out, speaking out, not always to a specific neighbor. Seth looked at me and hoisted a shoulder. I mimicked him and watched as he waited for the confusion and noise to subside.

Eventually, Chadad stood and the group quieted. He then turned to Seth. "One wife and no relations until after marriage? Is Jehovah so unkind?" The audience encouraged him with low growls. "We have many women and few men in Axelston. Do you expect them to be left alone, without a husband?"

Voices lifted in protest.

Seth lifted his hands for quiet. When their voices quieted, he spoke. "Jehovah cares for his sons and his daughters. He does not want his daughters to be alone. However, he stands firm on this, no relations until marriage. Unmarried women need not be afraid. Men who are worthy of them can be found for each woman. There is a solution. Jehovah does not give a command without making it possible to obey."

He bowed his head and prayed for Axelston. His voice filled the space. After his final "Amen" Seth stood with his head bowed for many long moments. People raised their heads, glancing from him to their neighbors. No one broke the silence.

They began to shift in their seats before Seth lifted his head to speak. "I am sorry, friends of Axelston. The answer to our prayer was long in coming and complex. There is a way to take care of your women as you follow this command, if you choose to be obedient."

He stopped and stared at them.

"Our situation can only be solved by obedience?" Nita tipped her head to the side and rolled her lips inward.

A low rumble of questions spread through the crowd. Seth waited.

When they were ready to listen, he spoke again, "Obedience solves all problems. Sometimes it takes longer for them to work out. Jehovah hears our prayers and will always answer. It is not given as fast as we would like, nor will it consistently be yes. Jehovah knows the right solution is often different than the one we think."

Seth gazed at the men. "In this situation, the challenge is more complex than just an imbalance of the genders in Axelston. Your men are using this situation as an excuse to be unchaste. They claim it as an excuse to have relations with those who are not their wives, causing unmarried women to sin. Repentance is needed by many in order to obey."

My heart beat wildly at the thought of these young women having relations with married men. They must not be able to hope for a better future. I understood, living as they did far from other villages.

"We will leave you to decide, for until you can obey, I am commanded to withhold the means of solving this."

Seth turned, took me by the elbow, and escorted me to our borrowed home.

~

"That was quite a pronouncement. Will the Axelston choose obedience?" I asked as Seth shut our door against the noise and gathered me into an embrace.

"I do not know. It depends on their humility and desire to change. The problem is tangled. Girls who have been taken by married men believe they love them. They will not want to leave them. Some of the wives do not know what their husbands are doing, though some do. Not all men of Axelston are participating in this sinful behavior, but there are enough."

"Is it that bad?" I shook my head. "I would not have known as I worked with the women today."

He held me tight, running his fingers through my thick hair. "They did not speak of it to me. I saw shock on their faces as I spoke this evening. They thought they could keep this a secret. You may want to prepare to leave. We may not still be welcome."

"Jehovah led you to believe this village would be successful for us. But ..." I retrieved our packs from the corner and shook the contents out. I refolded the blankets, laying them neatly in the bottom. I pulled our robes from the hooks on the wall, folded them neatly, and was tucking them into a pack when rap sounded on the door.

Chadad and Nita stood outside. As Seth asked them in, Nita observed my preparations to travel. "Are you leaving? We thought you were here to teach us."

"I am." Seth stood with the door open for them. "After that revelation, we prepared to leave in a hurry, if necessary."

"We need to visit with you." Chadad glanced at me and back to Seth. "May we come in."

Seth welcomed them in and closed the door behind them. Our visitors sat on comfortable chairs near the window. I finished folding my robe and lay it on top of my pack before sitting next to Seth.

Chadad stared at his hands for a long moment, and then moved his eyes up to Seth. "You surprised us with your knowledge of the actions of some."

Seth lifted a shoulder. "If it helps, the information surprised me, too, when Jehovah shared it with me. Men believe they can hide their disobedience from Jehovah. He sees everything we do. He understands the desires of our hearts. Because of this, He knows your people are not happy with the situation you are in and prefer not to be caught in these bonds of sin."

"Exactly," Chadad paused and frowned. "Most of those who engage in this reprehensible behavior, enticing young women into improper relations, are embarrassed. We separated to talk. Men of Axelston seek to know more of repentance. How is it accomplished?"

"You should have heard the ruckus among the women." Nita twisted her hands together. "Or maybe not. It was not pleasant. Wives accused the single women of enticing their husbands. We did not know which of our husbands are guilty, at least most of us do not. Some admitted to participating in unacceptable relations, but they claimed to be drawn into it by the men. Some claim to love the married man who took their maidenhood. We are upset with the situation. These women, too, desire repentance and do not know what is required."

Nita and Chadad gazed into our faces.

"Seth, Ganet, please do not leave us in this lost circumstance," Chadad said. "Help us learn how to repent. Help us learn how to obey and solve this problem. They wait for you in the square."

Seth gazed at Chadad and Nita, gauging their determination and intent, before nodding and taking my hand. "Come with me, Ganet. I require your support."

We followed Chadad and Nita to the center of the village. People milled as they waited. Some spoke quietly. Others sat in silence with heads bowed.

Chadad gestured to those standing to sit. Almost as one, they sat on the ground, expectantly facing Seth. Little children, who usually ran along the edges sat quietly with their families. Babies lay in their mama's arms, some with bright eyes focused on Seth. The remainder slept. Some husbands clasped their wife's hand. Others, gripped their fingers together in their lap. Young women and older girls sat in family groups, beside their papas and mamas. All waited for Seth.

"You wonder how I know of your hidden activities." He pitched his voice to be heard across the crowd. "Jehovah summoned me to leave my home and bring along my companion and wife, Ganet, in a preaching journey through the land." He paused to touch my shoulder.

"We were directed to come to Axelston to help the lost children of Adam and Eve. I am to share with you His love and His great desire to have you repent and return to His fold. As I prayed in preparation for this evening's meeting, Jehovah shared your sins with me. I must know. Will you repent?"

As one, the throng cried, "Yes! Teach us to repent."

Over the next hour, Seth taught of repentance. He taught them why and how this should happen. I watched two men, who sat in the back, stand and leave, followed by three women. They did not come back.

All the rest, old and young, sat concentrated on Seth. Expressions of sorrow changed to hope and a yearning for change. These humble people wanted the blessings and love of Jehovah in their lives.

"As you become clean in Jehovah's eyes, it is important for you to know this. Two other villages have problems opposite from yours. They have too many men. They heard of your concern and are traveling toward Axelston. They will be here in five days." Seth studied the crowd.

"How do you know they come? Have you been there?" a man called from in the middle of the group.

"From Jehovah. Watch and pray, that you—and they—will be obedient. Complete your repentance. Will you young, unmarried women be obedient and accept one of these men, if they are worthy? Will you men work with them, as they learn to obey the commands of Jehovah? Go to your homes to think on this."

A resounding "Yes" echoed as Seth bent to lift me from my seat and escort me from the square.

"Men come from other villages?" I latched the door behind us.

"I saw them. Men travel from the north and from the west."

"Are they good men?"

"I think … Yes, I think most of them are. They will need to be taught again of the commands of Jehovah, but many are honorable, I hope. We will have much work to do, as we continue to teach here in Axelston and those of the other places."

Seth pulled me close and held me tight for a long time.

Chapter Ten

Celebration

W e were busy during those five days. We helped with chores and taught. Many residents of Axelston were baptized on the Sabbath, agreeing to obey Jehovah's commands. They particularly agreed to the command to be chaste. They looked forward to the coming parties of men with hope. We gathered in the afternoon to hear Seth preach and to pray for those men who were coming, begging for them to come in peace.

Five days later, we waited for the travelers to arrive. A few among the citizens of Axelston mumbled their concern that no one would come, wondering if Seth spoke the truth, and men would arrive.

The men from the distant villages arrived almost at the same time, entering Axleston in the late afternoon, a band from the north and another from the west. They brought with them a wealth of furs and fish, hoping to influence Axelston to accept their young men as husbands for the unmarried young women.

The men entered the village square, walking through an aisle that opened as the people stepped back. In the center, as they neared Seth and Chadad, the groups realized they were not alone in their quest. With startled faces and some grumbling, the visitors stared at the opposing party, deciding whether to prepare for battle.

Chadad was ready. He raised his hands to calm the men and his people. "We hope you came in peace, for we expected you and are willing to discuss your proposal."

The leaders of the two parties blinked and stepped backward.

"You knew we were coming? How?" one leader demanded.

"We sent no message. How would you know of our purpose?" the second leader spoke a moment behind the first. The two stared hard at the other.

"How can we be sure you know why we are here?" the first asked.

Chadad gestured to Seth. "This man came to us last week to teach us the commands of Jehovah. He is a prophet, for he saw your coming and your purpose. Seth?"

"I saw you coming from the north," Seth pointed to the first, "and you from the west." He indicated the second. "You have many men and not enough young women to be their wives. It has been causing problems for you. Your villages sent you to Axelston when you learned they have a surplus of young, unattached women."

Even from where I stood, a distance from Seth, I could see their mouths drop and eyes open wide. Aviv, one who hoped for an honorable husband, nudged me. "The one over there," she pointed with her chin, "looks nice."

I followed the direction of her chin to the young men who arrived from the west. "Which one? They all look nice."

Aviv giggled. "The third one, on the far left. The one with yellow hair. Do you think he will like me?"

I glanced at him. He stared around at the young women, openly seeking. "Ah, yes. He does seem to be especially nice. Of course, he will like you, Aviv. Are you sure he will be the one who will treat you right?"

The look of joy on her face slipped for a moment. "I … I hope he will." The glow reappeared.

"I hope so, too."

"Look at that one," Ana whispered, pointing toward one of the young men who came from the north. "Is he not handsome?"

"Which one?"

"The one with dark hair."

"The one with dark hair and a straight nose?" I asked.

"Yes. I like his looks."

"Appearance is not everything. How they treat you is most important. You two should see what happens at the celebration. Wait, be patient."

I returned my gaze to Seth, glad to have a good man as my husband.

"Our daughters are not to be taken without a covenant of marriage," Chadad moved his arms up and down to emphasize his words. "We have taken upon ourselves a covenant to obey the commandments of Jehovah. Our daughters seek men who will do the same. Can you consider such a covenant?"

Each company of men faced inward, speaking hotly. I heard cries from them, such as:

"No, we cannot."

"What does this mean?"

"Women are to be taken!"

"What will happen to us if we do not listen?"

The men from the north turned to Chadad first, their answer ready. They waited a long moment for the men of the west to face Chadad again.

When all once again focused on him, Chadad nodded to the men of the north.

"I am Eylam, leader of this search. We of Seedar cannot commit our people to such a covenant," the crowd around them rumbled, "but we who are here are willing to learn of it." The crowd stilled.

"And you?" Chadad signaled the others.

"I am Tam. We, who are from Quillon, will listen. We would invite Seth to return with us to our home to teach our people.

"And ours," Eylam folded his arms and leaned back.

Voices of our friends in Axleston murmured. "How can Seth teach them both? They live in different directions. How can he teach them before we give our daughters to their sons?"

"I will teach you who are here. When it is time, my wife and I will travel to your homes and teach there."

"Now, however, we have a welcome celebration prepared," Chadad announced. "We will show you good places to camp. Then, please return and join us." Chadad clapped his hands in a signal to his people.

While the visitors were led to camping places, on different sides of the village, the women slipped away to retrieve great bowls of food prepared earlier in the day. Men tramped to the storage building, gathering long tables. Others scurried to their homes, returning with stools. The men from Seedar and Quillon joined in putting tables together and setting them in place.

I, too, fetched a desert made earlier in the day from our little guest house. I set it on one end of the table set aside for food and helped throw cloths across the tables. Children brought bowls and spoons, setting them in front of the stools. In almost no time, we sat down to a feast.

Aviv and Ana sidled next to the young men they desired. All the unattached young women surrounded young men they fancied. Of course, some chose the men Aviv and Ana liked. The few visitors were surrounded by giggling young women, trying to gain their attention.

"I hope there are more men back at their homes." I stretched my arms outward, away from Axleston. "There are certainly not enough here."

"No," Seth laughed. "These will have first choice, it seems."

The visiting young men laughed and enjoyed the attentions of the young women from Axleston. Later, during the dancing, one young woman after another softly cried out, "No. I will not go into the dark with you. I have made covenants to be chaste."

I raised my eyebrows. "Will this be a problem?" I asked Seth.

"We will find out tomorrow."

I counted the single women to see who continued to celebrate with the village. All but two were visible. Some sat in a group with young men. Aviv sat alone with her blond man. I hoped he would treat her well. Ana sat alone.

The party broke up late into the night, with the guests finding their way to their camps, alone. I watched Aviv's chosen young man escort her to her door, before he turned toward his camp. Seth took my arm and guided me to our temporary home.

~

Seth taught the men of Quillon and Seedar the commandments of Jehovah over the next days. I spent my days with the women. We cleaned, straightened, and dyed wool in lovely soft shades. With the hope of marriages for their daughters, new blankets were needed for them to take to their new homes. Lengths of fabric were to be used to create new marriage clothing. I spent my share of time at a loom, weaving.

Hope swirled around us, as mamas and daughters once again dreamed for a husband and a future. They talked of the anticipated bridegroom, wondering if he currently visited Axleston, or one who remained behind in Seeder or Quillon. Would he treat her well? Mamas struggled to fully trust these unknown strangers.

Seth joined me for dinner the first evening, exhausted. His voice was scratchy and nearly gone from all the speaking. I poured him a tall glass of tangy cherry and apple juice to soothe his throat. Expectant families took the individual visitors home to feed them. We were grateful for the moment to be together, alone.

"They have lots of questions," Seth answered my query. "They have not been taught about Jehovah. Quillon has an idol god, Zil, they sometimes worship. This has been a challenge for some of their young men. Seedar has not found anyone to worship, yet. They have been seeking a god to follow. Perhaps, they say, they have been searching for Jehovah."

"Do they believe?"

"Many do. Most from Quillon begin to reject Zil. Amir has already asked for baptism. He is much taken with Aviv and desires to marry her. Aviv's father will not allow such a marriage without his accepting the covenant. I do not know if his true desire is for Aviv, or for baptism."

"Is not Amir from Quillon? What does he say about their idol?"

"He has questions. He thinks Zil sent them here. I fear his conversion is hollow."

"Poor Aviv. She loves Jehovah, yet she pines for Amir."

"Perhaps her desires will bring her sweet tasting fruit." Seth kissed me tenderly, and then leaned back in his chair and rubbed his eyes.

"This is not the easy mission I dreamed of in Home Valley. I had no real knowledge of the sins men and women commit." I sighed. "The attitudes of the people in Geber astounded me. Why would they be so against us and the word of Jehovah? And now, we meet these people who were unchaste."

"And we are just beginning. Who knows what we will face in our travels?"

Seth continued to teach the men of Seedar and Quillon with mixed success. I worked with the women, weaving blankets and baskets, and reinforcing Seth's instructions. Aviv moved from excited joy to heartbroken sorrow and back again in one morning. Amir professed love for her, talking of baptism. Yet, he continued to question, extolling the glory of Zil and insisting he sent them to Axelston.

"My papa will not allow me to marry one who follows Zil. What am I to do?" Aviv cried.

"Pray the Lord will change his heart," I said, "soften his heart, and open his eyes. He may need to see Zil as false. This may take longer than you like."

I prayed Jehovah would soften Amir's heart, I hoped it would happen. Would it happen for Aviv because she wanted it or because I wanted it? What would Aviv do if Amir chose not to follow Jehovah?

"Will you pray with me? Jehovah hears you."

"He hears you, too. But I will join you."

I accompanied her into a small grove of trees, away from the others, and joined her in prayer. Aviv prayed earnestly, with great desire, but I felt no positive confirmation. I hoped the response would be "wait" rather than "no."

"What will you do if Amir chooses to follow Zil rather than Jehovah?"

Aviv hung her head and moaned. "I have no idea. I love Amir, but my new covenants with Jehovah are more important. I pray Amir's heart will be softened."

After two weeks, and two celebrations of the Sabbath, Eylam led the men from Seedar toward their home with a desire to teach the people of their village the things they learned from Seth. Seth promised Eylam we would join them in his village within the month. A few newly married girls from Axelston joined them.

Tam and his men from Quillon planned to leave the following day. Tam begged Seth to travel to his village first, promising his people would be ready. Seth could only tell him we would arrive as soon as possible.

Aviv, her face covered in tears, visited us the night before the men from Quillon were to leave.

"I need your help, Ganet, Seth." She stood in the middle of the room. "Amir begs me to be his mate, but refuses to marry me in the covenant. Papa will not allow it, for Amir will not agree to give up a belief in Zil and be baptized. What shall I do?"

I put my arms around her, allowing her tears to drench my robe, while Seth awkwardly patted her back. *What can I say? I would not marry one who does not follow the commandments of Jehovah. But, I am not Aviv.*

Eventually, her sobs ended, though tears continually leaked from her eyes. She lifted her head and detached herself from my arms. "Do you have any suggestions?" Her stare alternated between me and Seth.

We sat in comfortable chairs near the fire space.

"The decision must be yours." Seth picked up a small log and held it. "Only you can determine the right thing for you. However, as a servant of Jehovah, I must warn you, a mating with Amir, while he continues to follow Zil, will bring you sorrow and pain." He set the log on the fire.

Aviv watched the embers settle and flame around the log. "I understand. I hear it in the way Amir treats me. He refuses to allow me the right to an opinion. He acts as though I am already his mate, and his servant. I thought it to be cute, at first. Not now. I prefer to be appreciated, loved for me, allowed to think, and join in making decisions."

"You have your answer." I raised my eyebrows. "Just listen to yourself. Are you happy with Amir now, in the protection of your papa's home?"

Aviv slowly shook her head.

"How will you find joy in Amir's home?" Seth asked.

We allowed the question to settle in her mind, watching her mobile face express her sorrow.

"You are right," she cried at last. "I will never be happy with Amir while he follows Zil. I cannot marry him now. Perhaps, he will change?"

"You can wait for him to change, or you can open your heart to another man." Seth leaned forward toward her. "Either choice is difficult. The decision is yours, as is the responsibility for the consequences. This gift of choice is the greatest gift our God has given us, the greatest and sometimes the most burdensome."

"Burdensome? How?" Aviv glanced at me, then stared at Seth.

"If you can push the responsibility for choice onto another, then the following burden of the consequences is also theirs. Sometimes, it is a burden to see possible events following our actions. Still, it is ours to choose, our responsibility." Seth relaxed into his chair, giving her time to think.

I watched her face, bowed in contemplation. "What will you do, Aviv?"

She stood and rubbed her arms. "Go to my papa's house and stay there until the men from Quillon leave. I fear Amir will try to force me to join them. If he does, I will be lost."

Seth and I understood her fears. "Then, we will escort you home to be sure you get to your papa's safely." I stood and put an arm around her waist.

Seth escorted us to the door and reached for our cloaks. "I will have a word with your papa while we are there."

The next afternoon, the noise of extra people and the extra men and their camps, had quieted. The excitement of their visit subdued. A few men from Seedar and Quillon stayed in Axelston with their new brides. Some young women joined those from Quillon. Aviv did not. She stayed safely in her papa's home, away from Amir.

Seth and I stayed another week, helping with the harvest of winter grains and early vegetables in return for a share. Grain, fresh peas, strawberries, and other fruits and vegetables filled our pouches, along with fruits and vegetables I had helped to dry. I did not want to run out of food again.

We left Axelston, promising to return as soon as we could. We followed the north trail, taken by Eylam and his band.

Chapter Eleven

High Mountains

The trail north wound ever upward. It twisted and turned on itself to prevent our falling straight down the mountain. We were eager to reach Seedar. I looked forward to seeing the new brides and learning of their adjustment to their new home. Seth prepared to continue teaching of Jehovah.

We enjoyed our quiet time together. Our busyness in Axleston prevented this, and we sometimes forgot we, too, were newly married.

We reached a rise and stopped to give the horses an opportunity to breathe in the high altitude. The view of high valleys and green meadows caught my breath away. At this elevation, new leaves fluttered on the trees and soft, green grass grew everywhere it could. We traveled, once again, in the newness of growing things and gaped in wonder.

"New life, again," Seth breathed.

"How many early growing times do you think we will enjoy this year?"

"As high as we are, I expect this to be the last. The wakening of the earth to growth causes my soul to swell with joy. Jehovah has taught us He will return to this earth after His cruel death bringing a newness of life. This time of year reminds me of hope of new life for us all."

He kissed me deeply and we continued up the trail until the sun dropped to the top of the trees.

"Look!" I pointed. "Smoke."

Seth stood in his stirrups to gaze at the smoke. "Nothing to worry about. It signals a village."

"Do you think it is Seedar?"

"It must be. Eylam told us they live in the top of the mountains."

"Can we get there tonight?"

"Not safely. The sun sets rapidly here. We can make camp here in this little glen and spend one more night alone together, before facing all the questions."

"I like your way of thinking." I gave him a quick kiss on the cheek and guided Listella off the path.

We hobbled the horses near a tiny stream, wending its way along the edge of the tall grass. It would give us enough for a wash and drinks for ourselves and our horses. The sweet-smelling grass grew tall enough to make a comfortable bed. I helped remove the saddles and packs from the horses and wiped the sweat from them. I found my brush and gave Listella's coat a good brushing, then turned to brush Hester while Seth brushed his other side.

Seth dragged the packs a short distance into the grass, where he discovered a fire ring, blackened rock surrounding black ash.

"Someone else has used this place. One thing less for me to do." He dropped the packs with a sigh.

We set up camp and started a simple meal, and then hurried to wash.

"Eek! It is cold!" I leaped from the water.

"What do you expect?" Seth laughed.

"No bath for me." I pulled my robe over my head and scurried to search for a pot big enough to hold water. Seth's soft laughter reached me.

I carried the pot and our water bags to the stream and filled them with the cold water. I set the pot in the flames to heat. I could wait for a warm bath.

We bathed, ate, and banked the fire then lay back on our blankets to watch the stars brighten the sky. Their number and brightness amazed us. Vastly more stars twinkled up there than in the valleys.

"Do you remember when we met?"

"Met? When you were six and I was two? We did live in the same village." I waggled my eyebrows at him.

Seth laughed. "Yes, we did. And, no, not when you were two."

"You as a boy, maybe eleven. You always had your rock thrower with you."

"I was rather accurate with my sling at an early age. Still am. Good thing, too. I went to herd the flocks about then. One day in the hills, a lone black lion attacked my flocks. I reached into my pouch for a smooth stone I kept there." He moved with the memory, as though reaching to retrieve a stone. "I put it in my sling, spun it around, and let it go, straight between the lion's eyes. He fell, dead." With this, his arm fell from the air to his body.

"You dragged him back to Home Valley. I wondered how you managed to drag such a big lion from the hills."

"I found two fallen trees and tied my cloak around them. I pushed and shoved the lion for a long time before I managed to roll him across the log onto my cloak. Blackie, a friendly old goat similar to Pasha, the old goat mama and papa loved from their early days, let me attach the poles to a harness we often used when I needed him to help pull things."

"I cannot believe a goat agreed to pull a lion behind it."

"The rest of the flock did not like the smell. It spooked them, but Blackie did not mind. I led him and the rest of the flock followed us home, from a distance. Mama grumbled about the smell of the lion on my cloak. It took her forever to wash the stink away. She threatened to throw it away."

I chuckled. "I am sure Mama Eve did not appreciate the stench. All the girls wanted to to touch the lion's pelt. Many were frightened. Why would they fear a dead animal? I will never understand. You stopped so we could feel its soft fur."

"The boys were jealous. I had to fight a few battles because of it."

"I remember a bloody nose." I leaned close to stroke his nose. "What did you do with the pelt?"

"Papa helped me tan the hide. Then we made a cape for Mama. She still uses it in the rainy season. She pulls it over her head to keep the rain off."

I rolled onto my back to stare at the stars. "She wore the cape last year. I forgot it came from the pelt of your lion."

"Mama does not wear it often. She says it is too heavy. I think she believes she is 'showing off' to wear such a nice fur." Seth smiled at the memory.

He shook his head and leaned toward me. "You did not answer my question, Ganet. Do you remember the day we met?"

"Of course, I do. I watched you for years. You are the son of Eve and Adam, beautiful and tall, like none of the other boys. All the girls watched you, even dreamed of you as their husband."

Seth snorted. "Me? The girls dreamed of me?"

"Oh, yes, my beautiful goat herder. You were the dream of many girls." I giggled as his face colored a beet red.

I waited for Seth to regain his composure before I answered the question he had been asking. "I rode a young horse with my brothers, Gomer and Ravid, the day we met. I love riding."

"I remember watching you ride your goat when you were small."

"Gomer set me on our old goat, Spot, and ran beside me until I learned to balance on his back by myself. One day when he was not around to help me, I enticed him with a carrot to the fence and clambered onto him. I rode everywhere on him." My face shone with the memory.

"It was then I saw you. Your courage impressed me, such a little girl, riding an old goat." Seth pulled me closer. "Look, stars are streaking."

"There, and there. Lots. Wonder why?"

"Only Jehovah knows." We lay close, watching the stars streak through the sky.

"Mama did not consider me to be courageous," I broke the silence. "She battered me with words, 'You are a girl. Girls do not ride brazenly through the village on a goat, showing their legs.'" I pulled up my robe to show my legs.

Seth laughed and playfully ran his hands along my thigh. I slapped it away and continued, "Finally, Chayim took pity on me and found a pair of his old trousers to wear under my robe. Mama did not stop fussing at me until Gomer let me ride one of the old mares. Even that did not stop mamas fussing. No more goats for me after that. I think old Spot missed me, though, for he followed me for several months and off and on for years."

"Goats are funny that way. Mama tells stories of Pasha protecting my older brothers and sisters. She could concentrate on her work, secure in the knowledge that Pasha kept the small children safe. Even though Blackie helped me willingly, I never had one for a friend. My dogs, Scamp and now Blaze, were my best friends, until you. Wonder why we had no goat friends?"

"Too hard on your mama when Pasha died?" I suggested.

Seth thought a long moment. "No. After Pasha, papa sacrificed goats. No other willingly took on the responsibilities of children as Pasha did."

"Probably not. You had boys who were friends. I saw you with them."

"None close. They did not trust me, as the son of Adam. They would not accept me."

He never appeared to be sorry for himself, though I noticed his attachment to his animals. I squeezed his hand.

"On the day we met, I rode Listella for the first time. We were new to each other and she was young and extremely skittish. She startled at the least little thing, even leaves blowing on the trees. She stepped near a serpent causing it to rise up hissing and spitting. It alarmed her, no less than it surprised me."

Seth rubbed the back of my hand with his thumb. "Serpents startle most horses. She is not as skittish now."

"No. She settled into a stable ride, but then, Listella was young then. I had taken her on our first jaunt together outside our home paddock. In the newness of the situation and her edginess, the serpent was more than she could handle. She reared and ran out of control. At first, I clung to her, unable to do anything else. She plunged upward in the hills, through every bush she saw. Gomer and Ravid chased behind, shouting at us."

"Your arms and legs were bloody from the scratches. I heard a shout and looked up to see you racing toward the edge of the cliff. You shouted and dragged on her reins. I ran to intercept you and caught her head. I threw my cloak over her head to calm her. She stood snorting and stamping her feet, while you trilled in your excitement."

"That is the first time you called me Wild Woman." I poked out my lower lip in a fake pout.

"Because you raced recklessly up the hill."

"Because Listella spooked."

"I know. You called me Goat Herder. I was a goat herder, would love to be one now."

"If I remember right, I called you a stupid, smelly goat herder. You are not stupid. The excitement of the ride and my frustration with Listella caused me to say you were stupid when you called me Wild Woman. I must admit, you did smell of goats, dirt, and smoke. Whatever you thought about me, I was frightened. I knew about the cliff. Then my brothers took me home, one riding on either side of me. Did I ever thank you for being there to save me?" I turned on my side to gaze at him.

Seth turned his face from the stars toward me. "No, I do not remember any gratitude then. However, you can show your gratitude now." His mouth twitched into a grin.

"I can, can I?"

"Oh, yes. I can think of ways you can acknowledge it."

We giggled and played, joining in loving.

Later, we lay together, relaxing. "Oh!" Seth jumped. "Pacer Too, your lips are cold."

Pacer Too snorted and stomped.

"Go away Pacer Too."

He stomped again. Blaze whined and pawed at us.

"Both of you?" I asked. "What is going on? I lifted my head to see five boys sitting across the campfire from us. "Oh!"

"Oh?" Seth lifted his head from the blankets. "Oh. Hello." We sat up, pulling blankets around us.

The silence stretched between us until a boy pointed at us. "This is our place. Why are you here?"

"We travel to Seedar. We stopped here to rest before traveling the last distance in the morning." Seth reached out for a dry log and tossed it onto the dwindling flames. Sparks flashed and danced. "Did you plan to spend the night in this meadow? There is room for all of us."

The boys glanced at each other, murmuring words I did not hear. "No," the leader said. "You stay here. We will return to Seedar and tell them Seth will arrive tomorrow."

My eyebrows shot up. "How did—?"

The boys rose and drifted silently into the dark.

"—they know who you are?"

Seth lay his hand on my arm. "They expect us, remember?"

I stared into the trees where the boys disappeared when the earth shuddered beneath us and my insides quivered.

"What caused that?" I looked to Seth.

"I do not know. Mama told a story when she and Papa were in the hills. A mountain glowed with fire, then split and shook. They ran through many valleys before the shaking stopped and the earth stopped splitting into deep chasms. Perhaps this is similar."

I caught a glimpse of something bright over the trees, too big and too close to be a star. "Like that?" I pointed. "It looks like the mountain burns."

Seth stood and stared at the burning in the distance. "Perhaps lightning hit it and set the trees ablaze. All the top burns. Strange."

We prayed for protection and help in teaching the people of Quillon and settled in to sleep. Dreams of racing from burning mountains disturbed my sleep. I woke exhausted the next morning.

The   mountain   no   longer   burned.

Chapter Twelve

Seedar

The boys had shared the news of our coming with everyone. They all waited with Eylam to greet us. They stood murmuring to one another as they lined the street, watched and waited.

We dismounted from our horses when we reached Eylam, who greeted us warmly. He turned to the crowd, quieting them.

"People of Seedar," he said, "this is Seth and his wife, Ganet. He knew of our coming to Axelston and told them why five days before we arrived, though we sent no message. They taught us about Jehovah and his commandments. Seth, a son of Adam, learned of Jehovah from his birth. They are here to teach us as he taught the people of Axelston. Please give them your attention."

Seth took my hand and drew me close. "Father placed us on the earth to be happy. Happiness comes from loving companions—husbands or wives who support us. We learn love in families. Who among you have not argued with a brother or sister?"

Chuckles and laughter rippled through the crowd in a wave of understanding. I joined them.

"Yes," Seth continued, "Even I argue with my brothers and sisters. Even as we argue, we love each other. Some of my family left our village and valley in search of a different life. Some of your parents and grandparents were among these. Mama and papa did not stop loving them when they chose disobedience. They have not given up hope for them. Even today, they pray night and morning for their return. I heard their earnest pleas for the children and the grandchildren we never met. This includes each of you."

He paused, allowing the people of Seedar to consider and accept these words. Many turned to the person beside them, whispering to each other. Some nodded, others shook their heads.

"Marriage and children embody this love, proving it. Your village struggles with more men than women. That makes it difficult to have children." Laughter filled the square. "I want children. Ganet wants children. We hope children will be born to our marriage before many years."

I felt my cheeks redden. My bleeding continued each month, I was not yet with child. Eylam's wife, Sara, reached out to touch my arm and smiled. I appreciated her support.

Seth taught those people of Jehovah for nearly an hour when we broke to join them for lunch.

Sara and Eylam led us to a table. We visited as we ate. Men filled most of the seats, though a few women sat beside their men. Bina sat beside her new husband, love glowed in her eyes. She looked happy. Beside her sat an older couple, I thought must probably be his parents. Young men surrounded them. Brothers or friends still hoping for a woman to marry.

Some of the women from Axelston found us, offering us thanks. Bina slipped to my side at the end of the meal.

"Ganet. It is good to see you again!"

"How is it for you and Geb? You look happy."

"We are. He is kind to me and obedient to Jehovah's commandments. I ... I think I am with child already. I missed my monthly bleeding."

"Congratulations, Bina! Jehovah has blessed you." I was happy for her, though I felt a tiny stab of jealousy.

"Did you see the mountain?" She pointed behind us.

"The mountain that burns?" Seth did not turn to look.

"Yes. The men of Seedar say it is sacred," Bini said. "They say a God lives there. Can that be?"

"I have never heard of Jehovah living on a burning mountain. He is the only God." Seth rubbed his chin in thought.

Bina stared at the mountain. "I have not heard of any god living in a mountain. It seems strange. Some days the earth shakes and the fire can be seen high above the mountain. They say the god is angry."

"It is a mystery. Papa would have shared if Jehovah lives in a mountain. I think there is another answer."

We spoke of other small things. When she left, I sat still, unaware of the others. *I am not yet carrying a child. Am I less obedient? I try to obey. Is there a reason I do not carry a child in my womb?*

Seth touched my elbow and brought me back to an awareness of my surroundings. "Your time will come. Not all families begin quickly. Ours will come in time."

He understood my sorrow. It reflected in his eyes. Though we married only a few months earlier, we wanted a child and were saddened when my bleeding came the day before.

Over the next weeks, Seth taught the men and women of Seedar. They listened to Seth. As we worked together the next days, women asked me questions, while the men asked Seth during the times we worked together. The women believed more easily than the men.

Seth returned to our guest house each evening exhausted from teaching men who did not want to listen or learn. All I could do was feed him a warm meal and hold him close as I listened.

"They hold back. There is something they do not want me to know. They do not understand I know their secrets. Jehovah opened it to me."

"And you have not shared your knowledge with them?" I leaned close and set my forehead on his.

"Jehovah has not given me permission to share my knowledge. For now, I listen and share those truths of the gospel I am allowed. More soften their hearts each day. I find it difficult to watch them struggle. Agency is hard, especially for the teacher. Papa told me it would be challenging to allow all men the right to choose their own future and watch them live with the consequences of their choices." He tightened his arms around me.

"That is the challenge of this life, is it not? To make choices and live by the consequences?"

We sat together, holding each other close for a long, silent time.

I did not ask what he knew about these people. I did not want to know. Each day, I grew to love these people. The women accepted me as one of them. In time, I would leave them, but for now, I was one of them.

When it was time for birthing of young animals, the men appreciated Seth's knowledge of animals. He helped sheep and goats deliver their young. More than once, they called on Seth to assist with a difficult birth, whether it was a sheep, goat, cow or horse. During these times, Seth discussed application of Jehovah's laws in their lives.

Changes came slowly among these people, though the interval between planting and harvest flew past. We worked among them through the short growing time and into the warmth of the summer months. By then, many in Seedar took upon themselves the covenants of Jehovah. Men of Seedar traveled to Axelston to return with wives and strengthen Seedar. Others remained in Axelston with their new wives, strengthening that community.

Grain waved in the fields, growing heavy and near to harvest when Seth declared it time to move onward. My sadness at leaving new friends battled with my joy in moving forward with Seth, to find other grandchildren of Eve and Adam who needed the gospel of Jehovah.

We left early the morning after Sabbath.

Chapter Thirteen

Earth Shake

B lack.

Black darkness permeated my senses, with my eyes open or closed.

After many long minutes, I tried to lift my head. It pounded. I discovered my head spun less when I lay still. I tried to work out where I lay. What was my head resting on? Something hard and earthy smelling. I eased my hand up to touch beneath my head. Sticky blood. No wonder the pain increased when I moved it.

My heart thundered in my ears. I discerned no other sounds.

Where was I? What happened? Why was I there? I lay in the dark struggling to remember. My memory returned in jerks and stops. Eventually, I worked out some of it, feeling betrayed, silly, and horrified.

The people of Quillon sent a message to us, expressing a desire to learn of Jehovah. They requested us to leave Seedar and travel to Quillon suggesting some emergency. Reluctantly, Seth and I left Seedar two weeks earlier to travel to Quillon. We arrived late in the night.

Seth wanted to camp early the evening before. He preferred to arrive in the warm sunlight of day. I hoped to sleep in a bed. My back ached from riding and sleeping on the hard earth. I begged Seth to continue on. He warned me it was not safe to ride into an unknown village in the dark. Impetuous, as always, I plead to sleep in a bed. Against his better judgment, he listened to my pleas and we rode on.

"I should have listened," I mumbled.

Inside Quillon, we were surrounded by silent men who reached to grab us from our horses. Seth shouted. I screamed. A rough hand covered my mouth. I bit it. It jerked away. I screamed for Seth. The hand returned to my mouth. Another grasped my body, dragging me. I struggled and kicked. Something heavy hit me on the head. I fell limp into blackness.

Quillon did not desire for us to share the truths of Jehovah with them. That was painfully apparent. What did they want? Why did they lure us to their village?

My head ached from the injury. At last, when I could lift it without the blackness rising in my eyes, I rolled over and pushed myself to sit. I reached out, hands wide, attempting to discover some clue as to my location. One touched a rough-hewn wall. I pulled back with a small cry and a splinter stuck in my finger. I set my teeth on the splinter and pulled it out. With greater care, I stretched out my arms again, searching.

Baskets blocked much of the floor. I sat on one holding lumpy, dirt smelling potatoes, the cause for the earthy fragrance. I shared my holding cell with vegetables. I wiggled my feet on the floor until I found a flat place, praying it marked the path between the baskets to the door. I stood and stumbled forward, hunting for it with arms spread wide. I did not detect it.

I spoke to relieve the silence. "Why so dark in here?"

Sealing of storage buildings, in my limited experience, makes no sense. To prevent and protect against spoilage, air generally circulated through them.

"Where am I?" I did not expect an answer.

I wobbled, nearly falling. The lump on my head ached and made me dizzy.

Where was Seth? I fought down my growing panic. He would find me and get me out of this. I clung to my trust in him, and waited for the panic to subside.

Once more, I pushed myself up and slowly inched a foot forward, feeling for a smooth path leading to the door, there had to be a way out. Baskets were scattered everywhere. Some woman would not be happy with this mess.

My foot touched something round. I fought for a moment for balance. I shoved the round object aside and set my right foot on the floor. I brought the left foot forward, careful to maintain my weight on one foot until I had set the other securely on the floor ahead of me. In this way, with hands stretched wide and moving from front to sides, I inched along, probing for the entrance.

I realized I should have felt along the wall. "How big is this place? Have I been wandering in circles?" I moaned and put my hand to my head again. "All I know is my head aches. Where is Seth?"

I found the wall again. "Follow this, find an opening."

I mumbled to myself as I stumbled along. "No luck along this one. Try the next."

At the corner, I turned and traced it to the next one. At last, I found it. Wood set upright, different from the rest. Pinpoints of light tantalized me shining through. I found the handle.

"Open. Please, open."

I rattled the handle and struggled to budge it, pushing and shoving. It refused to budge.

"Seth! Seth!" I shouted until I could shout no more and my throat hurt.

He did not answer. What happened to him? Did the silent men of Quillon hurt him? I slid to the floor and sobbed.

I must have slept. I became aware of my hunger.

"No reason to be hungry, locked with the root storage." Although the vegetables absorbed the sound of my voice, I spoke aloud to break the silence.

I lifted the lids on the closed baskets, investigating. Potatoes overflowed one. Different varieties of root crops crowded others. I chose a small potato, a big carrot, and a turnip and wiped the dirt from them. I sat beside the door to eat and wait. Someone had to come for food.

My stomach stopped aching. I sat in the dark, praying. More light appeared. I jolted awake.

A whisper hissed through the opening. "Ganet, are you in there?"

I wanted to shout and scream, but the whisper warned me to speak softly. "Seth! Yes, sitting by the door."

"Yes. At last I found you. Move away."

I scooted to the side and listened to wood scraping against the outside. I heard him grunt and the sound of something heavy dropped. Finally, light blinded me as the door screeched free. I fell in to Seth's arms.

"Quiet," he warned. "We must leave here, now." The urgency in his voice quelled the questions waiting on my lips.

Drums beat somewhere near us. Beside the building, two men lay on the ground. Blaze stood over them. I could not tell if they were dead or injured. Did my gentle Seth do this? At the moment, I did not care.

He put a finger to his lips and shook his head. I trailed behind him in silence. Drums hammered louder behind us. I shivered. Nothing good could come from that.

Seth led me into a low shelter smelling of horses. I heard a familiar nicker. Listella leaned against me. Seth boosted me onto her and handed me her reins. He dragged himself onto Pacer Too and led the way out and toward the edge of town. Blaze tracked behind us.

A shout from behind urged Seth faster. I hoped we had escaped. I was wrong. Then men appeared in front of us. Seth led me around a corner. Men crammed that street, as well. We turned to retreat the way we came, but men surrounded us.

Terror overwhelmed me. I would not go back to the storage building. Pacer Too reared. His hooves slashed into the men nearest us. I clung to Listella as the horses plunged and reared. Blaze barked and snapped at the men, biting any within reach.

The men backed into a circle around us. Although the horses stopped dancing, they continued to toss their heads in agitation.

"You cannot escape us. We will sacrifice this woman to Zil." Amir stepped forward.

A shuddering chill rocked me.

"Not my wife. Jehovah will not allow it." Seth nudged Pacer Too to stand between me and Amir.

Amir snorted. "Your god cannot protect you from Zil who is all powerful. Jehovah did not keep you from us."

My fault. If I had not insisted we enter Quillon in the dark, we would not be here now.

Seth raised his hands. "In the name of Jehovah, I command you to depart."

~

Men shifted their feet. Some moved to leave. Early morning sunlight flickered on uncertain faces. Even Amir retreated a pace before setting his feet firmly. "Zil is greater than Jehovah. What do we have to fear from your words?"

The men stiffened and ceased drifting away and faced us again.

"What will you do now?" Amir sneered.

"I will not do anything. It is Jehovah who will overcome Zil."

Their laughter sounded strangely wicked, echoing eerily off the surrounding walls. When nothing happened to them, they inched closer. I waited for Pacer Too, Listella, and Blaze to react, but they stood still. Blaze growled, his hair standing up. Even so, he did not react when Amir gave the signal.

Hands reached out, grabbing the horses' harnesses. We were in their power, again, this time in daylight. I contained my scream. A quiver racked my body, leaving me barely able to stay upright on to Listella's saddle.

Whooping and shouting, Amir and his men led us back into Quillon, the drumming grew louder. My heart pounded with the drums, feeling like it might pound out of my body.

I glanced at Seth on Pacer Too. He stared straight ahead, almost unaware of his surroundings, lost in prayer. From this, I took hope. My heart slowed slowly and I regained control. I tightened my grasp on Listella's reins, waiting for a signal from Seth.

The men halted in front of a large building. The drums echoed through the wide, open doors. Inside, a man, dressed in bright greens and golds, faced a shrine covered with serpents. A gigantic green and gold serpent, larger around than two of Seth, twisted and heaved about his feet. It raised its head and gazed into my eyes and opened wide its giant maw.

I shuddered and drug my eyes away from it, looking instead at Seth. He no longer looked inward. A small smile twitched along the edges of his lips. My fear washed away. I would not be given to the monster.

Amir strode toward me. "Will you get off the horse on your own, or must I drag you?"

"Good luck trying to drag me off Listella. She or Blaze will prevent it," I glared at him.

Amir reached for Listella's reins, but she stepped aside and tromped on his foot.

Amir howled and jumped. "The beast stomped on my foot on purpose."

From the corner of my eye, I saw Seth's smile grow. "She did. You will not take my wife from her horse."

A sense of safety surrounded me. Hands reached for me. Listella whinnied and tossed her head, spiraling and treading on any who came too near. Blaze bit those who got too close to me. Wails and moans swelled through the air. I gripped onto Listella with my knees, glad of all the time I spent with her, both in the saddle and on her bare back. The shouting increased as the men danced away from Listella's feet.

"Should we run? The horses can get past these men," I asked Seth in a whisper.

He lifted a hand. "I want to say we should, but, no. Wait."

I sighed. The green and black serpent slithered toward the door, focused on me.

"I am not going to be sacrificed to their 'god'." Uneasiness settled in my stomach.

"No. Wait. Jehovah is with us. He will save us." He sat relaxed on Pacer Too, reins held loosely in his hands.

I breathed deeply, working to lower the pace of my heart. "Jehovah will save us. Jehovah will save us," I repeated.

Listella stood still, her breathing calm. Blaze sat at her feet. I clung to the assurance I felt from Seth and Listella. The men who surrounded us stirred and shifted away as the serpent slithered nearer to the open door. Their discomfort in the presence of the monster matched mine. Blaze growled.

"Submit to me!" The voice appeared to emanate from it. This could not happen.

"I am Zil. You cannot defeat me. I am greater than any other god. Give yourself up. Come to me." The sound mesmerized me.

I shuddered and swung my head back and forth several times, breaking away from the control. "No!" I shouted. "I will not allow myself to be sacrificed to you. I worship the One True God, Jehovah. He will protect me."

An eerie cackle emitted through mouth of the monster. Men near me shuffled their feet until it hissed, "Bring her to me. Now."

The men surged toward me once more. Listella's muscles tighten, ready to spring away. I tightened my legs against her.

"Now!" Seth shouted. "Now we run!"

Listella and Pacer Too bounded forward, slamming into the men in front of us.The horses wheeled right, soaring over men who fell to the ground. Blaze, too, bounced past them and continued running beside me. I briefly wondered why they fell, but was too busy holding on to think about it. Listella and Pacer Too raced through empty streets, surging over cracks suddenly appearing in the earth. We sped down one street, spun around a corner, and ran down another. It made little sense to me. I grasped to Listella's mane and let her run beside Pacer Too and Blaze.

We ran through the village and into the field, racing for the forest. I began to relax, until Listella, following Pacer Too, turned sharply and vaulted across a growing chasm. *Where did that come from?* I glanced over my shoulder to see trees whipping to and fro. My eyebrows climbed higher as I leaned my body closer to Listella's neck.

We clung to the horses. They ran up a hill and came to a stand. Blaze flopped down, his tongue hung from his mouth. We stared out at Quillon valley. Homes crumbled and fell. Fires swept through the broken and battered buildings. Trees bent near the ground before thrashing back to touch the earth in the opposite direction, sometimes crashing into each other and sharply breaking. Many snapped off just above the ground, falling and bouncing with the shaking. I wondered what would cause such devastation.

After what seemed like a lifetime, the earth and trees stopped shaking.

What was that?" I asked.

Seth shrugged his shoulders. "I knew Jehovah would protect us, but I did not expect a shaking. In the stories, Mama and Papa told me about on a day when the earth shook, nothing like this happened, although there was a mountain of fire, then, too. There were no others then, just them."

"An earth shake. I remember you telling me the story. Look at all the destruction. Did anyone live through it?"

Buildings still burned. A breeze blew the smoke and the sound of a woman screaming toward us. Her voice held a familiar tone, both the terror in it and the woman, one I knew.

Seth sighed. We turned to ride across broken landscape and through the devastation that had been Quillon.

Chapter Fourteen

Into the Flames

Fires blazed throughout the village. Few buildings were spared. Even the storage space that had been my prison burned. The fragrance of baking yams and potatoes mingled with the stench of burning bodies.

We picked our way past homes and other buildings. At the temple of Zil, the priest lay inside, charred. The serpent, speared with a sharpened huge tree trunk shaken from the roof, lay twitching half in and half out the opening, Amir's body clutched in its teeth. Men lay scattered across the square. Some died from their burns. Others died for no visible reason.

The woman's screams for help echoed between the smoldering buildings. Seth moved away from the dying serpent toward the scream. I shuddered and urged Listella forward

It came from the house on our right. We slid from our horses. I started to rush inside.

Seth stretched forth his arm to slow me. "We do not know the dangers of this place. We must move slow and careful."

"But the woman—"

"—could be a trap. Her life is important, Ganet, though not like yours, for me. I will lead the way. Place your feet where I put mine."

I brushed my hair behind my ear and ducked my head in acknowledgment. Seth turned toward the house. He pushed the door open and gazed in. I stood on my toes to peek past his shoulder. Aviv lay on the floor. A large crossbeam lay on top of her legs, pinning them to the floor.

She looked up and moaned, "Thank you, Jehovah. The right people came."

"I started to rush to her, but Seth stopped me. "Remember?"

"We are here, Aviv, hang on. Seth and I will free you," I called.

Seth stared into all the corners before creeping across the floor to stoop over Aviv.

"Be careful, Seth. They still want Ganet," she whispered.

He jerked his head up and gazed around us once more. "Are you certain, Aviv?"

She groaned and raised her head. "He slipped out the side door as you entered."

Seth nodded and beckoned for me to stand by him. He hoisted a length of a smaller broken log that had fallen from the roofing. He handed it to me. "Hold on to this, Ganet."

I took the unwieldy thing, wishing I had my belt knife. I watched as Seth bent to pull the beam from Aviv's legs. I leaned against a wall and scanned for danger. Seth groaned as he heaved it.

"Let me help," I said, moving toward him.

"No. Watch for danger. I want you to be safe."

I shrugged and stepped back against the wall. Seth strained to raise the rafter. The wood inched up away from Aviv's legs. I set my weapon aside and reached to pull Aviv from under the crossbar. Green and gold flashed near the door. Aviv shouted a warning. A man dressed in green and gold picked up my stick. I jerked Aviv from under the beam and ducked as he swung it at my head.

Aviv gasped. Seth knocked the weapon from his hands and dove toward my attacker's knees. A flash of brown and black flew past as Blaze leaped for the throat of my attacker.

Seth and Blaze knocked the man to the ground as the log swished above my head again. It bounced on the floor. I scrambled for it. Seth and Blaze wrestled with the man. Blaze jumped on him and knocked him over.

Seth grabbed his arms and held them behind him. Blaze growled a warning. In my frustration, I bashed his head twice with the stick. The man stopped struggling and lay still. Seth pulled him up, bruised and bloody, holding his arms behind him.

"Why did you attack this woman?" Seth's voice harder than I had ever heard it. "Why?"

The man stood, shaking, in front of Seth. "I am a priest of Zil. I am commanded to sacrifice the woman, Ganet. If I do not obey, I will be sacrificed."

"You know the serpent is dead?"

"I ... I saw it in the d-d-doorway," he stammered. "But Zil is more than the serpent. Zil is strong. Zil will take my life."

Seth glanced past the priest's shoulder at me, and then stared into his eyes. "Zil is a false god. He cannot take your life. Jehovah is a living God. He is the God of this world, and he loves you. What do you think of that?"

"I cannot trust you. Zil has been my god all my life. He will kill me."

"If you insist. You will stay here until we depart. After that, you may give yourself to Zil. Do you understand?"

The priest slowly bent his head in agreement.

"Tie him up!" Aviv urged. "Do not trust him. Rope is in the cupboard. Tie him."

Seth inclined his head in the direction. I found rope and brought it to Seth. Seth wound it around the prisoner's hands and feet and tied them.

"I leave you to Zil." He pushed him to the floor and strode over to us.

He assisted Aviv to stand. Bruises developed on her leg from the beam. She tried to step forward, and fell. Seth lifted her and carried her outside. I followed. Hester stood between Pacer Too and Listella.

"Where did you come from?" I rubbed his nose. "I have no carrots for you, but when I find some, I will be certain to share them with you. I am happy to see you again." I turned to Listella. "You, too. I will find carrots for all of you."

"Can you ride without a saddle, Aviv? We must leave and the saddles are missing."

"Of course, I can. I rode bare back in Axelston, when I helped Papa with the sheep. I can ride, if you help me get on a horse."

Aviv grimaced, holding in the pain, as Seth boosted her high enough to throw her good leg onto Hester and drag herself on.

"He is gentle but has not carried a person for years. He is our pack animal. But, he is all we have. You should be able to ride him."

Hester twisted his head to nuzzle Aviv's leg. "I will be fine. Do not worry. We should go."

I grabbed Listella's mane and Seth boosted me up and jumped onto Pacer Too. Blaze led the way as we picked our way through the burning remnants of Quillon. Neither Seth nor I turned to for another view. I do not know if Aviv did.

As we sat around our night time campfire, Aviv shared her story.

~

Amir returned to Axelston a week after we left. In his open, friendly manner, claiming to Aviv's papa his willingness to commit to Jehovah's marriage covenant. He wanted to be baptized the next morning, if Aviv's papa agreed to the marriage in the afternoon. Aviv recognized his deceit and begged her papa not to agree. He did not agree. Amir entered her room in the middle of the night, taking her away against her will.

"He growled horrible things in my ear the first night," Aviv told us through her tears. "He said I was only useful as a slave and a servant to men. Women are useless, except to be carriers of the new generation or as sacrifices to Zil."

I winced as Seth growled deep in his throat. Even Blaze snarled as he sat at my feet.

"Why did your papa not follow you and try to save you?" I asked.

"Amir forced me to leave a note telling papa I no longer choose the covenants of Jehovah. I am sure it broke Papa's heart. Why would he follow me?" She lifted her head, tears slipping down her cheeks.

"Amir insisted Zil is the true god, and Jehovah has no use for women, not even as sacrifices." She slumped with her head into her hands, shaking it. "He used me all night. Said he prepared me for my only value in Quillon—to be used by men, whenever they chose."

I set my hand on her shoulder, but she flinched away. "I am filthy. Not worthy. Do not touch me."

I eased my hand away. "No, you are a good woman, stolen—"

"I was taken in by that … that monster! He said he loved me. All he cares for is causing pain." Aviv pulled at her clothing. "Every time we stopped, he jerked me from the horse and took his sick pleasure in my body. The more I screamed, the more he liked it. As I rode before him, he muttered filth into my ears, taunting me, telling me what he would do to me when we stopped. I learned to accept his attentions in silence, all the time crying to Jehovah inside. Why did He allow this horror to befall me? Why me? Her voice rose to a scream as she looked about her wildly. Her screaming stopped and she let her head fall to her chest once more.

"Jehovah loves you—" Seth began.

"How can you say that?" Aviv raised her head to stare into Seth's eyes. "He allowed this to happen to me."

"Jehovah allows terrible things to happen to the righteous. In this, the wicked prove their obedience to Satan. Their penalty is just. Everyone has the right of choice—"

"Where was my choice in this? I did not choose to be abused!"

"No, and you did nothing wrong," Seth continued, his voice soft and soothing. "You are innocent in this. You were taken. Amir made the decision. He kidnapped you from your home, against your will, to make you a slave. He abused you terribly. The guilt is his. The punishment will be his."

"*His* punishment? How will he be punished?" Aviv raised a tight fist.

"Yes. Jehovah's judgment is just. In this life and in the afterlife, Amir will be punished." Seth gazed into her eyes until her fist slowly dropped.

"Aviv. Did you see his death? Did you see his body?" I stretched my hand out, stopped short of her arm, and let it hover.

Aviv slowly moved her head back and forth as fear swept through her. She jumped to her feet and spun to search for Amir, as if he still lived, still stalked her.

"The serpent pierced him with his teeth. He lay clenched in its jaws," I whispered. "The serpent twitched, speared to the ground by the sharp ends of roof beams. Amir is dead."

"You were not there to see Amir die," Aviv shouted. "How can I ever feel safe if I do not know for certain he died." She stood, fist clamped, staring back and forth between Seth and me.

"I saw him," Seth said. "His lower body hung from the monster's maw, trapped in a crevice that shut and crushed him in the shaking earth. The serpent held him in his teeth. Blood and gore coated him. He is dead."

"Are you sure? Absolutely certain?" Aviv quivered and she stared at Seth a long moment before falling to her knees. She put her hands over her face to cover her sobbing.

I reached out to touch Aviv's hair, but Seth touched my arm and shook his head. We moved to the other side of the fire, giving her space and time to herself.

"Are you sure of Amir?" I murmured. "He could have been unconscious."

"Not with all the blood and gore I saw. No one can survive a stabbing through the body, and the serpent stabbed Amir in multiple places in him. Aviv needed to know what we saw. I am certain he is dead," Seth said. "Or at least, I think he is." The last sentence was spoken so low I barely heard it.

Aviv's bruises healed as we traveled, but her mind had not healed. She was lost to us, rarely speaking. I tried to draw her out, talk of happy experiences in Axelston, with little success. At night, she tossed in her sleep, shouting at the men who abused her in her dreams.

We scavenged food as we rode. We lost the packs with our food in Quillon. Hester joined us with only his halter and reins, nothing else. We made do without the supplies in them. Nothing could entice us into a return trip into that horror.

After riding through the hills for six days, and taking one of them to celebrate the Sabbath, we reached the next village, Migid. Adam taught there earlier, with success. Among all the many people who refused to listen, the people of Migid had listened and obeyed.

Their healer, Rafaela, took Aviv in. She had journeyed between Migid and Home Valley, where she learned healing from Eve. I remembered seeing her there. Rafaela gave us little hope for Aviv, but promised to do all she could for her. Aviv's illness had settled in her mind.

While there, my head began to ache. Sometimes the intense pain prevented me from opening my eyes. Seth massaged my neck and placed cool cloths across my forehead. These helped them to ease. Rafaela prepared packets of medication that helped some. The pains returned at inopportune moments. I learned to live with them.

We stayed in Migid long enough to work with them and trade for new packs, filled with food, bedding, pans, and other supplies for our travels. I tucked a bag of herbs into one of the packs for later use.

We visited Aviv one last time. I threw my arms around her unresponsive body and told her I loved her, Jehovah loved her, and even her sad Papa continued to love her. I kissed her on the cheek and stepped back. Her only indication of hearing me was silent tear wending down her cheek.

We left Migid and traveled west, hoping to find another village more like Axelston or Seedar, filled with people willing to listen

Chapter Fifteen

Illness

Seth and I knelt together in prayer each evening and morning. We asked for directions. Which village waited for us? Where should we go to preach?

Seth followed the directions that came as impressions. We climbed tall mountains, traveling in a north and westerly direction. The difficult journey led us high above the tree line before we discovered a pass to take us to the other side.

We froze most of the time. White flakes fell from the sky, burying the ground. We trudged through this—snow, Seth called it. Many days we frequently dismounted to give the horses a rest. Seth led Pacer Too, I gripped Pacer Too's tail and followed in his footsteps. Blaze forged his own trail or stepped behind Listella and Hester.

My headaches continued, sometimes so bad I could not ride. When they struck, Seth took Listella's reins allowing me to focus on hanging on to her saddle. In blinding snowstorms, the pain intensified, debilitating me. Seth worried about me, while trying to find a path through the snow.

My bleeding ended. I was with child. We were excited to finally have a child coming to us. Seth protected me, aware of my actions, and protecting the child. Some days I stopped several times to slide off Listella and lean over the snow as the food I ate earlier refused to stay down.

Seth wrapped me in blankets during the day and coaxed fires from the wet wood at night. We snuggled close, trying to stay warm. At least, as we waded through the snow, our movement warmed us, some.

I woke up almost every night, screaming. My dreams were crowded with fear, locked again in the storage house amongst root vegetables. Huge glowing eyes moved toward me. A beam of light shone on them. The serpent, Zil, slithered toward me, its mouth open wide to swallow me. I woke screaming. Seth held me close, speaking soothing words and rocking me gently.

This dream returned many times, sometimes more than once in a night, interrupting our sleep. Even awake, I saw the eyes, the maw opening to swallow me. Between the dreams and the headaches, I lost strength. My body grew thin, rather than putting on weight.

Seth feared for me and the child. At last, one evening he pulled me close and lay his hands on my head, praying to Jehovah for the dreams and headaches to end, and that I would be healthy so the babe could grow strong and I would be healthy.

Peace filled me. The frightening dreams ended. The pains in my head eased until I rarely thought of them. Jehovah answered our prayers.

We labored through the pass for weeks, climbing higher into the mountains before descending into a valley. Spring greens dotted the land. Tiny flowers and the beginnings of leaves on the treas warmed my soul. New life burst all around us and within me.

When we reached a stream, we stopped early. We could not bathe in the icy water, so we dipped it into a pot to heat it. We braved the cold air to shed our clothes, a bit at a time, and wash.

"Ganet, you are changing." Seth stared at my stomach.

I grabbed my robe and stretched it in front of me. "I know, I am fat."

"Not fat." He plucked the robe from me and gently touched the growing bump. "Beautiful." He tugged me into a tight embrace.

My sisters and other women in Home Valley had babies. I watched them grow, their bodies change during the months they carried a child within them. Still, it surprised me to discover the little lump, already.

I thought back to my last bleeding time, trying to work out how long it had been. Was it before Quillon or later? No, it started when we were there. I remembered the discomfort of the moss between my legs as I woke in the storage building.

Did it return after then? Seth and I were together one night, while Aviv slept. When did this happened? How long before the child's birth? I did not remember. We had lost track of the sun and moon while we were in the mountains.

"It has been more than three months, nearly four," Seth said. "I have been counting."

How does he know what I am thinking?

"I am bigger than I expected."

"Perhaps our son is big?" He raised an eyebrow.

"Perhaps. At least, the sickness is nearly past."

Seth laughed. "I certainly hope so. We can travel much faster if you are not stopping to lose every meal."

"Listella is growing wider, too. She does not pause to lose her breakfast." I patted her neck. "A colt grows within her."

Seth laughed and patted Pacer Too. These two enjoyed their time in Seedar. You may be more comfortable on Hester before long."

"Not yet. I love my Listella, even as she grows wide with her child."

We rode into a valley, searching for signs of human life. Animals crossed our path and we saw animal tracks, but we saw no signs of humanity. I searched for spring growth to add to our diet as we made our way down the mountain side. Seth made a new sling and used it to hit rabbits for dinner. He did not attempt to kill anything larger. We did not have space to carry the meat, the time, or a way to preserve it while we traveled.

Seth skinned and rolled the rabbit skins in ash bark to dry and protect them. Each morning after prayers we shook it out and pulled on the edges to stretch the skins. Seth formed frames of green wood and tied the skins to them, then secured the frames to the packs on Hester's back.

"I will make you a fine cloak to keep you warm," he said.

"A cloak of rabbit skins?"

"They keep the rabbit warm. They will keep you warm in the cold. You will see."

I shrugged, still not sure.

As we traveled lower down the mountain, we found berries to eat. Most of the supplies we brought from Migid were gone long before. We depended on finding food along the way.

One evening, I felt a flutter in my tummy. Over the next few days, the flutter became stronger. A few night later, as Seth lay beside me, he rested his hand on my stomach. He jumped.

"Oh! What was that?"

"The babe likes your warm hand. He kicked you."

He put his hand back, waiting for another kick. When it came, Seth's face twisted into a funny little grin.

Each day after then, when we stopped, Seth rested his hand on my belly, waiting for the babe to welcome him.

Seth had developed a cough. First it was a small cough, but within a few days it became a harsh, ragged cough that bent him nearly in half. His face burned and he struggled to stay in the saddle.

"The ... The v-v-v-village is j-j-j-just ahead, I n-n-know it. T-t-t-tie me onto Pacer Too, w-w-we must g-g-get there s-s-s-soon."

Seth's teeth chattered so much I feared he would bite his tongue. I found an old blanket and tied him to his saddle. The day before, I discovered a willow tree, cut some bark, and steeped it. This medicine now filled a small water skin. I helped Seth take a big drink of it, then took Pacer Too's reins and led him and Hester down the mountain side.

I feared for Seth's health. He did not improve. He hacked as he slept on Pacer Too's back. Cold rain fell. Seth needed to get dry or he would never recover.

I located a little cave and directed the horses into its shelter. I untied the blanket around Seth and balanced him to prevent his falling off his tall horse. I made a warm bed for him and settled him in. Blaze crawled next to him. Even wet, the dog would warm him. Dry leaves and twigs littered the floor, providing me with a promise of a small fire and heat.

I unloaded Hester and unsaddled Listella and Pacer Too. They would not wander from the safety of the cave. I threw my cloak over my head and stepped into the downpour to search among the tree litter for pieces of drier wood to keep the flame burning. I gathered an armful and hurried inside, shaking the rain off. I shivered as I bent to touch Seth's forehead. He burned.

Seth would not get well if I did not get him dry. I scraped leaves away to make a safe fire space. I found rocks and set them in a circle to contain it. I gathered the dry leaves and twigs from the cave floor into the center and bashed my knife against my fire stone over and over until a little spark flew out. Before I could bend to feed more dry leaves to the tiny flame, a gust of wind swept in, dousing it and blowing leaves everywhere.

I sat shivering, refusing to allow the tears to form in my eyes. I had no time to give in to the frustration. Not now. The baby kicked in sympathy.

~

I leaned over and scraped the leaves and twigs back into a pile. Before trying again, I scooted around to block the wind with my body. I picked up the fire stone and my knife. I struck the knife against the stone repeatedly until a tiny spark leaped from it into the pile of tinder. I bent and gently breathed on it, watching the flame grow. As it burned, I boosted in larger sticks until, at last, I added two larger logs. I sat back on my heels and expelled a sigh of relief. Seth usually did this, his fires started in one try. In my parent's home, the fire never went out.

I rejoiced to see the fire for a moment. Then Seth moaned. I leaped up and rushed to his side. In the firelight, his face reflected red. He hacked, even in his sleep. I dug into the large pack for the smaller packet of herbs Rafaela sent with us in case of need. I needed something now. My knowledge did not include finding healing plants, if there were plants available and big enough to use.

The packet included written instructions for basic use inside. I carried it all to the fire in order to see better. I unconsciously opened my cloak as I scanned through the list of uses.

There, cough. I tossed back my hood to see the writing easier. I was finally warm. I located the instructions for cough and chest soother:

'Soak equal parts (a small pinch) coltsfoot, mullein, com-frey, and mallow root in cold water. Bring to boil over low heat and allow to steep. Drink hot. May add honey. Drink three times a day.'

Rafaela would not have sent instructions like this without the herbs. I searched through the packet, sorting the smaller packets. Mallow root, mullein, coltsfoot. Where was the comfrey? I found camphor, gentian, violet, and basil, but not the comfrey. Eventually, I encountered it, on the bottom, of course. I fished out the comfrey, set it beside the other required herbs, and dumped all those not required for Seth's medication into Rafaela's container and put it aside.

Seth sat up and hacked, his face ashen under the red of his fever. He lay back, not even waking to cough. I splashed water from the skin into a small pot. *Half empty. Is there a stream nearby? Can I catch some from the rain?*

I returned to my recipe and reached into each packet, taking a pinch of each one and dropping it in. 'Soak in water,' I read.

I removed my cloak and hung it on a high rock protruding from the cave wall above the entrance. The draft from the wind lessened, warming the space. I returned the individual packets to the pack and lay it beside my pack. I kept the instructions where I could read them.

I examined Seth again. He burned. I woke him and assisted him to sit while I held a cup of willow tea for him to drink. I helped him lie down and sat holding his hand, willing him to heal.

The fire burned down, much of the wood I had gathered with it. I dragged my cloak from the rock and threw it over my head. I trekked into the rain for more, making several trips to carry arm loads inside. We needed more than I could carry in one trip.

After my firewood gathering exercise, I studied the herb mixture. It looked soaked to me. Now what? I reread the instructions. *'Bring to boil over low heat.'* I set the pot into the low flames and waited for it to boil. I shoved another log near to dry. It would go into the fire when the medication boiled.

I dug into the pack searching for something to eat. Seth's illness prevented him from hunting rabbits or anything else to eat for several days. I discovered bits of dry meat and other bits of edibles we somehow missed. I poured water into another pot and set it in the fire near the medicine. Into the second pot I dropped in a small piece of dried meat. I scraped the hairy roots from a carrot and sliced it in with the meat. An onion, discovered and pulled the day earlier, and two wrinkled potatoes from the pack joined the meat and carrots. The scent of the soup cheered me. I realized I was hungry. Hot food would benefit Seth, too.

The medicine boiled and I took it from the fire and allowed it to steep. Its smell did not gag me, nor did it entice me. I probed deep for honey. I danced when I spotted a small jar. I would mix bread if we still had flour. Too bad we had none. I dripped a few drops of the sweet, sticky liquid into the hot concoction, and licked it from my fingers. I dribbled a bit into the cup and carried to Seth.

"Seth. Seth, darling."

He hacked and coughed, and lay back down, still asleep.

"Seth." I nudged him in his ribs. "I have medicine to heal you. Please sit up and drink this."

He sat, in a drowsy stupor, and drank the liquid I held to his mouth with a grimace.

"A little more, please," I urged.

Obediently, he swallowed, before coughing again. He lay down, immediately sleeping.

"Jehovah, please bless my Seth," I prayed. "Heal him. Help this medicine work. I am lost and have no support without him. He is my greatest love and your servant. Please, please, heal him."

I watched him, wishing he would rouse long enough to feel the baby kick. As the time passed, he hacked less and breathed easier. Jehovah blessed us both.

The fragrance of soup stimulated me. I tested the cough medicine, confirming it stayed warm without boiling away. The soup smelled delicious. I dished some into our bowls, pushed in another log to the fire, and took it to Seth's bed.

He stirred awake. "Where are we?"

"In a cave. I had to bring you out of the rain. You needed to be warm and dry. I found this place and started a fire."

"Ummm. Feels nice. How long have we been here?"

"Almost all day. I had time to build a fire and prepare both medicine and soup. Do you feel well enough to feed yourself?"

He tried to shove himself up to sit, but failed. "No. I guess not."

"It is fine. I will assist you. I have done this."

I dipped his spoon into the soup, blew on it, and nudged his mouth open with the edge of it. He swallowed the warmth.

"I have not been fed like this since for a long time—since childhood."

"Big people require support sometimes, too. I fed my sister during her last illness. I have practice." I scooped another spoonful and hoisted it to his mouth, dribbling a bit on his chest.

"Practice?" he yelped. "You need more."

"I am doing just that, practicing. Here. Eat more."

Between bites he asked, "How is baby?"

"He kicks harder every day."

Seth reached to touch the bump on my stomach. "Kick for papa?"

The babe kicked his hand, making him smile.

I managed to feed us both without spilling, much. I offered a bowl of the soup to Blaze. His hunger had not been sated for two or three days. Seth turned on his side and coughed, though not nearly as hard as earlier. He needed an additional dose of the medicine, later.

I banked the fire and stared out the front of the cave. Rain fell through the trees. I lay next to Seth, pulling my cloak around us, praying for him to heal soon.

Chapter Sixteen

Rescue

Rain fell two more days. I sat in our cave tending Seth and the fire. The deep cave protected the horses. Each day I gave them a measure of the precious grain and water. All the rain and we were running out of water. I dashed out with a large pot and set it in an open space away from the overhang of rock and drooping limbs.

Three times I rushed out to grab it up and bring it in to pour into the almost empty water skin. Some sloshed over the side the first try. After that, I took greater care to ensure none fell outside the skin.

I stretched the soup to last longer, dropping water and a small handful of grain in. Little remained to eat. I dosed Seth with medicine, alternating between the willow tea and the chest concoction every few hours. While we waited for the storm to end, his fever dropped and his cough almost disappeared. For this, I added my thanks in my morning and evening prayers. On the second evening, Seth joined me in prayer.

"We will have to leave our comfortable cave tomorrow, whether this ends or not," I said as we stared past the trees into the rain.

"And slog through all that mud?" He wrinkled his forehead.

"We must. The firewood is nearly gone. There is nothing left to eat after we eat the last of the soup in the morning. I gave the horses the last of the grain today. They need more to eat."

Seth frowned and dropped his hand into Blaze's fur. Faithful Blaze stayed close to Seth as always.

"Your cough is almost gone. I would love to stay here another week, but we cannot live without food." I threw my hands out in frustration.

"Everything is gone? How long have I been sick?"

"More than a week. I tied you to your saddle a week ago and tried to continue on. We have been in this cave three days, since it began to rain. I hope there is a stream not muddied from the runoff. It has been difficult to catch water in pots and fill the water skins"

"Food and fire? All gone?" His eyebrows lifted.

I nodded.

"How did you start the fire? Have you ever started one?" He drew me closer.

I shrugged. "I watched you and others. The wind blew it out the first time, but I shielded the spark with my body. It had to be done, so ... so I did it."

"I am proud of you. You helped me. You prepared the mixture to heal me. You built a fire. You carried on in the storm. I am proud."

I lay my head in his shoulder. "I did what had to be done."

Though his cough had nearly gone, I heated the chest mixture for him to drink before we allowed the blaze to die out the next morning. A fine mist dripped on us as we left our cozy cave. I dragged my cloak over my head to keep the raindrops from dripping down my back. We stopped under thick trees that kept most of the moisture away while the animals grazed on the sweet, new grass.

We trekked on and soon were wet and miserable. Near mid-day it ended, leaving deep mud for us to trudge through.

"We need meat to eat. Keep your eyes open for a small animal. At this point, something not so small will do. We cannot be choosy when we starve." Seth probed in his bag of smooth stones for his sling.

"Anything? Even that big sheep?"

A mountain sheep stood on the rocks in front of us.

"Yes. Especially that."

For once, Blaze did not growl or bark. Seth tucked a round stone in the sling and spun it around and let it fly. The mountain sheep dropped to the base of the rocks.

"You hit it!" I shouted.

"You doubt my skills?" He growled. My face fell until he laughed at me.

"You tease!"

We ran through the mud to the dead animal. Seth pulled his knife from his waist and slit its throat, allowing the blood to drain. Seth skinned and cleaned the carcass. I discovered a pocket of dry needles and leaves beneath a thick, long needle pine. Broken limbs laid beneath the pines, some dry enough to burn. I gathered these to a wide flat rock where I struggled to build a fire.

The blaze caught on and grew. Seth brought me a hunk of roast. Our hunger drove us to cut thin slices from the roast as it browned. Blaze gulped down the raw strips we threw to him. He caught most in the air. The baby leaped within me as the fragrance of cooking filled the tiny glen.

A little stream wandered past, clear enough I dipped our skins in to fill them. Hot meat and water. What more could we want?

We decided to camp while we dried it and preserved the hide. I hoped the extra time would give Seth time to regain his health.

While the thin strips dried, I searched the area for anything edible growing. I uncovered new greens above ground and beets, carrots, onions, and turnips under the ground, left from the previous year. This provided us with more to eat than we had for a long time. With so little to eat in the past weeks, even this little bit would be more.

Food strengthened both of us. Seth's cough improved and he regained some of his energy. Even the horses improved in their looks. Hair started to grow in the bare patches across their bodies. Blaze's ribs no longer showed through his fur, which had thinned. He spent time chasing, catching, and eating rabbits and other small animals.

We continued to bow before Jehovah in prayer each morning and evening, thanking Jehovah for the food. We begged for help to find people on this side of the mountain. We knew they were here. Seth had been directed this way.

On the morning of our third day there, while we checked the drying meat we heard a shout, "Hello the camp!"

We looked at each other. I reached for my belt knife while Seth's sling found its way into his hands. After our experiences in Quillon, we took no chances.

Seth called back, "Hello. Who are you?"

"Hunters. We saw your smoke. Can we come in?" Three men on horses appeared at the edge of the trees, hands in the air to show they held no weapons.

"Get off your horses and come in one at a time," Seth ordered.

They slid off their horses, and each man took his turn to raise his arms and lead his horse into our camp. Seth held his sling ready while I checked each hunter for hidden weapons. Blaze stood guard, his teeth bared.

"Our hunting spears and bows hang on our saddles. You may take them," the first hunter told me.

I removed his belt knife then reached behind his saddle and collected his spears. I pointed to the far side of the fire, "Sit."

As each one arrived, I searched him and removed his weapons, from his body and his horse, before sending him to sit with his friends. When all were seated, I led their horses away and tied them to trees across the glen away from Pacer Too, Listella, and Hester.

The men sat watching me as I piled their spears, bows, and arrows far away from them, across the campfire. *If they make a wrong move, I can throw these into the fire.*

"What brings you this high into the mountains? It is cold for hunting." Seth said at last.

"We heard one comes to teach us of Jehovah," the first one who entered said. "We came to find him. While we are here, we hunt animals for our families. Do you know of this man?"

I stood beside Seth and stared at them, not trusting their message.

"What would you do with this person if you find him?" Seth asked.

"Escort him to our village. We have prayed for one to teach us. We live in Lib. Our leader, Lechish, is a good man. He dreamed of a husband and wife struggling through the snow in our mountains. He would teach us of Jehovah. Are you him?"

Seth glanced at me, then turned to the men. "I am he. I am Seth, son of Adam. Others came to us, speaking of peace and desiring to learn of Jehovah, only to turn on us. Because of

this, we must remain cautious of strangers seeking our teachings."

A shiver of remembered fear played across my heart.

Our visitors exclaimed at this news. "Who would attack a
son of Adam, a messenger of Jehovah?" They shook their
heads and shrugged their shoulders.

"For our caution, we apologize. We were sent by Jehovah
to share his gospel to a village in these mountains." Seth
shrugged.

The men smiled and nodded. One stood and asked permission to retrieve something from his horse. I believed I
removed all the weapons, so Seth allowed it. Blaze followed
with teeth bared as he dug into his pack and returned with
travel bread.

"You have meat, but little to go with it," He said. "We offer you bread, that your hunger, and ours, may be filled." He
bowed over it slightly and offered it to me.

I received it with a nod. Seth cut the slices from the roasted
sheep and offered a slice to each man. The few vegetables and
berries I found were gone. The bread tasted good with the
sheep. The babe within me leaped and kicked.

~

Danel, Adad, and Zamir led us down the mountain the next
day. Seth and I took turns sleeping and guarding against possible treachery.

We had piled the now dry meat into Hester's nearly empty
pack. We stuck the spears in the pack bindings, handles pro-

truding outward to be easily retrieved by Seth or myself in case of attack.

We traced a track so dim I feared they were leading us into a trap. It would have been almost impossible to discover this faint track without the three who led us.

Two slow days of travel later, smoke rose over buildings huddled close, several plumes from each long building. My forehead wrinkled as my eyebrows crunched in. Why were there so many fires in one building?

Men and women joined together in a loose semi-circle, watching us ride toward them. I experienced a deep sense of relief to see welcoming in their faces. This village looked positive. No obvious show of men controlling women appeared. Zamir climbed off his horse and hugged an older couple.

"Papa, Mama. We found them. This is Seth, son of Adam, and his wife, Ganet."

A cheer rose from the crowd of villagers, then settled to quiet watchfulness.

"They were starving on the edge of the snow line, though Seth killed a mountain goat. They crossed the high passes alone, seeking a village who would accept Jehovah's teachings, as He revealed to Seth." Zamir waved his hands toward the high mountains, then back to Seth.

The woman moved forward. "Welcome to Lib. We have been waiting for you. I am Ora."

"And I am Lechish." The man joined Ora. "We feared you were lost. I dreamed you were coming through the mountains many weeks ago. When you did not arrive, I sent my son, Zamir, with Danel and Adad to find you."

Adad and Danel dismounted and went to Zamir's side. Seth stepped down off Pacer Too's back and came to help me. My body felt heavy, my mind unclear. I reached for Seth and fell into his arms.

"She is not well?" Ora asked.

"Too long hungry, the child requires more than she can offer." Seth wrapped me in his arms and held me up.

"Child? She is with child? How could you bring her across those mountains in her condition?"

I shook my head to clear it. "I chose to join my husband. We did not expect the snows. I am fine, just tired."

Voices flowed past me. I stood, a stone in a stream, trying to listen, too tired to attend. Seth lifted me into his arms and followed Ora into a building. She drew back blankets on a bed while Seth pulled off my cloak. I sat on the bed while he removed my foot coverings. He helped me lie down.

A woman handed a bowl of thick, warm soup to Seth. He gently spooned it all into my mouth. I lay with my eyes closed, savoring the complex flavors gently thrust into me, and the soft, warm bed.

"Sleep, my love. You can meet these people later." He tucked the covers up to my chin and kissed my nose.

I woke to the glow of a low burning fire, warming the air surrounding the bed. Smooth walls of branches surrounded me on three sides. My eyes followed the branches as they bent into the roof, ending in an opening allowing the smoke to escape. Interesting.

A delicious fragrance drew me from the last clutches of sleep.

I pushed myself up to sit on the side and stared. My cloak hung next to Seth's on the wall, held there on a kind of a hook. I saw my foot coverings beside the bed and bent to pull them on. Everything spun around me. I tucked my head between my knees and waited. When the dizziness ended, I pulled them on and stood. I quivered inside. I struggled with the feeling of helplessness. I had always been strong and independent.

I used the walls to support me and felt my way out of the chamber to an open space. Women sat around fires. I thought they may be cooking. Children ran up and down the lengthy, central space, dodging fires, extended legs, and playful slaps. A few men sat together around a fire. I thought the others were outside, for I heard the murmur of men's voices.

I watched the activity as I gathered my courage. One of the women looked up and caught my eye with a smile. She detached herself and made her way to me.

"You are awake!" she said. "You were very tired. I am Tora."

"I am Ganet."

"I know. Seth told us. He told us of your courage on the ride over the mountains and how you cared for him during his illness."

"How long did I sleep?"

"Through yesterday afternoon and all of today. We are preparing the evening meal. You must be famished."

"Starving. I wonder how my hunger did not wake me earlier." I inhaled the enticing aroma of cooking. "Is there anything I could eat now, or will I need to wait for the meal?"

"Come with me." Tora casually flopped her arm over my shoulder. "I can find something for you."

"Food sounds wonderful, after I relieve myself. Where—?"

"Come with me."

I leaned my weight on her and let her lead me through the maze of fires and supplies and pushed open a door.

"You can relieve yourself in here." Tora pointed to a round seat with an open center above a hole. I heard water flowing below. It must carry away the refuse.

"Here is water to wash your face and hands when you finish." She lifted a lid and dipped a basin into the water within. She set it on the shelf near the entrance.

"Take your time, make yourself pretty for Seth. I will wait for you." Tora stepped out and shut the door behind her.

I never experienced such convenience. I expected the water to be cold and touched my fingertips into the bowl. Warm! I splashed the it on my face. Soap rested in a small bowl. I scrubbed the dirt from my face, arms, and legs. It felt lovely to be cleaner. I used a length of cloth hanging from a hook to dry. I drug my fingers through my hair, trying to remove the knots and tangles.

Tora waited nearby, leaning against a wall, when I left the room. "Thank you. I feel much better."

"Good. You look better. I will find a brush for your hair." My stomach gurgled loudly. "After we get you some food," she laughed.

We walked back to the fire.

"Ganet is hungry," Tora announced.

The women made a place for me to sit, exclaiming at my extended sleep.

"Anyone would be hungry after sleeping as long as you have."

"Especially one carrying an unborn child."

"Are you rested, yet?"

"Poor thing, to be so tired to sleep through three meals. Of course, you are need food."

Tora nodded toward the woman sitting beside me. "This is Marta. Beside her is Amina, Danya, Chita, Rona, and Vered." Each smiled, nodded, or said "hello" as Tora named her.

"Thank you for welcoming me." I ducked my head to hide a tear.

Chita reached into a basket and brought out a thin, round, flat bread. She dipped a spoon into the pot hanging over the fire for a mixture of meat and vegetables, which she folded in the center of the bread.

"Here, eat this." She handed me the wonderfully tasty smelling concoction. "But wait a bit for it to cool. It is hot."

I blew on the mixture inside, and took a small bite.

"Yum! Delicious." The babe within me stirred. "Even my little one likes it."

The women laughed with me. I finished all they gave me and drank a glass of goat's milk before I began to stare around.

"You are all so kind." I turned to look all about me. "But where are the men? Where is Seth?"

They giggled. "He will be along. More? Vered asked.

"Yes. No. I want more, but I want to eat with Seth."

They giggled. "He will be in soon." Rona glanced toward the exit. "Men often eat with each other, as women eat together, around our own fires. Do they not do this where you come from?"

"We eat together, men, women, and children, families and friends."

Some of my joy leaked away at this news.

Chapter Seventeen

Lib

I heard Seth laugh and turned to see him in the midst of a crowd of men. He searched each fire ahead of him. I watched and waited as he made his way through the middle of the building to where I sat.

His eyes found mine and his smile suffused his whole body. The corners of my mouth lifted as he broke away from the men and wound his way toward me. I stood in time to be lifted into his arms and twirled around.

"Ganet! You are awake. And out of bed. I worried for you." He breathed into my ear. "I missed having you near. Is the babe well?"

My joy spilled out in a laugh as he set me on my feet. "He is, feel." I pulled his hand to my belly where the babe kicked.

Seth moved closer, his eyes open wide. "I am glad you are with us again. I need your support."

"Is something amiss?" I searched his face for signs of a problem.

"Nothing big, but there is an undercurrent I cannot swim alone."

He kissed me deeply, as though when we were alone. My new friends tittered. I did not care.

When we were alone again in my chamber, I asked, "Did you see the looks from the men as we ate?"

"I saw them watching us. I wondered why no other man ate with his wife."

"They do not eat with their men." I tugged my foot coverings from my feet, and bent to drag Seth's off.

"You do not need to remove my foot coverings." He leaned forward a hand on my shoulder.

"I choose to be part of your life, to help you, even to remove your foot coverings."

He kissed my forehead. "You should get more rest, go back to bed." He stood to assist my undressing.

"I will, if you join me." I stepped to the bed and sat on it, patting the bed beside me.

"I am to meet with the men again. I am teaching them of Jehovah's love. However, I will lie with you for a while, if you will lie down now."

I plopped onto the narrow bed and scooted over, making room for him. He eased himself next to me, curling around the bulk of my stomach. We lay together, the babe leaping at his touch. We kissed and lay in a close embrace.

Seth slipped from my bed as sleep claimed me. He returned, much later, moving slowly so as not to wake me. I roused enough to reach out and pull him close. He groaned and snuggled closer.

"Is this place like Quillon? Do the men—?" I whispered.

"No. They do not act in that way. They worship no false god. They have a true desire to learn of Jehovah. They just have strange ideas about their women."

"I wondered—"

"Not now. We will speak of it tomorrow. Sleep."

I woke again to the sounds of children playing and the fragrance of cooking grains. Seth had left his scent in a depression beside me. I clambered from my bed without the room spinning on me. Food boosted my ability to think clearly and walk about the day before. I wanted more. I dressed and managed to leave the chamber without clinging to the walls. I even found my way to the amazing relief room and returned to the fire, determined to help Tora and Marta prepare a morning meal.

They made room for me and gladly accepted my assistance. I loved learning their new ways of cooking, different from how mama taught me. They teased my awkwardness. I worked harder to do it right.

"Why do men not join you for meals?" I asked Tora.

"I will tell you later, outside." She grimaced and raised a shoulder. "It is the way of our village."

I lifted an eyebrow in question.

"Later."

Everything here is later or outside. Why can we say nothing inside? Who are they afraid of?

I assisted in cleaning the dishes after the breakfast meal, and then ambled past other fires, waving or stopping to visit, in my course to the open door and out of the long house. Bird songs filled the air. I walked into the trees, watching robins flutter to the ground and pick up bits of leaf and twigs, before flitting up to add them to their nests. Jays screeched at me. I glanced to see their nest above my head, smiled, and stepped away. Bits of green poked through the leaf litter, promising a colorful display of blossoms. I inhaled the fragrance of new life.

I heard steps and turned to see Seth treading through the leaf litter. My heart leaped to see him. He saw my gaze and flashed a smile. His step quickened and we met with arms encircling the other.

"What are you doing here?" Seth asked.

"I wanted to breathe fresh air. We have been traveling so long, I miss being outside. What have you been doing?"

"Planting with the men. I came to find you. I want you to see something."

His eyes almost glowed with excitement.

"What? You have not been excited like this for a long time."

"You will not understand until you see. Come with me."

Seth took my elbow and guided me over a fallen ash, out of the trees, and through the fields. We crossed tilled, but still unplanted, land to the edge. We took care to walk in the furrows until we arrived where men gathered around something. *Was this the something Seth wanted me to see?*

The circle opened, bringing into view a square box perched on top of two slices of a thick tree. A long, narrow piece of wood extended from the box, ending in the dirt. I expected it to fall apart any moment. Heavy bags of seeds sat inside it.

"We need these nearer the top of the field." A man waved in the direction.

"Good." Seth nodded. "Ganet can see it in use."

See what in use?

I remained silent and watched two men bend and lift the long piece of wood by the cross piece attached to the end, invisible as it lay in the dirt. They tugged on it. I wondered what good it would do. With only a small grunt of effort, the round wood slices rolled and the box above it moved with it, heavy bags of seed and all, behind them. I watched with wide eyes as the two men pulled the object across the tilled soil to another location, and dropped the wood pieces to the ground. Men who followed reached into the bags of seed, filled their own, and began to spread the seed.

One man stayed with us, observing my amazed stare. "Do you like it?"

"What is it?" I whispered.

Seth and the man laughed briefly. It did not sound derisive.

"That is a cart. Do you like it?" Seth waved toward it.

"Yes. It is interesting. Is seed all it can carry?"

"No, it will carry whatever fits in the box." The man waved his hands to imitate the dimensions.

"Ganet, this is Elam, the designer of the cart. He is married to your friend, Tora."

Elam hesitated briefly, and then extending his hand and taking my small one in his meaty paw. "I am glad you are feeling better. Tora has been worried about you."

"Thank you. I am feeling some better. It is good to be out-doors again. I feel closed in after traveling so far."

We began to trudge along the edge of the field together.

"We should join them in the planting." Seth pointed to the men with his chin.

"The women are not helping? Are there enough men they are not needed?" I gazed across the tilled dirt and back at the small line of men.

Some villages had more than enough men, others required the women to help plant. In Home Valley, everyone joined in, basking in the warming sun and the crowd of friends.

"Cooking the food is woman's work, not planting or grow-ing it. Men must encourage the plants to grow, as they must hunt for game to eat." Elam ducked his head, reciting the words formally.

I looked at Seth and raised an eyebrow. He gave me a slow nod.

~

"Who, then, cares for the animals? You do have sheep and goats? Cows and chickens? I know you have horses." I slipped my hand into Seth's as we picked our way toward the cart and seeds.

"Females care for the chickens and goats. We have no sheep. Cows are milked by the women and girls, bulls are herded by the men and boys." Elam kicked a clod.

"You do not like this separation of responsibilities?" Seth glanced at me from the corners of his eye.

"No. It is silly for women not to be allowed to touch the seeds. They cannot hurt them."

So, that was the problem.

"What caused it? Was it a natural distribution of work between men and women?" Seth slowed his step.

"No. No. Our village elder, Gavi, never liked women." Elam spoke slowly, and then hurried on. "When his wife died years ago, he went into the hills. On his return, he claimed to have had a vision. Men and women were to be separated. Women are necessary, but dangerous to bring too close. You two are permitted to sleep together, you are not from here. Men can only sleep with their wives in the small outer huts. We must live separately in the long houses."

I recognized the name. Gavi was one of Seth's many brothers who left Home Valley when he became dissatisfied with the commandments of Jehovah. He never returned to visit his mama or papa. I glanced at Seth. He shook his head slightly. I stayed quiet.

"There are few huts for husbands and wives," Seth said. "Does it not cause problems?"

"Yes. However, we should talk about this later." Elam nodded toward the workers. "We have work to do. Ganet, do you want to watch? I suppose they will allow it."

I looked at the men casting seed side-by-side in front of us. "No. I do not wish to cause you any more problems. I will return to the women and assist the women prepare food for you men." I allowed sarcasm to leak into my voice.

Seth lifted a shoulder and I nodded before turning to make my way across the field and toward the long houses and the women.

I joined them in toiling over hot pots sitting above the fire to launder clothing. I washed mine and Seth's, and then aided in washing other's garments. Mothers, sisters, and wives cleaned their men's clothing.

Few single men without a mother or sister to provide cleaning services lived in Lib. The others traded the responsibility of laundering for them the week, unless a specific girl chose to indicate her interest in him by laundering his garments for him. I watched as they argued over who should wash Adad's attire. Danya grabbed Upaz's clothing to wash. Her friends giggled and elbowed her in the ribs.

We scrubbed everything and spread them across lines hung inside the long house. When I hung our laundry on the lines, I begged exhaustion and stumbled to my bed to rest.

My strength ebbed, leaving me with less than I ever felt, and nothing I did helped. The babe within me kicked, but his energy ebbed along with mine. With a twinge of fear, I lay back thinking it may be best to allow the others to do the difficult work and cut back for a while, at least until I regained my health.

Each day I rose to find Seth gone. I participated in a portion of the assigned labor. As we worked, I answered their questions about Jehovah and shared the things I knew, for as long as I could sit up to be with them. They listened. I heard their discussions outside my chamber where I dragged myself to rest in my chamber earlier each day.

At night, Seth entered my chamber, removed his robes, and slipped into bed with me. He stayed all night. We would whisper together, share the joys of our growing child, and discuss the ways his teaching of Jehovah's laws affected the people of Lib.

We were relieved when the babe's strength increased, kicking strongly to settle our minds that he grew. Mine declined while his improved. For that, we were grateful.

I managed to help prepare the morning meal for a time. Every day, men gathered with us in the women's long house. They assisted with the cooking, carried wood, and water for us. Tora told me of some who left the fires and woman's work to aid in the planting, weeding and watering the fields. Seth and I applauded the changes each night in time alone.

In the three months we stayed in Lib, although I ate well, my health continued to fail. I could no longer struggle from the bed on my own, not able to help with preparing meals, cleaning, or laundry.

Occasionally, Seth carried me out for fresh air after the morning meal. There, both boys and girls led herds of goats to the hills. Boys and girls gathered eggs and milking cows. A few men walked hand in hand with their wives into the fields, tools casually hanging over their shoulders to weed together.

Seth shared the greatest change with me: men joined their wives in the sleeping chambers at night, beginning with Elam and Tora, quietly enjoying their marriage rights. Children slept on pallets near their parents or in a nearby chamber. Women moved into the men's house. A few families chose to claim the single huts as their own.

My health continued to decline. Confined to my bed, Seth feared for our child and worried about me. Men and women sat with me, a few at a time, asked about Jehovah, when I was strong enough to answer, and waited in silence when I slept.

Late one night, he laid his hands on my head and whispered a blessing of health for me and the child. I regained some strength afterward, enough I could once again sit in my bed a short time each day.

~

Seth rushed to my bedside one afternoon, his eyes alight. "Listella has given birth. She has a lovely little colt."

He helped me as I struggled to sit. "At last, poor thing. She was so big, I worried for her. What does he look like?"

"Dark, like his mama, with white socks on his feet and a white blaze on his nose. He is a robust little thing."

"Take me to see him." I tried to get out of bed, but my weakened strength prevented it.

Seth scooped my bulk into his capable arms and carried me out to the barn. The beautiful little colt leaned against Listella, who nursed him. She allowed me to pet both her and her babe. I murmured soothing words to her and congratulated her on the birth. She turned her big head and nuzzled me. I felt her love.

Seth saw me struggling to keep myself upright beside her and swung me into his arms and carried me to my bed.

"Thank you, Seth, for taking me to see her."

"He smiled and brushed a lock of hair off my forehead. "Of course. You needed to see them."

Not many days later, as I dipped hot oats from my bowl to my mouth, an intense pain ripped through my lower stomach, where the babe lay.

"Oh." I held my hands over the pain.

"What?" Tora asked. She stayed near me over the past three seven-days, especially as my strength declined, attuned to my needs almost like Seth.

"A pain knifes across the babe!"

"Ah. It is time, then. I thought it should be near." She touched me. The hardness accompanying the pain softened. "The pain will return, along with the hardness. Do not fear. I will help you."

"Thank you, Tora. I fear I am not tough enough to expel the child from within me."

"You are stronger than you think. Your weakness comes from your starvation while the babe needed the food to grow. Eat now, while you can. Soon you will not be able."

I scooped the honey covered oats into my mouth and savored it. Another pain streaked across my stomach, hardening the muscles. I managed to set the bowl on the table beside me and bent into the pain.

"Another?" Tora rubbed my back until it relaxed. "Harder, too? This one is ready to be born. Good."

I finished my oats before a constricting pain hardened my belly. "Oh," I whispered.

Women joined us in my sleeping compartment, laughing and telling stories between my pains. I recounted what I could remember of Eve's first birth, alone except for Adam. The women responded with "Oh's" and "Ah's" at all the appropriate places. I stopped to press on my stomach and bend into the pain each time it returned. They ripped through me more often and stronger.

Dov, Marta's son, left the women's house during an intense pain. After an intense pain, Seth's comforting hands massaged my back.

I turned. "Oh, Seth. You are here."

He reached to give me a hug from behind. I smiled, until another pain crashed into me.

"Sit by her head and hold her hand." A smile filled Tora's voice. "Watch and learn. There may be a time you must do this alone, as your papa did for your mama."

Seth pulled a stool close to the bed and held it. He massaged my back and stomach, mopped my forehead, and offered words of comfort over the long time my body struggled to expel its burden. Amina brought a torch for light, replacing it twice.

In spite of my loud cries of pain, I heard the women's house quiet and settle, then begin to rustle again as people rose to begin a new day. I wondered how the children and women, with their men, could sleep through my noise. I tried to prevent the cries. I succeeded, sometimes better than others.

Sometime during that long day and night, between the moans, cries, and intermittent screams, Seth placed his hands on my head, prayed for Jehovah to relieve the pain and help the babe move from within me. It dropped lower. The pushing exhausted me.

"One more push, Ganet," Tora called from somewhere in the blackness. "This one should do it. The head is nearly out."

A pain rippled through me and I pushed with a gigantic moan.

"Great work. The head is free. Wait a second." I felt her do something to ease the pressure. Another clenching pain rippled. "Push, Ganet, push!"

I pushed until the babe slid out. Seth gripped my hand and stood to see the child. "A girl, Ganet! We have a girl!" He bent to kiss me.

"Girl? And you are happy?"

"Very. There is no reason for me to want a boy first. I am happy she is here. You both live. Now you can regain your strength."

I sighed. "I can do that."

Tora lay the babe in my arms.

"Oh, she is wonderful." I traced her cheek with the back of a finger.

Chapter Eighteen

Home

I hoped to grow stronger each day after Lilah's birth, though I did not. My strength did allow me to walk a bit every day with her in my arms. The days I managed to reach the door and sunshine filled me with joy, even if Tora needed to send for Seth to carry us to our chamber and bed.

Seth carried Lilah and me and set me on a rock by the stream, now warmed in the early harvest sun. I watched as Seth baptized many of the men and women of Lib, beginning with Lechish and Ora. They affirmed Seth's teachings and encouraged the inhabitants of Lib to approve of husbands living together with their wives and participating in the educating of their children.

Over the next weeks, Seth continued to teach the people of Lib, ensuring the commandments and love of Jehovah were understood and accepted. I sat near the women during the day with Lilah and answered their questions. In my weakness, taking care of Lilah's needs and visiting with the women sapped my strength. I sat for short periods of time before Tora or Seth led me to my bed.

In the evenings, Tora and Elam joined Seth and me for dinner, talking and laughing together around the evening fire. Sometimes we went outside to watch the stars. The darkness of the women's house drew me down, I begged to spend time in the fresh air.

One morning, Seth carried me outdoors where the women busied themselves with the weekly laundry. He lay me in an open-air bed.

"Now you can rest in the sunshine with the women."

Tears of gratitude flowed as I kissed him.

"Tora and I agreed you may get better faster here in the company of others with Lilah."

My glow matched the sun. I appreciated its benefits and the clean, fresh air, but in my weakness, healing did not come as fast as Seth and I wanted.

"Do the women accepted our teachings?" Seth asked one night.

"They do. They are happier. They talk and laugh about their husbands in a way they never did before. They ask what and why less. Their discussions are more like what my mama and yours would have. How is it with the men?"

"They work hard to provide for their families. They always have. They desired to be part of the lives of their wives and children, though hidden by the rigid restraints forced on them by their false prophet, Ayah." His voice roughened.

I set my hand on his elbow. "Did you learn what happened to Ayah?"

"He fell off a cliff herding sheep. The fall killed him. In their sorrow, and to honor him, the men of Lib left them all in the mountains, no longer caring for them."

"How silly, blaming animals for Ayah's death. He was responsible."

Seth turned on his side toward me. "No, they did nothing. Ayah fell, alone up there. No one knows how it happened. Adad and his friends begin to gather in those sheep who will return."

I nodded. "And their understanding of Jehovah's commands? Can we perhaps go home?"

"How can we? Your lack of strength prevents riding the distance. I want to take you home. Your mama and mine know how to assist you to regain your health. Tora admits she and the others have run out of ways to help you."

"They are wonderful to me, but I am a burden. I miss my mama and yours. They will want to see Lilah. They can provide me with what I need to grow stronger. Is there any way? Are these people ready? Can they stay strong in the gospel of Jehovah without you? I would not ask to leave, if they were not."

Seth took a long moment to think. "They absorb the commands of Jehovah. They need to sacrifice, but I have not the proper Priesthood to sacrifice on my own. I must return to visit with papa about this." He pulled me into his arms and held me close. "I do not know how we will get you there, but I will find a way."

Days later, Seth supported me in a slow stroll with Lilah in my arms. We passed my bed and crossed toward the barn.

"What is out here? Do I get to see Listella and her colt again?"

"You could, but I have a surprise for you." Seth grinned.

"A surprise for me? What?

"It is a surprise. You will have to wait. Only a few more steps."

We turned the corner. A cart, larger than the one in the fields, waited by the barn.

"This is your surprise." Seth spread his arms wide.

"A cart?"

"Look inside."

I handed Lilah to Seth and stretched on my toes to peep past the high sides inside. A comfortable bed sat on top of a pile of grass. I turned to Seth with wide eyes.

"Yes. We can go home."

"How? You cannot pull me in this."

"No. Elam traded us this and two bullocks to pull it for the colt, if you will trade."

"The colt? Is he ready to be weaned?"

"Not quite, but Elam feeds him with soft mash. He loves it. He will be fine without his mama."

I threw my arms around Seth and Lilah. "When do we leave?"

"Tomorrow is the Sabbath. We leave the next morning. Elam drew me a map of a better way to get through the mountains and home. We should arrive by harvest."

"Thank you, Seth." I kissed him deeply. "Where is Elam so I can thank him?"

"In his shop, building more. You can thank him this evening. Now, you must rest."

As he assisted me to my outdoor bed, I reminded him of the things we needed for our journey.

He laughed. "I know. I have much of this gathered, with Tora's help."

During our Sabbath worship, Seth formally appointed Lechish to be the leader of their branch of the gospel. One after the other, men and women stood to testify of their love for Jehovah. We knew this village had a stable beginning.

Early the next morning, we shared our good-byes to our friends. Tora and the other women cried to see us leave. They knew I needed the care of my mama to bolster my healing. They presented me with little toys and clothing for Lilah and treats to help me on our trek. Elam and Tora promised to follow soon, bringing a cart for Papa Adam and Mama Eve. He offered to teach the men of Home Valley how to build some of their own.

I set Lilah into the cart with her toys and Tora gave me a big hug. Tears fell as I climbed in beside the baby. I would miss these friends.

Listella snorted. She and Hester suffered the indignity of being tied behind the cart. Seth rode Pacer Too beside the bullocks to guide them.

We traveled south through a low pass out of the valley. Though rough, the cart made it possible for us to travel. Each evening when we stopped, Seth found fresh grass to pile inside to soften our ride. Elam added a cover to protect Lilah and me from the sun and rain. When it rained hard, Seth joined us inside.

Five weeks of plodding behind the bullocks brought our little party, at last, to crest the hill leading to Home Valley.

Chapter Nineteen

Carts

L ate in the afternoon, we plodded down the hill toward the village in Home Valley. Children saw us coming. As always, they came running to welcome strangers. When we were recognized, boys ran to tell our parents. By the time we arrived at the orchards, both of our mamas and papas appeared, racing toward us.

My mama won, dragging her dapple-gray mare to a sudden stop. She jumped off and ran to our cart. I handed Lilah to her and crawled from the back. Seth and I found ourselves engulfed by hugs and love from our families. Grandparents, aunts and uncles handed Lilah around, giving her loves.

"What are you riding in?" Papa Adam asked.

"A cart," Seth answered.

"And what are those round things?" my papa pointed.

"Wheels."

"Wheels? Who thought of wheels?" Papa Adam stooped beside the cart to examine them. My papa joined him.

"Elam, who lives in Lib, watched trees roll down a mountain side." Seth squatted next to our papas and gestured and pointed "When slices of them are cut, and two are secured in the center, they roll together. It took little time to imagine this. He has developed the wheels, making them lighter and stronger, while making them roll easier. He connected two sets to the box for this one, to make it more stable. As he built them larger, he learned men and animals can pull them."

"Like our goats hauled logs for us so many years ago." Mama Eve touched the crosspiece leading to the animals.

"Elam remembered stories Gavi told of your goats and started with a small cart, convincing a goat to tow it. He developed bigger ones, like this one the bullocks are pulling. He is building even larger ones. This is the first one he covered. He hopes to have carts to travel with baggage over great distances, even in the storms. This one worked well for us."

"It could help with trading between villages," Papa Adam said. "It may help us to share the gospel, as well."

"Elam and the men of Lib use small ones to assist with the planting and harvesting."

My papa glanced toward the fields. "That would be a help."

"Ganet and Lilah rode in this cart from far away Lib. Elam saw we needed to come home, but could not, with Ganet's poor health. He traded this cart for Listella's colt."

"Ganet's poor health?" Mama pounced on the words. She peered into my eyes, lifting up an eyelid. "You are not well. You are pale and struggle to stand. You should rest into your cart. Joram, help Ganet into the cart."

Though I protested, papa gently lifted me onto my bed.

"What has happened, little girl? You weigh no more than a feather." Papa searched my face.

"The baby, the journey ..." I shrugged and redirected his thoughts. "Are these carts not wonderful?"

Papa looked to Seth. "Is this the only one? How is it made?"

"Elam says he can make more like this one, larger or smaller, depending on the needs of the user. He plans to travel to the villages between Lib and Home Valley, offering these to others." Seth's voice carried to us. Papa joined the men in the discussion about the carts.

"Give them to others as he gave one to you?" Papa Adam brows rose, skepticism filled his voice. "I cannot see Elam spending his time to create these ... Um, did you call them carts?"

Seth nodded.

"The time spent to create these carts. He would not have time to plant or harvest his crops, or tend his animals. How does he care for his family?"

"I traded for this one. The people of Lib work together. They are happy to trade with Elam. Early on, he struggled alone. He built the first one during the dark and cold season of the year. When he brought out the cart to haul his bags of seeds, the others laughed, until he carried three times more than they could."

Papa Adam snorted. "I suspect they stopped laughing then."

Seth stood. "Yes. The others were interested in trading time for carts. While he built, they planted, so they would have enough to bring in the harvest. Now they use them for both planting and harvesting."

We listened to the discussion for a while. Both mama and Mama Eve were interested in the new contraption.

"Ganet is not well. Shall we return home and continue this discussion?" Mama stared at the men.

All the others stepped into stirrups and mounted their horses. Papa Adam refused to give up the baby and sat Lilah in front of him on his tall red stallion.

Papa Adam and Papa rode ahead with Seth as he directed the bullocks, continued the discussion about the wagons. Mama and Mama Eve followed behind, riding beside me.

"What happened, Ganet?" Mama eyed me. "You are not the healthy, robust girl I sent with Seth."

"I suffered a long and difficult delivery with Lilah. It took most of a day. I thought she would never be born and we would both die in the trying. When Seth gave me a blessing, I felt her move. It did not take much time, then, for her to be enticed out of her comfortable nest into our world."

"A difficult delivery can be hard on you, for sure." Mama frowned. "But certainly not a reason for such weakness. Were you sick?"

"Before we arrived in Lib, we starved." I recounted the tale of our journey through the snow and Seth's illness. Mama and Mama Eve were relieved to hear when we were found by the men from Lib. "I guess I went without food too many days then, more than was good for me or Lilah. Perhaps an illness claimed me, as well."

"Lilah is a big baby. Her delivery must have been hard on both of you," Mama Eve said.

"Once her head came out, the rest came out with no problem. Her head stuck, I think."

"We will get you strong again." Mama reached across the cart wall to pat my head.

Mama Eve nodded.

Seth and I stayed with my mama and papa. We slept in the same room I used as a child. Mama petted me with my favorite foods—and gave me nasty medicines. She insisted they would help me regain my health. She cared for Lilah while I slept, bring her to me for feeding and short periods of play. In time, I regained my health and stamina.

Seth worked in the fields with the others, helping with the late harvests. He joined in threshing, winnowing, and gathering food into huge baskets and jars. He came to me the first evening, covered with dried bits of plants and dirt. I sneezed and he laughed, and then left to wash it away in the wash room.

Besides helping with the harvest, Seth spent part of his days with his papa, sharing with Papa Adam the stories of the villages we traveled to and those we taught.

It took me many seven-days to regain enough strength to walk with Seth to visit with Mama Eve and Papa Adam in their home. We shared a pleasant evening. They played with Lilah. Papa Adam bounced her on his knee and sang silly songs. Mama Eve crooned and rocked her to sleep, and set her in a basket. We ate and regaled them with stories of our adventures.

Papa Adam frowned when he heard how unkind the people of Geber were to us. He and Seth had discussed the idol Rivka stuffed into our pack. When we repeated that part of the tale, his jaw tightened and Mama Eve growled. They experienced our joy as we told of Axelston and Seedar and their acceptance of the gospel. Her face paled when I mentioned the serpent-god Zil that wanted me as a sacrifice."

"So that is what became of the serpent," she murmured.

"What serpent, mama?" Seth placed a hand on hers.

"The serpent the Destroyer convinced to tempt me in Eden. I never saw it again, though his image adorns the cane the Destroyer carries. You said it died?"

"I saw him pinned to the floor of his temple," I said. "The sharp end of the roof log pierced his head. It did not move."

"It is dead. I am sure of it," Seth added.

Mama Eve breathed a sigh of relief. Papa Adam patted her hand.

I grew stronger each day. At first, Mama only allowed me to walk outdoors with her help, or help from my brother Gomer, papa, or Seth. A seven-days after our visit with Mama

Eve and Papa Adam, she let me go out alone, with Lilah. We wandered the village, a bit farther each time.

When I walked all the way to the orchard for a fresh peach, I saw Elam and Tora coming.

~

Elam, always good as his word, arrived with two bullocks pulling a huge cart, filled with smaller ones. I watched from trees until they were almost beside me before I stepped into the open. Elam stopped the animals and Tora ran to envelop me in her arms.

"You made it home! And, look how far away from the village you are. Are you alone?"

"Mama is a good healer, though her medicine is nasty." I stepped out of her hug.

"May I take Lilah?" she asked, reaching for the baby. "Look how she has grown."

I surrendered Lilah to Tora and walked with them into Home Valley. Seth saw us coming and ran to get his papa. They met us in the central square.

"Adam," Elam said after the introductions, "I brought you three carts to aid in your planting and harvest. I came to assist the men here learn to build their own."

"Thank you," Papa Adam said. "This will be a great help to us. How can you manage to give this gift to us? How do you take care of your family?"

Elam waved at the carts. "These come as a gift from Jehovah. Because of him, I learned how to build them. Each one is better than last. The wheels, for instance: I cut away the center parts to make them lighter and stronger. Many desire my carts and can use them for multiple purposes. I am here, willing to share my knowledge with others."

"We will be happy to learn from you. Thank you for your generosity."

The men embraced and led the bullocks with the carts into the barn, the murmur of their voices floating behind. Tora and I strolled to a seat in the square to catch up on the news of Lib.

Elam spent his days with the men, teaching them about carts and wheels and how to put them together. Seth participated, knowing the knowledge would be necessary when we returned to our travels for Jehovah.

Tora and I participated in the activities of women. One morning, she joined Eve and me in painting new jars she planned to store oil or grains in or to carry water from the well. I watched Eve and Tora examine the brushes, made from hair gathered from clipping the horses' tails, tied to a small stick and cut to an even length. They dipped the brushes into a yellow paint Eve had developed using yellow earth found in a distant part of Home Valley, ground into a fine powder, and mixed with water and a small amount of fat.

Tora painted a strong and beautiful design on a large grain jar. I painted an oil container with a simple pattern using black paint. Each had been filled with a slurry of maize and left to absorb until the vessels were sealed. Preventing moisture from seeping into the precious food. Each one waited for paint, otherwise ready for food or water. Tora exclaimed over my simple work, though hers was more intricate. We set them in the sun to dry.

Tora and Elam stayed with us through two Sabbaths, where they shared in worshiping Jehovah in prayer and song. We climbed to the altar on the hill. Seth and Elam pulled me in a cart, giving me the opportunity to participate, as I had not yet gained enough strength to hike up the hill. Seth joined Adam, participating in his first sacrifice in two years. Tears of gratitude dripped from my cheeks, grateful for the opportunity to be reminded of the coming sacrifice of our Savior. Papa Adam continued in his usual calm, though with an unquenchable smile. Elam contained his quiet excitement, happy to be with Tora there to experience the rite.

Tora and Elam left the following day, planning to call on other villages on their path home, expecting to arrive there before the rains and mud prevented travel. I stood waving as they departed, grateful for their visit and sad to see them go. I cherished Tora's friendship.

We stayed through the rainy season. My strength improved enough I was able to once again manage my own home. We moved into an empty guest houses with Lilah. She grew more each day. It became a challenge to keep her safe. She scooted around the house. Like all little children, she was drawn to the bright, flickering flames. Each day, Papa Adam's design for safe fire spaces in every home filled me with gratitude and keeping Lilah safe.

I healed and grew stronger, warm in the love of our families. I wanted to believe we would stay in Home Valley, no longer journeying from place to place, sharing the words of Jehovah. While I knew this could not happen, I enjoyed the stability of home.

"We depart from here when the crops are planted," Seth told me one evening after a long day planting. We sat on the wide seat in the open air beside the front door while Lilah slept in her basket.

"Depart? I suppose we must."

"You like being here near our parent's, I know, but my mission to teach our brothers and sisters is not yet ended. I can leave you here and return each year to visit—"

"No!" I cried. "I love living here, safe in a home near our families, but I do not want you to leave me and Lilah behind. I am strong again. I can journey. Elam's cart removes many of the problems."

"You choose the demand of journeying over staying here?" Seth's jaw dropped, opening his mouth a bit.

"I do. I prefer to be with you. You need me to share with the women while you teach the men. Without me, your challenges in Axelston, Seedar, and Lib would have been greater."

"You consider Axelston easy?"

"Less difficult than Quillon!" I laughed at this outrageous thought.

Seth joined me laughing. "Yes. You are correct. You are necessary. Your assistance made the difference."

"When do we depart?"

"When the grains are planted. I will confer with papa about which direction we should travel. I depend on his revelations from Jehovah to know where to go next."

"Will you be given the right to sacrifice in other lands?"

Seth leaned back in the seat. "I do not know. Jehovah, only, determines who can sacrifice. Does he find me ready, yet? I do not know."

"Either way, we will be fine. Though it may make things more uncomplicated, we survived without sacrificing over the past two years."

"I will not give this up to stay in the safety of home."

In the next three weeks, Seth helped to finish the planting while mama and I planted vegetables in her garden. In the evenings, we gathered the items we required for our journey. We packed them into the cart Elam gave us in Lib. Seth spent time with Papa Adam, discussing the future of our mission. The days passed faster than I thought.

Seth leaned close and took me in his arms. "I am happy you want to go with me," he whispered, "I would miss doing this." He kissed me deeply and thoroughly.

Chapter Twenty

Burning Mountain

The day came when we were prepared to depart. The cart carried more than Hester ever could. It particularly had the benefit of keeping Lilah secure. We kissed our mamas and papas, and watched as they kissed Lilah a last time.

I set her into her basket, filled with toys to distract her. She sat in there, kicking and playing. I climbed onto my sturdy, chestnut colored Listella, while Seth mounted his tall, black Pacer Too. Though the cart held many things, Hester joined us, as usual, laden with goods, trailing behind Seth. The ever-faithful Blaze ran along beside the cart, watchful now for Lilah, and for Seth and me.

We waved to our loved ones and set our course north in the direction Papa Adam directed. I turned to wave again as we neared the top of the hill, and then turned forward, eager to face our next adventure.

We followed the same paths we did after we were married two years before for a distance. We traveled slowly, as we now had Lilah to consider. She explored everything in the cart making a mess of things, except when she napped. Eventually, we put her in the saddle in front of Seth or me, the only certain way to protect her. We fastened a strip of wool around her body and ours, to keep her in the saddle, as we had fastened in Rivka's children. We wanted to keep our daughter safe.

Like Eve had with Absalom so long ago, I connected a length of cord to her, tying it to her tiny stomach, knotted behind her where she could not undo it, the other end tied to my ankle, each time we stopped. It kept her near. Seth laughed and reminding me we missed a friendly goat to care for her. In his place, Blaze watched over Lilah for us.

As she learned to walk, the little girl worked to twist the cord to the front and play with the knot until it loosened. As it loosened, Lilah stepped out of the loop and toddled away. Blaze always grabbed her by the back of her dress, lifting her like a pup, and brought her to us. He recognized an unseen fence encircling each camp.

The trail branched after three days. We journeyed on north, rather than turning west, as we had earlier. We trekked across hills and through mountains. One morning, I packed all our clothing, food, and extra supplies into baskets and tied them tightly to the edges of the cart.

"Why are you taking the time to do this?" Seth stood with his hands on his hips. "Our baggage has always been protected."

"Yes, but something tells me they need to be protected today."

Seth shrugged and helped attach our supplies to the cart.

We had not gone far when we saw the glowing mountain across the valley. Red fire leaped from its tip in the same way sparks bounded from our campfire. A nasty smell blew from it into our faces.

"What is that?" I whispered.

"I do not know, but I do know we do not want to travel close to it. Look." Seth pointed toward it. "Fire boils down the sides like an overfull pot."

We watched for a long moment, grateful to be far away, until the horses grew restless. We turned and led the bullocks from the mountain. The cart bumped and bounced. The animals struggled to maintain their footing. Seth slid off Pacer Too, and grasped for his saddle. Blaze barked at him.

"The earth shakes."

I gripped Lilah between me and Listella and held on to the horse with my legs. Seth lifted himself onto Pacer Too and prodded the bullocks to move faster, though they did not require much prodding. Their eyes rolled in fear. The cart banged against their feet. Hester ran with us, his packs rattling and banging against his body. Blaze barked at the heels of any animal that slackened its pace.

We raced across the shaking and breaking surface, leaping sudden crevices opening in front of us. I expected Lilah to scream in fear, but she tried to push me back, laughing. This continued for a long time, carrying us up a hill and out of the valley before the animals calmed and brought us to a stop.

I climbed from Listella and handed Lilah to Seth. I hurried to look into the cart. I feared I would see our few possessions strewn across the broken landscape.

Nothing fell out. Only one skin dripped precious water down the side of the cart onto the ground. I grabbed it and turned it upright, searching for the hole. I found no hole. It had become untied at the neck.

"You listened." Seth put his hand on my shoulder. "I would have left our supplies loose to be tossed out across the land. You heard the voice of warning."

A trickle of warmth heated my chest. I listened and obeyed. And our equipment remained inside the cart. Seth set Lilah in her basket and drew me into a tight embrace.

"We must be aware of the fire mountain and stay far from it. It is dangerous," he whispered into my hair.

I could only nod.

Lilah stretched her arms to us, begging to join our affection. I lifted her into my arms and held her close. Seth examined each of the animals. One bullock picked up a stone in his foot. None of the others were injured.

Seth lifted its foot and pried out the stone with his knife. I soaked a few of the herbs Mama Eve sent with us and wrapped it around its foot. Then we knelt beside the wagon to offer a prayer of thanks for ours and our animals' and our belongings.

I prepared a small meal for us while Seth led the animals to a brook trickling nearby. While they drank, he moved upstream to refill our water skins. They grazed on the sweet green grass while we ate.

"Do we continue on, or stay here for the night?" I looked at the enticing green grass, trees, and cool stream.

Seth looked to the sky. The midday sun stood high. "Continue on. We need to find shelter."

The sun shone in a clear sky, but the day no longer felt clean. It tasted different, in some strange way. I nodded and repacked the cart. Lilah fell asleep and I lay her in her basket in the cart, allowing it to rock her as we plodded on in search of a safe camp.

We passed a pretty clearing surrounded by tall trees.

"Here?" I asked.

"No. The trees will fall in a storm."

We passed a rocky outcrop, with an overhang suggesting protection from rain.

"Here?"

"No. The rock will fall. The animals can be hurt."

What was Seth looking for?

At last we saw a black spot in the hill ahead.

"There." Seth pointed.

Darkness drew near. Lilah cried in hunger. Huge, dark clouds built up above us with flashes of lightning. I looked forward to escaping the oncoming weather. Seth led us into the blackness of a cave large enough to hold all of us and the cart.

We removed the saddles from the horses and were removing the harness from the bullocks when a great clash of lightning, followed by a crash of thunder opened the clouds in a river of rain. I appreciated Seth's foresight. We would have been drenched in the previous camp sites.

Seth built a small fire, using dry wood we carried in the cart. We found logs left by an earlier traveler. We sat on a big one. Another huge log, charred on the ends, lay in the middle of the rock circle. Seth drug it out until the smaller flames were big enough to accept it, bringing us light and warmth. For a third time that day, we knelt to offer thanks to Jehovah for His protection.

~

Five days later, we saw the smoke of another community. The villagers of Seacum welcomed us. We appreciated their warm welcome, although they were not interested in obeying the commands of Jehovah. We stayed with them three months, working with them in the fields and gardens, weaving and sewing, sharing the blessings of obedience. Few believed. They were not antagonistic, like the people of Geber. They received our labor, but not our knowledge.

Jehovah led us onward to other places, some north, others east of Home Valley. In each of these, some heard and believed, some listened politely and never accepted, like in Seacum, and others chased us from their villages without allowing us to speak. We trekked east a distance before the command came to Seth to travel south again. The sons of Cain in Nod were specifically denied our presence and the guidance of Jehovah's word.

A few communities participated and became obedient to the commands of Jehovah. In our journeys, Seth ensured that we never starved. He feared further difficulties similar to those of Lilah's birth. In Kor, families obeyed the words of Jehovah. There, Galya tended to me when our son, Aviv joined our family. Although not everyone in Kor agreed, we returned to visit with Galya and her family as we journeyed through the land.

More sons and daughters were born to us. During those years, we rode many days to stop for a short time among a new group of people. Occasionally, we stayed most of a year, teaching and sharing with communities who wanted to learn of Jehovah and return to his ways. More often, however, our stays were only a few weeks or months. Usually, when the time arrived for me to give birth, we were in a friendly village. Once, Seth and Lilah worked to help the babe arrive in a cave while it rained outside.

We returned to Home Valley about every second year. There, Adam and Seth met together, discussing the joys and sorrows of our mission. Each visit, I wondered if our release from our requirement to teach our brothers and sisters had finally arrived. The disappointment, or joy, consumed me for a seven-day or more, and the mission continued.

In all our migration, Seth widely avoided the burning mountain. We viewed it in varied stages, often it appeared as

the other mountains. The boys urged us to hike closer. Seth
refused.

Chapter Twenty-One

Zamir

We returned to Lib when we could, enjoying the companionship of our friends there. Tora and Elam welcomed us each time. Over companionable meals, we shared stories of our journeys. Seth and I told stories of service to Jehovah, teaching His gospel or encountering those who refused to believe. Their tales included providing carts to all who desired to learn. They, too, encountered unfriendly men who preferred to steal objects without gaining the knowledge required to build or repair their own. We sorrowed together for the wicked men and women.

Our family consisted of seven children when we returned to visit Lib. Tora and Elam greeted us warmly. They, too, now had sons and daughters, nine in all. The sons worked in his shop building carts and now larger wagons. The colt we traded, now a strong stallion, presided over a herd of mares and their young. The people of Lib continued in valiant obedience to the laws of Jehovah enabling the village to grow. Some chose to live as extended families in the long houses, while others chose to live in individual homes. All were accepted, regardless of their living conditions.

We were given a guest house for our family during our stay there. Seth traveled with Elam or one of the young men, leaving me and the children in the safety of Lib. It became a stable home for a time, a pleasant change from all the journeys.

Zamir came by to check on me, when Seth contacted nearby communities. We needed no man to check on us, for Aviv, at thirteen, offered the protection of a man and brought me firewood and water.

His habit of arriving there when the older children were gone unnerved me. He had a way of timing his visits to coincide with the afternoon naps of little Adah and Zebulon. Almost always, they were the only ones with me. I tried to be courteous to Zamir, at first, until these calls became too deliberate to be coincidental. He stood at my door, waiting for me to invite him in. I never did. Rather, I kept his interviews as short as possible, declining all his attempts to assist me.

Then, one day, it changed.

"You are too nice a woman to be left alone like this." Zamir, in a sickly honeyed voice, referred to Seth's most recent expedition to nearby villages.

"Alone? With seven children? How can I be alone?" Sarcasm filled my voice and I raised my eyebrows, glad my broom sat next the door beside me.

"You need a man to keep you company."

"Company? Seth does that quite nicely, thank you." I folded my arms underneath my breasts.

"Seth? He is frequently gone. How does he take care of a fine woman such as you, Ganet?" Zamir leaned against the wall, closer to me than I wanted him to be.

"Just fine."

He angled nearer, the smell of garlic on his breath gagged me. I stepped backward, stretching past the door frame for the broom.

"You need a real man, not one who leaves you behind." He inched closer.

"And you think you are man enough for me?" I found my broom.

"Yes, I do." He stepped forward and grabbed for me.

I brought my broom around and cracked him against the knees. He skipped backward.

"Why did you have to go and do that?" Zamir snarled. He attempted to capture my broom.

"Go away!" I shouted and waved the broom in front of me. "I want nothing to do with you."

"Too bad, Ganet. I want lots to do with you." He grasped my wrist with one hand and jerked the broom from me with the other.

Icy panic pumped through my veins.

"No!" I endeavored to pull my hand free, he held on tight.

With my free hand, I slapped his face, hoping surprise would force him to let go. Instead, his grip tightened. I raked my nails across his face. His fingers dug into my wrists. He caught the other hand in his. I bent to bite the fist holding me. I refused to be taken by this smelly little man. He was stronger than he looked.

I frantically searched the space near my house, seeking someone to help me. No one moved. It was devoid of all life except, Zamir and me. I kicked him in the shins, over and over, screaming as loud as I could.

"Stop this, Ganet. No one is here to save you." He dragged me toward the door.

Seth left the day before for a seven-day-long visit to another village. Lilah and Aviv took the three children younger than them to Ora's home, where she taught them to read and write, before hiking to the fields to assist in the harvest. Again, only two-year-old Adah and baby Zebulon were home. No help for me. Where were the women who so often passed in front of my house? I prayed for Jehovah's assistance.

I screamed a high piercing scream, aimed for Zamir's ear.

"Stop fighting," he grunted. "You are mine."

"I am not." I continued to struggle, managing to extricate a hand from his grasp.

Zebulon cried.

"Mama?" Adah stood behind me, rubbing sleep from her eyes. Zamir clasped a hand across my mouth, another encircled my body, ripping my dress. I bit his hand and kicked behind me. He lifted me from the ground and pushed me through the door, knocking Adah aside.

The sound of a rap on a ripe melon filled the room. Zamir's grasp on me loosened and I stumbled back. He fell, knocking me down and landing on me. I screamed and struggled to kick his weight from my legs. In a frenzy, I batted at the hands stretching toward me.

"No. Get off. Go away." I shouted.

"Ganet, Ganet. It is me, Seth."

I quit hitting him and, instead, fell into his arms, sobbing. "Seth! Where did you come from? I thought you were traveling. Oh, Seth!"

He pulled me from beneath Zamir and comforted me. His gentle words buzzed in my ear. I could not connect a meaning to the buzz.

The words acquired meaning as Zamir stirred at our feet. He sat up, rubbing his head.

"What are you doing here? You are supposed to be half way to Seedar."

A growl sounded deep in Seth's throat. "What are trying to do to my wife?"

Zamir shrunk into himself.

"I woke in the night with a warning that I was needed here. I rode Pacer Too as fast as I dared, arriving in time to see Ganet struggling to get away from you. What right do you have to attack my wife?"

Every bit of me quivered. Adah wailed. I scooped her into my arms and stared at Zamir, waiting for his answer.

"You leave her far too often. She needs a real man to take care of her." Zamir sneered my way.

"And you are a real man?" Seth spoke in a quiet, hard voice.

"I am better than you."

Men came at a run. They were late. Seth had stopped Zamir, already.

"We heard screaming." Danel gasped for air. "We came as fast as possible. We work in the farthest field today."

Seth nodded. "Zamir knew."

The men encircled Zamir, preventing his escape.

Seth faced Zamir. "You knew they were in the farthest fields and I traveled during this seven-days. You waited for such an opportunity to attack my wife."

"She has been friendly with me," Zamir whined. "She encouraged my attention."

"I never wanted your attention," I growled. "I was polite. You would not leave me alone. I have a husband and sons."

"She smiled at me in a special—"

"I smile at everyone. I smile those special smiles for Seth, only for Seth, never for a snake like you."

Zamir began to edge out of the circle, but Tal snagged him. "You will come with us."

The men yanked him out of the house and away. He strove to hang back, dragging his feet. As they turned a corner, Adad smacked Zamir on the back of his head, where Seth had hit him. "You will walk."

~

I stood stiff in the doorway. Seth turned toward me.

"I did not invite him in. I never asked for his assis—"

He enveloped me in his warm embrace. I fought back a shudder.

"I know you did not encourage him. I heard your screams and shouts as I rode in. You are innocent in this."

I settled Adah in my left arm and wrapped my right arm around Seth. "You believe me? You know you are the only man for me?"

"Of course, I do. You have been by my side for all these years. You are my wife. I know you."

"And you are mine. I desire no other." I set Adah on her feet next to us and wrapped both arms around Seth. I could no longer prevent the quivering.

Seth lifted me in his strong arms and carried me to sit on the sofa. Adah padded behind, sucking her thumb. I became aware Zebulon had stopped crying. Seth sat beside me and stared at me until I returned the look.

"I have seen Zamir follow you, not only with his eyes. I have been aware of his attentions for many days."

"Y-y-y-you h-h-h-have?" I stammered through my shivers. I felt stupid, to have been so unaware of his attention.

"I have. Zamir is not a good man."

"N-n-no." I clenched my teeth in an attempt to stop the trembling.

"Just listen, you do not have to answer. Not yet."

I nodded.

"Zamir will not forget this. You left bloody scratches on his face. His wife will know. She is not a forgiving woman."

I shook my head. *No, Vered was not forgiving. She will be angry. Will she be angrier with Zamir or me?*

"We will attend the harvest festival. Lechish requested for me to lead the prayers of thanks for the recent abundant harvest. However, Jehovah spoke with me again. We must take our family and travel north."

I nodded.

"We depart after the Sabbath."

Tears soaked the front of my robe. "I do not want to be the cause of our leaving Lib."

"Zamir did this, not you. You are innocent, not the cause of our going. The command came last week. I planned to share it with you when I returned from Seedar. Our early departure is caused by Zamir."

I tipped back to gaze at Seth. "Will you still go to Seedar?"

"Not now. We will go together. It is time."

Zebulon cried out from his basket. Seth gently pushed me into the sofa and got up to get the baby. I sat back and closed my eyes.

I woke wondering what time of day it was. The room was gray in the near dark. I sat forward and brushed my hair away from my face, wondering where Seth and the children had disappeared. An enticing aroma floated from the kitchen. The front door opened as I stood and stretched, planning to see what was cooking. Adah and Chaviva bounded into the room, followed by Seth and the other children.

"Do you feel better, mama?" Pili asked.

"Yes, I do." I stretched my arms out to enfold all seven of them. Seth joined us, wrapping his arms about us, too.

"Glad sleep helped," Seth said.

"Mama, we have dinner ready." Lilah chirped. "Come into the kitchen."

We all trooped to the kitchen. Chairs scraped on the floor as we joined together around the table as a family. Seth offered thanks to Jehovah for the food and blessings of the day.

"And thank you that our mama is safe," Chaviva chimed in.

The talk and noise of a family filled the cracks in my joy. *Zamir is crazy if he thinks I would leave this for him. Besides, Vered needs him.*

My thoughts continued like this, until evening prayers and the children were sleeping.

"Zamir is locked in the potato storage building for now." Seth dropped into my thoughts. "He will face a public trial tomorrow, if you are up to it."

"So soon? I thought they would wait until the crops are all harvested."

"Everything is harvested, Ganet." Seth reached to cover my hand with his. "Only the winnowing remains. They wait for the grains and beans to dry before the winnowing will begin. Can you face him tomorrow?"

I searched within me. *Can I face him tomorrow? Am I strong enough?*

"What do you think, Seth? Will he be able to make me look guilty? Can he make others believe I invited him to visit? I was cordial. I am kind to all, both men and women. Is this bad?" My heart began to race.

"No, Ganet." Seth put his hands on my shoulders and began a soft massage. "You are known as a kind, friendly woman, pleasant and kind to all. I spoke with some of the men. They noticed Zamir was not with them, gathering the last of the dry beans. Zamir has made a habit of this, shirking his obligation to help in the fields to stalk you. No one expected him to attack you. In his self-absorption, he believed you would cheerfully succumb to his sick ways. He did not expect you to scream."

"Vered will hate me. Her jealousy of women is understood, perhaps with reason, though few women favor Zamir. I do not want to be perceived as a home destroyer, one who entices married men."

Seth dropped his hands from my shoulders to my waist and drew me close. "You will not be viewed as a destroyer of homes. You did not entice him, remember? You did not request him to come here."

I took several deep breaths. "You believe me? Really believe me?"

He tightened his embrace. "How can you doubt? I understand you like no one else. We have been married almost twenty years. Never have I known you to look at other men. I trust you. There is no reason to stop trusting you now."

I leaned against Seth, allowing my fears to flow into the back of his robe. He held me a long time, murmuring soft words of encouragement.

"I can face Zamir tomorrow if you are with me. You will stand with me?" I peered at him.

"Yes, I will stay with you. Normally, I would be part of the judgment, as a Priest of Jehovah. However, you are my wife. My judgment in this would be biased. I will stand with you."

"You will lose your position, because of me. Can we just leave, now?"

"No, darling. I would lose my position if I did not stand by you. Nor can we leave Lib without facing him. We would both lose trust from these people, which would spread where ever we travel. Do not fear. It is Zamir who should fear."

"What will happen to Zamir?"

"I do not know. It depends on how he responds. If he confesses and asks for forgiveness, it will be better for him."

Chapter Twenty-Two

Trial

E arly the next morning Seth placed his hands on my head, offering a blessing from Jehovah. It comforted me.

I preferred that our children stay at home, packing for our move. I did not want them to be confronted with the trial. I worried about what Zamir would say. Seth overruled me.

"They need to be there. They have a right to stand up for you, a right to know you were falsely accused. They need to see Zamir admit his lie. The people of Lib need to see them support you. If they do not, some may believe your guilt."

"You believe I am guilty?" My voice raised half an octave.

"No. I know you are innocent. There are those here who are watching for us to slip. We need to stand against them."

"One weasel can cause so many problems?"

"Especially when the weasel is Zamir."

Lilah took charge of Zebulon, Aviv brought Adah. Seth reminded the others to stay close. We marched to the village square and stood in a little knot, arriving ahead of most of the villagers. I watched the villagers arrive.

Vered entered not long after we did and took up a position across from us. She glared at me. I felt her venom.

Most of the women, and some of the men, came to offer me their support. A few of Vered's friends glowered at me and then trekked to visit with her. Vered moved a little, maintaining clear sight between us.

The square filled with the people of Lib. Boys and girls ran, shouting and laughing, as they did. Older boys gathered in gangs, pushing through the crowd, teasing the girls who stood together in twos and threes. Our children stood quietly, waiting and watching. The sound increased until it sounded like a pride of lions on the plains.

The assembly stopped speaking as Lechish, Ora, and Danel appeared, followed by three big men who pushed Zamir in front of them. Zamir walked with his hands tied behind him. He stumbled, regained his feet, and forced himself straight to walk towards the front and in the center. Men and women moved back, making space for him. Children ran to their parents.

Lechish lifted his hands to silence the already quiet throng. "We are here to decide the fate of this man, Zamir, whom we discovered trying to force his way into the home and life of Ganet, wife of Seth, son of Adam and Eve."

The crowd rumbled and Lechish stopped speaking until they settled.

"Zamir, what have you to say for yourself?"

I sucked in my breath, fearing his answer.

Zamir lifted his shoulders in a shrug and straightened his back. "I am not guilty of the crime for which you accuse me. The temptress, Ganet, enticed me with her smiles, her kind words, and the sway of her hips. I arrived at her house after Seth's departure. She invited me in, leaning close, allowing me to peek down her dress." He leered in my direction.

"I never invited him in, never leaned close, never allowed him to peek. I kept my distance," I growled.

"Hush, Ganet," Seth whispered. "You will have your turn."

I closed my mouth and listened. The effort to stay quiet forced me to roll my lips inward.

"I went often, when Seth traveled. She asked me to cut her wood or bring her water."

I shook my head back and forth in disagreement.

"She wanted me, desired my body. I could tell." Zamir turned from the crowd to stare at me. Titters scattered through the throng. My skin crawled. "Yesterday, I knew Seth traveled once more. Her offspring were away, studying, we were alone. But this temptress deceived me. She changed her mind. When I offered to take care of her," Zamir frowned, "she screamed. There was no reason for her to make such noise. I would have left if she asked."

A rumble rippled the press as men and women commented to their neighbor. I heard, "She tempted him," and "Ganet would not do that," and "She is always kind, would she be a temptress?" I went cold, though my neck and face betrayed me. Embarrassed color rose in them. I glanced at Zamir, who smirked at me.

"Quiet! Quiet. Please!" Lechish demanded, raising his hands into the air.

The cacophony lessened, slowly dropping to nothing.

"Ganet, do you have anything to say?"

All eyes focused on me. I gulped and glanced at Seth. He nodded and walked me to the center, near where Zamir stood. In a frantic daze, I thought, *'What do I say to combat Zamir's lies?'* A calmness overwhelmed me. All would be well.

I flashed a smile for Seth, not knowing what I would say. "Zamir speaks the truth." I paused as women gasped and men cleared their throats. "He knew when Seth traveled. He tried to visit me every time. He came to my door, when my older children were gone, offering to help."

The crowd rumbled. Lechish shouted for silence.

"That is the end of any truth to what Zamir had to say about any interactions between us. I refused his every suggestion of help. My children are old enough to carry water and cut wood. Lilah, Aviv, and the others, ensure there is sufficient for our family, even when Seth is here."

Faces turned toward my children, who nodded.

"When he visited, I felt uncomfortable. I was pleasant. He tried to draw closer to me, but I always backed away from him. I am not fond of his garlic breath." I brushed my hand across my nose. The villagers laughed.

"I respect Vered, whose cooked garlic keeps her husband from other women." Again, they laughed. I glanced to see Vered. She showed a mixture of pride and embarrassment.

"He came to our home once more yesterday, suggesting he could 'take care' of me better than Seth. He suggested Seth's actions were amiss when he left me alone. Alone, with seven children? I hardly consider that to be alone."

The crowd twittered. I heard a dark rumble from the men.

"He stepped closer to me. I stepped back and reached for my broom. He suggested I needed a man like him. I asked him to leave. He refused. Rather than him sweeping me off my feet, I whacked him in the shins with my broom." More sniggers. "That wiped the honey from his mouth. He growled and grabbed at me. He tried to hold me close. I kicked him. I bit his hand. I fought him. Look. He bears my scratches on his face. If you examine him, you will find bruises on his legs and bite marks on his hands."

A large men man bent to examine his legs, then pulled his hands apart to stare at them. He faced the leaders and nodded. "She is right. He has bruises and bite marks."

I continued. "He did not let me go or leave me alone. I screamed. No one was near. Regardless, I screamed again and again, until my voice hurt. Zamir held my hands," I lifted them to show the bruises on my wrists, "and warned me no one would hear me. He knew everyone harvested in the farthest field."

Men grumbled. Anger filled their rumbling.

"Zamir grabbed me and covered my mouth. He lifted me and pushed past my little daughter who woke to my screams. Seth surprised us both, hitting Zamir on the head and knocking him onto me. Shortly after, men ran from the fields to investigate my screams. I never invited Zamir to come to my door. I have never been interested in him as anyone other than as a resident of Lib."

I closed my eyes, wondering where those words came from. Seth joined me and encircled my waist.

"Is there something you would like to add?" Lechish signaled to Seth.

"Yes." Seth guided me to our family and returned to stand in front of Lechish, Ora, and Danel.

"I have been aware of Zamir's attention and interest in my wife. Aviv told me of his visits when I was gone. Ganet is innocent, unaware of the intentions of wicked men. Her focus has always been on me. She does not recognize when other men flirt with her. I have seen Zamir watch my wife, follow her with his eyes, even follow her through the village."

The murmur rose and Seth waited.

"I stopped him three days ago, before I left for Seedar, and warned him to stay away from my wife. He sneered at me and told me he would go where he pleased. I asked Elam to watch out for Zamir and his attentions toward Ganet. Sadly, yesterday Elam joined you in the far field. He told me he thought Zamir was harvesting with them—until he heard Ganet scream."

Other men stepped forward to speak for me, supporting Seth. They, too, were aware of Zamir's interest in me. They testified of what they saw when they arrived at our home. Tal shared how Zamir cursed me as they removed him from our house.

Danel, Ora, and Lechish bent their heads together to discuss. The responsibility to judge lay on them. They must decide what would happen to Zamir. Or to me, if they believed Zamir spoke truthfully.

~

I sat with Zebulon to nurse him while the torrent of words spilled past my head. I focused on Zebulon and Adah, who pushed herself tight against me. Seth and the other children stood near, forming a protective circle around us.

Zebulon finished eating and fell asleep in my arms. Seth reached down and assisted me to stand as Lechish called for silence. Lilah took the baby from my arms and Ovid lifted Adah to his shoulders, waiting to hear the decision of the leaders.

"Zamir, you will stand," Danel said.

He stood and flashed a frown in my direction.

"Ganet, if you please?"

I moved to the other side of the leaders. Seth stood beside me, his arm around me. Like Zamir, we faced the throng. Lechish, Ora, and Danel also faced the crowd.

Ora spoke first. "We have seen much of the same behavior Seth shared. I have seen Zamir shadow Ganet and other women about the village. In this, we accept the testimony of Seth."

"We heard Ganet scream," Danel added. "Those screams sounded like cries of alarm, not teasing. Her fear pierced through my body. In this, too, we accept the testimony of Tal and the other men."

Lechish turned to Zamir. "Zamir, do you have anything to add?"

"The slut lies." Hands covered his mouth, one held a gag where he could see. He understood the threat and quieted.

"Zamir, you prove yourself to be an unrepentant liar." Lechish pointed his finger at him. "You have one last opportunity to speak the truth."

He shook the hands from him and drew himself as tall as his short body would stand. He lifted his hand and pointed at me. "Ganet is a child of the Destroyer, tempting me with her body, her smile, her kindness. If I am guilty, so is Ganet." He stood a long moment, pointing at me, and then he dropped his arm to his side.

"You show no repentance," Lechish continued. "We cannot allow one who is so willing to force himself on a woman, to remain in our village."

The community residents looked from one to another with a wary stillness. Zamir began to stutter. "I-I-I"

"Silence," Danel demanded.

Lechish continued. "You have until the sun reaches its zenith to gather your possessions and depart from Lib. You may never return. We will send messages to the surrounding villages, detailing your crime, so no other woman will be attacked by you."

Zamir opened his mouth.

"Do not say anything. You have no time to argue. The sun is near its zenith. If you delay, you will be taken to the boundaries of our village by force."

"I will go with him!" Vered shouted.

"You are welcome to do that. Regardless, you have only until the zenith. By then, you will be gone, with or without your belongings." Lechish spoke with certainty.

Zamir and Vered barged through the crowd toward their home. One or two women trailed behind, moving slowly. No men left.

We watched the sun draw closer to the zenith, wondering if Zamir and Vered would leave on their own. The sun stood less than a finger width from zenith before a buzz of excitement filtered across the press. It separated, allowing Zamir and Vered to ride past, towing a pack horse, loaded high with their baggage, behind them. Zamir threw the pack horse lead rope to Vered and rode toward Seth and me.

"You win this time, slut," he spat, "but beware. You will not always live within the boundaries of this little place. I will find you and get my revenge." He hawked and spat a green gob that landed at my feet.

"We do not fear you, Zamir. Jehovah is our protector," Seth said.

Zamir growled and turned his horse, plodding to his wife. He snatched back the lead rope and kicked his horse, thrusting his way through the crowd to the path leading from Lib. Boys and men tracked them, ensuring they were well on their way away from Lib.

Men and women came to where we stood to exchange comfort with us, and then returned to unfinished chores. Seth took my arm and escorted me through the clearing mass home. Our children accompanied us.

Seth shared our plans to depart with Lechish and Ora after Zamir's trial. They were sad to see us leave and unhappy it would happen so close after Zamir's misconduct. I understood their concerns. However, we obeyed Jehovah's commands, and we had been commanded to depart from Lib.

Lilah, Pili, and I spent the next few days quietly packing our belongings into large baskets. I quivered at the thought I might see Zamir again. Though I trusted in Jehovah's protection, headaches began to plague me, along with nightmares.

We celebrated with Lib a subdued harvest festival. The excitement of the trial became an uneasy truce. Some of Vered's friends made a point to inform me of their intense anger. They blamed me that their friend had been forced to leave. The dividing line between the few who supported Vered and those who supported me was obvious and palpable.

Near the end, Seth called for the attention of the festival goers. "My friends, I am saddened to see the divisions, especially as they were caused by the behavior of a wicked man toward my wife. Even before the recent events, Jehovah commanded us to travel north to teach another community of His gospel of peace. Peace in Lib will return when our family is gone. Allow your love for each other and Jehovah to seal the chasm building between you."

A buzz of chatter filled the village square. Seth allowed it to run its course.

"Tomorrow is the Sabbath. We join you tomorrow in worship one last time before we depart the next day."

"No!" Tora cried out. She rushed to my side. "You are allowing that weasel to drive you away?"

I shook my head. "You heard Seth. Jehovah commanded us to move on, even before—"

"Before Zamir. Yes, I heard. I will miss you. Please come back, when you can."

I laid my hand on her arm. "And I will miss you. We will return, when Jehovah allows."

"Will you need assistance with packing?" Typical Tora, always ready to help others.

"No. Everything is packed. The girls and I have packed our few possessions over the past couple days. We do not have many possessions. We will fill both wagons Elam graciously gave us. We are grateful for his kindness in providing us with a second wagon, and yours."

Seth called the children to him. I gave Tora a hug and we left the village square.

Chapter Twenty-Three

Miracle

We traveled north, over the pass we used so many years ago, when Seth and I first came to Lib. We were better prepared this time with enough food and warm clothing for everyone. As a wiggly, curious boy, Zebulon, at seven months, threatened to crawl from his blankets. Chaviva helped, playing with Zebulon and keeping him inside the wagon.

I found myself gazing in the surrounding brush and trees or turning in the saddle, searching for a glimpse of Zamir. I had a constant sense of someone watching me. The thought of his threat of retribution left me quivering.

"Where do you think he is?" I tossed my head back and forth, searching the trees behind us.

"Who?" Seth knelt beside me, pounding stakes into the dirt to hold up our tent.

I shrugged and handed him another stake.

"Do you mean Zamir?"

My teeth chattered. "Y-y-y-yes. I can f-f-f-feel eyes on my neck."

He folded me onto his lap and crooned in my ear. "He will not climb these mountains, it is too steep and difficult for him. You are safe with me and the children. Do not fear."

I heaved a great sigh. "Do you really think this is too hard for him?"

"I do. He would not even climb up to work in the high fields. No, Ganet. You are safe."

I sat in his lap until my heart slowed and my breathing settled. I scooted to the pile of stakes and handed him one. "If we are to be warm tonight, we need this tent."

The headaches returned, stronger than ever. Some days I could not open my eyes without losing everything I just ate. Lilah packed cool cloths over them and behind my neck.

"What is happening to me," I moaned in the dark as Seth and I lay in each other's arms. "Why have the headaches returned with such strength?"

"They come after you have fearful experiences—after they tried to sacrifice you to the serpent. Zamir caused a similar reaction. He tried to take you without your consent."

"But, he failed. You came to save me."

"And the fear of it lingers. It surprises me you have not woke us all with your dreams. I hear your moans, your cries to be left alone."

"I am strong. Yes. I dream of him, and you always come in time to save me."

"Do you need a blessing from Jehovah?"

"Yes. I did not realize he is the cause of my problems."

Once more, in the darkness, Seth placed his hands on my head and offered a prayer, blessing me with a release from the pains in my head and the bad dreams. Once more, the pains eased and the dreams ended.

The rough path narrowed frequently, often only wide enough for a horse. Seth and Aviv bent to move rocks and trees, or fill dirt beside them to build the space up for wagons to pass. Even the little ones joined in. The long, arduous journey became colder as we neared the summit.

At the summit, all nine of us stood together gazing in awe across the world from the tops of the mountains. Near the bottom, we saw the greens of the warm season. Toward the middle of the slope, trees dressed in brilliant reds, golds and oranges of harvest season. Nearer to us, trees set in ranks nearly naked, with one or two leaves clinging to the shivering branches. Dark green pines dotted amid them all, dark shadows on the landscape. We stood above the trees among rocks and low bushes.

The first snow fell on us as we plodded down the slope toward the protection of the trees.

"Mama, I am cold," Pili cried, shivering in the bed of the front wagon, with blankets piled on top of her.

"It is." I glanced around, thinking.

"Jump down and walk." Seth bounced. "We are warmer when we move. All of you, jump down and walk beside the wagons."

Aviv grinned from the front where he led the bullocks as the others piled out. I wrapped a blanket around Zebulon and carried him until he squirmed from my arms to the ground and toddled through the snow, holding my hand. Lilah laughed as he lifted his little feet high above the white stuff. It soon melted under their feet. We were grateful for fur lined boots. They laughed as they played, trekking onward, until the cold drove them into the wagons to huddle together under a pile of blankets.

We struggled for many days. Fires built from wood we brought with us, melted the ice in our arms and legs, preparing us for another day of marching in the frigid air. We built a small fire to hold the heat inside our tent and cooked over an open campfire outside, except during the blasts of white during blizzards.

We trudged from the snow into mud. We crawled onward out of the cold season, into harvest, until we turned north to take another pass through another set of mountains. Once again, we hiked into snow. At odd moments, I still felt the prickle of someone watching me. I turned to search the trees and bushes for Zamir. I never saw him.

One morning we stared toward the smoke describing a village.

"People, at last," Ovid sighed.

"Will we stop here?" Lilah's hand screened the sun from her eyes.

"Will we, Papa? Will we?" Pili tapped Seth's arm.

"We shall see," Seth whispered. "Not all families choose to hear the word of Jehovah. Let us kneel and pray that these people will listen."

Lilah lifted Zebulon and Adah from the wagon to join our family circle while Seth poured out his soul to Jehovah, begging Him to soften the hearts of the residents of the village. "Our family traveled many days through terrible terrain. We suffered along the way. We followed your command to travel north. Please bless this community."

I added my "Amen" to the fervent prayer, feeling warmth spread from the center of my heart into my stomach. This place would be receptive to Seth's message. We made our way slowly into it.

~

The leaders of Laish welcomed us to their village, expressing an eagerness to learn of Jehovah's commandments and love. Our children bounced into the large guest house we were guided to, ours to live in while in Laish. We unpacked our few possessions and stored them neatly. The younger ones begged to run outside to play in the snow.

"You must remember to stay close to a brother or sister, never be alone." I said as I shoved Adah's feet into her warm boots.

Chaviva drew his eyebrows together, an expression he made when trying to understand. "Why, Mama?"

"We do not know these people, yet. Until we do, you must be careful and on your guard."

Pili bumped him on the arm, "Listen to mama. She has her reasons." She looked at me. "Right, Mama?"

I nodded. "Stay with a brother or sister, but have fun."

"We will, Mama." Aviv grabbed a warm, fur-lined cloak and tied it under his chin. "Come on, let us go!" He herded the others out into the bright sunshine and cold, leaving baby Zebulon and Lilah with me.

Seth came in with news of a gathering later in the evening, as an introduction of us to the people of Laish. This kind of meeting assisted in coming together as friends and neighbors.

The fragrance of food cooking over fires spread across the village. They were happy to enjoy an unplanned gathering. Lilah and I searched through our meager supplies for something different to add to the meal. We found dried grapes and an end of cinnamon bark.

At the appointed time, we dressed in clean clothes and prepared to join them. Lilah carried a pan of cinnamon rolls. The delicious aroma leaked past the covering.

The children bounced in excitement, happy to join new friends discovered in their hours of play in the snow.

"Remember," I warned, "do not be alone tonight. Stay with Papa, me, or someone in the family."

"Right. Be careful," Seth said.

They agreed to our request and trooped out the door toward the common hall. Seth and I followed more slowly. Seth with Adah on his shoulders, to keep her feet dry, while I carried Zebulon.

"What are those?" Pili pointed to long, white, carrot shapes hanging from the ends of the roof along the building.

Seth scrutinized them. "No idea. We will have to ask." We followed Pili through the door into the warmth and noise of all the families of Laish. We were prepared to offer news from other villages and participate in the good times.

Smiling faces welcomed us. Com, Laish's leader, and his wife, Dorit, greeted us with open arms and a brush of their lips on our cheeks. I hid my shudder, even as I smiled and returned the greeting. *Why the shudder? Seth is here. I am safe.* I covered my shaking with smiles and friendly words as each person greeted us with a hug and a kiss on the cheek.

After dinner, our younger children joined the others, running noisily around the hall. Some ran into the night air, returning to place cold hands on another child's neck. Squeals echoed in the cavernous room.

The men gathered on one end of the room. Lilah joined me with the women gathered a short distance away. I made a point to sit or stand so I could see, checking for Seth often. I listened to them talk of their families and the hunt planned by the men.

"Our crops fill our storage buildings, providing enough for us and to share with those who journey through Laish, though we are short on meat." Ela looked my way.

"Why travel into the mountains with your children in this weather?" Dorit asked. The question reflected on their faces.

I could no longer sit quietly and listen. I must speak. "Time for us to move. Jehovah commanded us to go north, so we did."

"Time?" Hana stared at me, an incredulous look on her face. "In the beginning of the cold times?"

"We are obedient. Jehovah commanded us to move. We did."

"When the snow fell?" Ela crunched her eyebrows together.

"It did not fall when we left. The weather changed on us as we traveled."

"It would. But when you left your last village, it was late in the year, was it not?" Hana asked.

"There were reasons."

I looked at my hands. I could not disclose the embarrassing cause of our precipitous leaving. I wanted these women to like me, not be fearful of me, always thinking I planned an attempt to steal their husbands. Lilah brushed her hand across my shoulder.

"Leave her alone." Yemina spoke sharply. "It is none of our business. She chooses not to share."

I glanced at her, grateful for her support. She smiled and gave me a little nod.

A girl slipped to the knot of chattering women and whispered in a woman's ear. Fear crossed her face as she followed the girl outside.

~

Her scream echoed from outside and penetrated the building, stirring everyone into motion. The men, who stood nearer the exit, rushed out first. We women followed on their heels. A boy lay in the snow, surrounded by what sounded like the distant buzzing of a beehive—men and women staring at the child, each offering a suggestion.

The boy's parents knelt beside him, touching him, calling to him. Seth looked to me. I nodded to his unspoken question.

He pushed through the crowd, stirring up the beehive of noise, and touched the boy's papa on the shoulder. I could see him now. Red streaked from a gash in his head. Beside him lay one of the long white carrots of ice, one end covered in the boy's blood.

Seth stooped next to the boy and his mama and papa. He felt his neck and cheek, lifted an eyelid, and brought his ear close to his mouth, listening. He shut his own eyes and prayed for the boy. He murmured something to the parents. The mama covered her face with her hands and cried. The papa's face frozen in stunned disbelief. Two men assisted Seth and the boy's papa to pick him from his icy bed and carried him, trailed by his mama, to a house.

I followed at a discrete distance with the women, silently praying for the boy to live. As we passed the ice carrot, I bent down to lift it. Its cold heaviness surprised me.

The sorrowing family shut their door after the men who carried their son. Soon, all but the parents and Seth left the boy in the home, participating in a silent vigil. Even the children stood, uncharacteristically still.

We waited in the bitter cold until late into the night, waiting for news of the boy. Some mama's drifted away, taking young ones in out of the frosty air with them. Lilah touched my shoulder and gestured with her head toward the guest house. I agreed. She gathered her brothers and sisters and directed them into the warmth of our temporary home. I waited for Seth with the others, knowing my children were well cared for.

Aviv slipped his hand into mine. I drew my eyebrows together in question.

"Lilah has the little ones in bed. We thought you needed some company," he whispered.

I squeezed his hand in gratitude.

People stamped their feet and moved to stay warm. In all this time, no one spoke, whispering only necessary communication. We silently waited. The moon rose over the mountains and mounted high into the sky, looking as though a big bite was taken from it. The moonlight reflected off the snow, creating long shadows.

Ovid draped a warm blanket across mine and Aviv's shoulders, kissed my cheek, and hurried inside. Little puffs of white filled the air above us. And still, we waited.

A woman brought mugs and a jug of hot soup, handing each of us a mug and pouring the hot soup into it. I nodded my thanks to her and watched the other men and the few women who still waited, over the steaming rim. She finished her rounds and hurried to the warmth of her home.

The moon had started its downward course when the door to the house opened. Seth stepped through and came toward me. The papa followed, quietly closing his door.

"Our son lives. Seth called upon Jehovah. He asked Him to allow our son to live. His breathing slowly returned to normal. He woke, and is with his mama, sipping a mug of hot soup. We thank you for your support. Meyer lives."

The silence shattered as men and women expressed their amazement. Seth reached me and Aviv and put his arms across our shoulders. Men and the few women who remained turned toward us. Questions filled the air.

"Our God, Jehovah, is the God of love." Seth's usual full voice sounded scratchy and sore. "He has healed Meyer. It is late. We will speak more of this tomorrow."

Seth turned us toward our temporary home. Voices called behind us, questioning. Seth walked on. He held our elbows, but we held him up. A door closed behind us.

"Meyer's papa went inside," Aviv whispered.

"Good," Seth murmured.

We helped Seth through our door and to the bed, where he lay with his arm thrown over his eyes.

"Seth?" I asked. "Do you want something to eat?"

"No. I am too tired to eat," he mumbled.

I pulled the blankets from beneath him and tucked them around him. I then checked on the children. Lilah and Aviv sat in front of the fire, whispering together.

"Will Papa be well?" Lilah's eyes opened wide.

"He will be. I have seen this before." I leaned against the edge of a table. "Calling upon Jehovah for such a long time takes much energy. He will be well in the morning."

She twitched her shoulders and ducked her head.

I caressed her face. "Thank you for bringing the little ones home and putting them to bed, Lilah. And you, Aviv, for your support." I set a hand on his elbow. "You two should go to bed and get some sleep."

Lilah and Aviv nodded and turned toward their beds. Aviv went to crawl into bed with the other boys. I heard Chaviva grumble in his sleep about the chill. Aviv would soon be warm with them.

Lilah slipped into bed with the girls. I heard small sounds of the sleepers, until she quietly shut the door. Zebulon slept near the banked fire in our room, warm and safe. I kissed his chubby cheeks. At last, I crawled into bed with Seth, seeking the warmth surrounding him.

Then, when I no longer stood in the icy night air, my teeth decided to rattle together. I cuddled next to Seth's body.

"You should have come inside sooner to get warm." Seth slid his arm under my head and pulled me near.

"I wanted to show my support for you. I did not expect you to be so long."

"No. You would not." Seth closed his eyes. I thought he drifted into sleep, but he spoke again. "You did not know we carried a dead child into the house. Meyer's mama and papa heard somewhere that if a man of God prayed, the sick would be healed. They begged me to stay and pray."

Seth drew in a deep, ragged breath and lay in the dark with his eyes shut another extended period. I wondered what more he would say. *A dead child who now lives?* No wonder Seth is exhausted.

"I prayed." His voice scratched at the silent darkness. "His mama, Betta, joined me. Even, Corin, his papa, gave in and joined us. His were fervent."

Seth sighed. "As we prayed, a small voice told me to blow the breath of life into his mouth and push the air out by pressing on his chest. Corin blew the air in. I pushed it out. All the while we prayed. We breathed, pushed, and prayed."

"And I joined in prayer outside," I said.

He pulled me nearer. "I wondered why we did this, until we heard Meyer take a broken breath. His frayed breathing came and dropped away, over and over, until he opened his eyes and spoke. 'Mama,' he said, 'why are you crying?' She swept him onto her lap and tears fell on his back. 'Because you were dead and now you live,' she cried."

"How long before you came to tell the crowd?" I stared at a slice of moonlight crossing his face.

"We waited for Meyer to grow strong enough to sit and eat the soup brought to the house, earlier. By then, we knew he would live. My strength was gone. I was grateful to see you and Aviv. I could never walk this far alone."

"I knew." I brushed Seth's hair back from his eyes.

"Oh, Ganet. Meyer was gone from this world. He had no breath. No beat of his heart. And, now, he lives! Jehovah is a mighty and loving God."

Chapter Twenty-Four

Laish

Not long after Seth found sleep, the sun rose. He did not. Lilah woke with the little ones and tended to their needs until I got up, sleepy-eyed. I sent her to bed. She stayed up as late as I had, waiting for Seth to return.

"Food smells wonderful." Seth came to the table with his usual bounce in his step, though it was still early. He bent to kiss me before he sat. "It is a beautiful day. Did you see the sun shine on the snow? Beautiful."

I half-expected him to rise bleary-eyed and groggy. Not my Seth. One of the many reasons I loved him.

Chaviva and Ovid banged the door open, arms filled with firewood.

"Papa, you are awake!" Chaviva called as he dropped the wood onto a pile near the fire space. "Men are outside waiting to hear from you."

Seth looked up from his hot wheat. "Men, son? Why would men be waiting to hear from me?"

Chaviva shrugged. "Something about last night, I guess. I do not know. Shall I tell them you are awake?"

"Not yet. I need food. Have you eaten?"

Chaviva gave his papa a good morning hug. "Yes. Lilah fed us earlier. We let you sleep. Did you sleep well?"

Seth nodded as he returned to his cooked wheat.

I sat beside him, watching him eat. "What will you do to-day? The people of Laish will want to understand about last night."

He spooned another bite into his mouth, taking time to think. "I will teach them of Jehovah. What happened last night is between Meyer, his parents, me, and Jehovah. It was a sa-cred experience. I asked Corin and Betta to say nothing. I pray they will maintain my confidence in them."

I leaned on my elbows, resting my chin on my hands. "When the people ask, what will you say?"

He looked up. "I will say we prayed and Jehovah an-swered. They do not know the boy did not breathe when we carried him into his home. They only need to know Jehovah healed the boy. He did."

"You will miss the opportunity to teach of Jehovah's great power?"

"Miracles and blessings such as this do not always build faith. They cause people to search for more miracles, instead. They do not recognize the small miracles that abound in their everyday lives. No. I was given to know this is not to be noised abroad, but kept near to my heart, as you are, my love." He leaned close, kissing me.

Seth washed and prepared himself, and then strode out the door to meet those who waited with questions. His voice reached me through the door, "It is much too cold to spend time in discussion here in the open air. May we enter the village hall and enjoy the fire as we speak and learn together?"

The murmur of voices dwindled as they clumped through the ice and snow to the hall. Soon, the only noises outside were the whoops and calls of boys racing in the snow and the occasional yelp as a snowball landed.

The girls and I organized our belongings and dressed in our warm cloaks to explore our new surroundings. Adah held fast to Pili's hand, skipping through the snow beside us. Zebulon sat on my back, watching the world with his big, blue eyes. We walked a distance before Yemina opened a door, wrapping a cloak around her, and joined us.

"We wanted to explore and discover how Laish is laid out." I waved my hands in explanation. "Would you like to give us a tour?"

"You did not see much yesterday. Less last night in the icy darkness. Come. I will show you." Yemina pointed out the houses of the families who lived in Laish. "You recognize the village hall?"

"I do. What happened last night?" I asked. "How was the boy injured?"

"Sometimes, the icicles loosen and fall, especially when children run around them. Sometimes, they bump into the icicles often enough they cause them to fall. One fell on Meyer last night. The blood on the icicle indicated he was hurt badly. Yet, today, he is with the men, listening to Seth. What did Seth do?" Yemina searched my face.

"I do not know. I waited outside with the others. I was not there. Seth said they prayed and Jehovah healed the boy."

"Jehovah healed him?"

"Yes. He heals the sick."

"It would be good to know this Jehovah," Yemina murmured. She pointed to a building straddling a stream. "It is too cold here to wash our clothing outdoors, most of the year. We built this building to keep it out." She opened the door.

Inside, fires burned on a stone floor. A great pot filled with bubbling water hung over each one. A woman stood near a hot pot with a long-handled hook. She reached out with the hook and tilted the pot until the water poured into a waiting black pot close by. She filled the black pot half way and pushed the boiling pot upright.

The woman dipped another pot of water from the stream running through the building and refilled the pot. She added one more small pot of cold water to her smaller pot and chopped soap plant into it. She shoved her clothing in and began to clean it.

"It is better than freezing on such a bitter day, and you can still have clean clothing." I glanced appreciatively at the bubbling pots.

"We froze or wore filthy clothing in the fiercely cold season of the year. Then Dorit thought of this. Our men were ready to have clean clothing again and willingly aided us in building the wash building."

"Dorit is wise. Are the fires always burning?"

"Only one small fire, to keep this place warm. It would require too much firewood. We light the other fires and clean our clothing only once every seven days. We each have a time to come use the water. Usually more than one woman is in here. I washed earlier. Leta is the last today. Then, they will be extinguished."

"How do you keep the water from freezing over in this frigid weather?" Lilah stood beside the gurgling stream.

"It often freezes. The men check on it more daily, especially when the ice grows thicker. We are happy it is deep and fast moving, preventing the ice from reaching the rocky bed below. If that happened, we would be without water. This is the only place water flows during the coldest parts of the year."

Relief flooded through me with the knowledge we would no longer have to seek clean snow to melt for water. I made a mental note to show Aviv, Ovid, and Chaviva where to find fresh water.

"Where do you dry your clothing?" I searched the area for drying clothing.

"We take them home and hang them near our own fires." Yemina waved her hands. "This prevents problems of mixed up and lost clothing."

I understood the challenge.

"May we clean our clothing?" I asked. "It has been many weeks since we had time, fire, and water to clean our clothing properly."

"Certainly. You will want to bring your washing soon, while they still burn."

It made sense to me. "Is there anything else I should see?"

"Not now. The rest can wait."

We walked together to collect packs full of dirty clothing to clean. Lilah and Yemina helped lug them to the washing building. Little Adah followed behind.

Much later, and after much hard work, we toted it all home again. Zebulon slept on my back. Chaviva saw us and ran to help Adah home. There, we spread the clothing around the house to dry in front of our fires.

Over the days and weeks, we shared in the women's daily activities, cleaning and weaving, among others. They lost their distrust of me, taking me into their confidence, allowing me to join in with them.

Seth met with the men, teaching them of Jehovah. In the afternoons, the women and older children coming together with them. Many listened. Many believed.

~

The snow lasted longer than I expected, longer even, then in Seedar. We greeted warmer days with joy, though it heralded a period of intense activity. The growing season was short high in the mountains.

Seth and the boys assisted the men with plowing, planting, and harvesting the crops and shearing the animals. The girls and I joined the women in preparing the seeds and the womanly chores of spinning and weaving cloth and baskets, feeding families, and caring for children. On the warmer days, we opened the wash building doors to allow the steam out and cooler air in.

When we created pots, it surprised me to see the way they hardened and prevented moisture from entering the clay ware. After it dried, we set it within great squares of mesquite wood and set it into blazing hot fires. They burned over two days. When the fires cooled, we brushed away the ashes. The pots, now hard, did not absorb water or break as easily. I stored the information in my mind, for when we returned to Home Valley.

Seth taught the people of Laish as often as they would listen. During this season of the year, they worked from dawn until dark, falling into exhausted sleep soon after dark. They gave him a few hours on the Sabbath to remember Jehovah.

Near the end, Aviv helped him dam an offshoot of a stream. The water filled in behind it, making a pool deep enough for Seth to baptize those who were ready. Everyone in Laish sat around the pool to observe the sacred rite.

Seth took a day between Sabbaths to visit nearby, smaller villages, taking baptized young men with him. Many listened and became followers of Jehovah, joining with us in Laish for Sabbath worship.

We gathered for a grand feast. Women provided pots of specially prepared foods, including breads, cakes, and honey.

We thanked Jehovah for the richness of the harvest and sang songs of praise. All enjoyed a wonderful evening.

That night, white flakes drifted across the mountains. We woke to white blanketing fields, gardens, orchards, roads, and rooftops. Chaviva and Ovid whooped and ran into the whiteness, gathering it into balls and throwing it at each other and the other boys who spilled out of their homes to play in the snow.

We spent the long, dark days of the cold weather, often with families of the village, sharing stories and listening to Seth teach of Jehovah. Men frequently broke icicles from the edges of the roofs to prevent injuries. Seth taught the men to build carts and wagons, using ours as a pattern. They created new tools for use in the growing times. I assisted in spinning and weaving, sewing and cooking.

Though the dreams rarely affected me, the headaches continued to debilitate me. As I recovered from one of these terrible bouts, Seth sat next to me on the bed.

"Ganet, I have prayed and thought about this pain for months. Do you think, perhaps, the pains return because deep inside you refuse to forgive Zil and Zamir?"

I sat beside Seth. "Zil? No. Zil's devotees blindly follow his priest's commands. They listen to the Destroyer. To hold onto anger against the Destroyer is pointless. While as we stay far from Quillon and Zil's disciples, I no longer fear him."

Seth put his arm around me, "That is wise. It has been years since your sleep, and mine, was disturbed by the eyes and maw of the serpent."

I shuddered and hoped those eyes would not plague me at night.

"But, Ganet," Seth continued, "what about Zamir?"

I turned inward, wondering. *Jehovah expects us to forgive, if we wanted to be forgiven by him. I make mistakes. I need this almost every day. What of Zamir? Thoughts of Zamir brought quivers of dismay and dread. No. Forgiveness was not complete. How could I be forgiven if I held a grudge against him? Were the pains in my head caused by repressed lack of forgiveness.*

"Pray with me, Seth," I asked. "I require help to forgive completely. I thought I had, but I find I have not."

We knelt, praying to relieve the apprehension, anger, and loathing of a man no longer a part of my life. Forgiveness came after many days of prayer, overcoming my fear of him. I did not dread seeing him again.

"Seth, I hope to find Zamir, let him know he is forgiven," I said at last.

Seth pulled me into a tight hug. "In time. You will have an opportunity, some day."

The guest house became our permanent home. We spent happy times there as a family. Adah and Zebulon grew. Adah began to help with small chores. Zebulon toddled around, getting into things and needing constant attention and care. Gratefully, his brothers and sisters loved him and cheerfully kept him safe. The children made friends among the young of Laish and a nice young man named Omer visited Lilah frequently.

The cold gave up its grip on the mountain once more and tiny green shoots peeped through the last of the snow. It melted and the air warmed enough to plant once more. Our family participated in sowing fields and gardens, grateful for all we received from Laish.

When the seeds were in, however, we gathered our possessions and loaded them into our wagons. The time came again for Seth to report to Adam about his successes. We extended sad farewells to our friends in Laish, promising to return when we could. Then, early in the morning we hitched the bullocks, climbed onto horses and into the wagons, and set off for Home Valley.

We returned over the mountains we had crossed two cold seasons ago. Our struggles through the ice and snow then prevented us from appreciating their beauty. We pointed out waterfalls, trees, and flowers to each other as we traveled. Leaves on trees opened above our heads, small flowers bloomed at our feet, and vines draped across rocks, each adding to the beauty of the land we crossed.

The joyful reunion we anticipated with our family as we neared Home Valley became a reality. Our horses and wagons entered the village surrounded by shouting children. Mama and Eve rushed from their homes to throw their arms around us. While we lived in Laish, we told stories of our families. Still the little ones hung back, not remembering these people.

Their shyness soon ended as Papa threw them into the air and Adam swung them in circles until they were dizzy. Everyone laughed watching the little ones. We ate, talked, and shared the stories of our recent adventures.

We settled in one of the larger guest houses. Crops in the valley were green and growing, some ready to harvest. Seth and the boys helped. All of us participated in the celebrations.

I remembered the skills of the women in Laish and shared their methods of baking clay ware to prevent moisture from absorbing through them. With cries of wonder, we replicated their process, and discovered the benefits.

Mama Eve turned a jar in her hands. "This will save maize for eating, rather than using it to cure our pots and jars."

Seth met most afternoons with Adam, sharing the successes and failures of his teachings in the villages in the mountains surrounding Laish. Eve invited me to join them, both with all our children and sometimes just the two of us. During those visits, we discussed our future and the directions we should travel to teach others of Jehovah's love.

Chapter Twenty-Five

Honor

We stayed in Home Valley until the fields and gardens were planted the next year. Though we were saddened to leave our beloved families, the time came to return to teaching. Once more, I expected another child. We faced the rising sun and traveled, toward other villages and people who forgot or never knew the love of Jehovah.

Over the next years, we traveled throughout the land, returning often to Laish, Seedar, and Lib. Our family continued to grow. Our sons were good men, helping Seth in his teachings. Some grew tired of the traveling and settled in a village we visited and raised their children.

Omer found us and convinced Seth to allow his marriage to Lilah. They settled in Laish, providing us another reason to see Laish as often as we could. Her sisters met good men and married them. Our children scattered across the land, helping their communities to remember the commandments and love of Jehovah.

We returned to Home Valley when we could, allowing Seth to meet with Adam. I enjoyed meeting my parents and family. While Seth and Adam met together, I visited with Eve, sometimes with our younger children, sometimes I left them with mama or one of the older daughters whose husbands lived there.

One visit stands out in my memory. We had been teaching our brothers and sisters the gospel of Jehovah for forty-four years. I met with Eve while Seth prayed at the altar with Grandpapa Adam. When they returned, they glowed.

Eve and I stood to welcome them. Seth strode over and enveloped me in a warm embrace. His shivers startled me. He held me close a long time with tears dampening my shoulder. I reached up to wipe tears from his face.

"Jehovah honored Seth." Adam released Eve from a tight hug. "He visited with us this day. I have been instructed to ordain Seth to the office of High Priest, to join with me in the responsibilities of the High Priesthood. He, too, is a prophet and seer."

Seth bowed his head. I understood his tears, his quaking, and his shining. He just came from the presence of Jehovah! I kissed him. His kiss sent quivers through me. I clasped his hand and sat near to him as we spoke with Adam and Eve.

Seth spent the next days preparing himself and a ram for sacrifice. It reminded me of the days before our marriage, watching him, then, preparing and bathing a ram. He participated in a ritual bath every day and spent hours in prayer, fasting during the days, eating only a small meal at night.

The next Sabbath, we all trekked to the altar on the hill to observe. Seth and Adam performed it together. The rite touched my soul. We had not participated for many months. Seth held the lower priesthood, without the right to sacrifice alone, since before our marriage.

After this sacred experience, Adam spoke to those who attended. "Seth, come stand by me."

Seth smiled into my eyes and stepped over the children to stand beside his papa, Adam, our High Priest.

"Seth has been honorable in his efforts to share the gospel of Jehovah in his many teaching expeditions, with Ganet and his family." Adam looked at me and smiled. "He holds the lesser priesthood, as do many of you honorable men. Seth has been honored by Jehovah. I am to ordain him to the office of High Priest. He will have the duties and responsibilities of this office, including the ability to perform sacrifices with and for those who live far away. Can you support us in this action?"

A chorus of yeses echoed across the valley.

"Are there any who cannot?" Adam asked.

No one raised their voice in opposition. Seth bowed his head. I glanced around at the others to see their joy, though some appeared troubled.

Adam recognized the cause of their troubled faces. "I will not live forever. Jehovah knows the beginning from the end. He knows I need help to carry His commands to my children.

Seth has done this for many years, teaching people and bringing them back to a remembrance of our God. Those who live far away lose the opportunity to remember or learn of His love for us." Adam watched them nod in agreement.

He continued, "The earth fills with people. Those far away lost the opportunity to observe and participate in sacrifices. Seth can teach them of Jehovah's great love. I hoped for years he would receive this honor. Now he has the authority to sacrifice."

Adam shared more with us before the rite ended. As people left, many stopped to offer support and congratulations. Awe filled our children and grandchildren who were with us.

"I am still your papa," Seth told them when we were the last ones beside the altar. "I will always love you, always desire your obedience to Jehovah."

Tuvya stepped close. "You will not change?"

"No, son. I will not."

Tuvya hugged him and pounded him on the back. The other children and grandchildren followed, hugging and congratulating their papa.

We entered the village to an impromptu feast being prepared, set out on large tables on the village green. As they completed the preparations, my papa and mama joined Seth, and me in Adam and Eve's home. Adam blessed Seth with powerful, yet simple words of authority. He offered a blessing that burned into my heart, never to be forgotten, too sacred to be repeated. At the end, Seth grabbed for his papa's hand to

be drawn into a loving embrace. We embraced him and offered words of love. Our eyes shone with unshed tears of joy.

We joined the villagers and our family in the green, eating
and celebrating the blessings of our God.

Our caravan left not long after. Bullocks pulled three wagons, each driven by one of our sons. Little ones rode in the
wagons, others rode with Seth and me on strong horses. Pacer
Too and Listella returned to Jehovah years earlier. We rode on
their offspring.

Herds of cattle and sheep trailed behind, herded by sons on
horses. We no longer depended on others to support us. Rather, we shared what we had with those in need.

Our travels led us to communities where Seth had found
success, teaching his brothers and sisters of the love of Jehovah. In many of these villages, Seth performed a sacrifice to
help them worship Jehovah.

Chapter Twenty-Six

Vase

As many of our children obeyed Jehovah's commandments, we were filled with joy. However, a few chose to marry non-believers. They promised to help teach them of Jehovah and become believers. It did not happen. We sorrowed as too many united with the non-believers.

Our family grew to twenty children, some born easier than others. Because each birth became more severe, I wondered if this was the last every time. I prayed about this often, begging Jehovah to reduce the struggle or ease the pain if I the requirement continued for me to bring children to the earth. Adam promised us a son who would obey and choose to observe the arduous responsibility of spiritual leadership. I struggled.

When we returned to Home Valley for Adam and Seth to confer, I was with child again. We determined to stay until after the birth. Between the greater challenges and my age, I wanted to be near my mama for this delivery.

Seth and I settled into a guest house with our younger children. Our daughters, Haya and Amit helped me in the house and with their youngest brothers and sisters. I spent many days in bed. When not in bed, I visited friends and Mama and sewed little things I could create quietly.

I woke early one morning to the forgotten, but familiar pains in my stomach, squeezing in an effort to expel the child. Seth sent Tal to collect my mama and his to come assist us. They brought my sister, Susanna and Haya to assist, as well, while Amit herded the littler ones to mama's house to be entertained by papa.

After a long and difficult delivery, a son emerged, red and quiet. Mama instructed Haya to hold him by the heels and massage his back and throat. I lay watching, holding my breath until he drew a breath and cried. I exhaled, allowing tears to flow. Eve wrapped him in a woven blanket and lay him in my arms.

Still too weak to hike the hill to the altar, strong sons pulled me and the babe in a small cart to the altar on the hill eight days later. I wanted to be there for the naming and thank sacrifice for this son, as I had been for the others. Seth led the sacrifice, then took the tiny boy in his arms to name and bless him.

Seth named the boy Enos and prayed for him to be blessed with obedience to Jehovah's commands, as he had blessed all our children. Other sons obeyed, but none chose to serve as Seth had in the priesthood. They chose to raise horses, build wagons, or activities that made it burdensome for them to travel and teach. We prayed he was the one to follow Seth.

Seth received a command to support his papa in Home Valley. His responsibility no longer focused on traveling from place to place to teach. He traveled, briefly, sometimes with Adam, other times with younger men. His purpose changed from reaching out to find new communities to obey Jehovah to returning to those we taught earlier, supporting and building their faith.

Over time, I returned to the normal activities of women—cooking, cleaning, making pots, weaving leaves and fronds into baskets and lengths of wool into cloth, sewing and mending clothing, preparing food for storage, and much more, always keeping Enos close. I listened to the women talk, and complain. I thought about their problems and considered how I could help them. An answer came.

One day while Seth traveled with Adam, I joined Eve in completing pots. Enos played with the clay, shaping it into animals. The pots had cooked in hot fires, as the people of Laish showed me, the heat held inside great ovens, making them hard and non-porous. Now we painted them and planned to return them to the hot ovens.

"Your design is interesting." Eve stopped painting to look at my work. "White fluffy clouds, green triangular trees, and brown earth. What do you plan to add in the space between the trees?"

"A wolf and a bear."

"Why a wolf and a bear?" She leaned back. A startled look crowded her face.

I understood her question. I preferred almost any other animals to bears and wolves, except serpents. "I remember the story you told the young ones—the story about when the wolf and bear protected you."

"A wolf, two bears, and a pair of mountain lions. Frightening."

I nodded and speculated if another bear and a pair of mountain lions would fit in the small space I left between the trees.

"I believe it will assist us in teaching the women." I closed my eyes, remembering their complaints. "We need share with them the marvel and immediacy of Jehovah's protection in time of trouble. Many women are left alone when their husbands hunt. Hannah and Lillith are alone now, and their time to give birth draws near. I believe this pot will remind them of Jehovah's love for us."

"Teach the women?" Her forehead wrinkled as she considered my concern. "Yes. Good plan. It will be a good visual reminder. You are right. We should help them learn." Eve thought a moment. "Ora and Zira will give birth soon, as well. Is anyone checking on any of these women? Will they have support with the babes?"

"None I know of." I shrugged. "The men leave us behind to care for families and animals. We have much to do. Can we not work together, support one another?" I dipped my brush into black paint and began to work on a bear.

"Perhaps." Eve paused to think about the problem. "We can gather the women of Home Valley to share what we know with them and ask for suggestions."

I lifted my brush and glanced toward grandmama. "That would work. Tomorrow? Perhaps after the men and others are fed? They can bring the little ones with them."

"We can visit with them at the well this evening when we go for water." She set her pot aside to dry.

"Where shall we meet tomorrow?" I examined mine and daubed paint on a spot I missed, before beginning on a lion.

"Lovely work, Ganet. It tells the story beautifully in art. We can meet in my home."

"Your house is nice, Eve, but is there enough room for all the women?" I began to mentally count them.

"Perhaps not. We can meet in the tabernacle, I'll ask … Oh. Adam is gone. It will have to be in the village green. Everyone fits there and the children can play nearby."

I finished painting and surveyed my pot. The wolf joined the bears and mountain lions, standing guard in the trees.

We gathered our pots and placed them inside the waiting oven, moved hot coals around to ensure even heat, and closed and locked the door. When we were certain all was right, we walked side by side to the well.

~

After husbands settled into evening activities the next day, fifty-seven women of Home Valley gathered with Eve and me on the village green including Haya and Amit. The women chattered and visited with friends as they sat in comfortable seats on the grass. Enos and the children who joined us found close places to play near their mamas. He sat by me, playing with his little clay animal.

I opened the meeting. "Sisters, women of Home Valley. Eve and I brought you here because we are concerned for you. We do not always enjoy the support of others when our men are gone. We have heavy burdens of home, children, and animals. We work alone or with our children in the fields when the men are gone."

A buzz filled the air as heads nodded in agreement. I paused a moment as the noise quieted before continuing.

"Ora, I see your birthing time comes soon. Has Yagil returned from his hunting trip?"

A flush of embarrassment crossed Ora's face. "No... No. I do not expect him for another week or two. We hoped the babe would wait for his papa." She shook her head and peeked at her swollen stomach. "Now, I doubt Yagil will be back in time."

A murmur rose above the green. I paused, allowing them to share, and then raising my hands for quiet.

"Ora needs a friend, a sister, to watch over her, to be there to help with the birth of this baby. Is there one who lives close to her, anyone who will take on this duty?"

"I will be there for her," Zilphah volunteered. "Ora is my neighbor. She helped me with my last two. This is her first. I will watch out for her and assist in the birthing."

Excitement buzzed across the green and several hands shot up.

"I will help."

"I live close, my daughter will assist with her chores."

"My sons will water her garden."

"And mine will weed it."

An impressive list of support for Ora grew.

I regained their attention. "Ora is not the only woman in Home Valley who could use care and love."

The sounds of women swelled as they shared examples of neighboring women in need. I raised my hands again to quieten the women.

"Zira, too, is close to giving birth. Hannah and Lillith spend long days alone with great responsibilities. Eve," I gestured in Eve's direction, and then toward myself, "and I believe each of us can work in pairs to be aware of two or three other women. All of us have the desire to be supported. No one can stand alone." I turned to Eve. "Even when Eve was alone here in Home Valley, she was not alone."

Voices filled the green, questioning, wondering. When the women settled in to listen, I reached behind a nearby tree and retrieved my freshly fired vase.

I signaled to Eve. "Grandmama Eve, please share with these women the story on my vase."

Eve stood to recount her story.

"Just before Bilhah's birth, Adam took Absalom on a short walk about overnight. The first afternoon, as I sat under a tree to weave, the hair on my neck lifted up, warning me of the presence of evil. The Destroyer, that old serpent, lazed against a tree across the clearing, observing me. Earlier, Adam's priesthood sheltered me, but he traveled far away."

Eve shivered. "Before I could even think to make a noise, two tall black bears, a wolf, and a pair of mountain lions maneuvered themselves between us, teeth bared and snarling."

Eve waited as the women bubbled with wonder.

"You may wonder that the animals did not attack me. They are my friends, and have always been. When they came, I was uncertain of their intentions, until I saw the direction they faced—toward the Destroyer. They followed him from Home Valley and away from me."

Eve shrugged. "The next day, Adam and Absalom returned with Bark, our first dog. We are sure he was the cub of the he-wolf who guarded me. A serpent killed Bark's mama. We never knew, but suspected her death came in retribution for the defense of his papa. We do know two things: the wolf and his friends defended me, and we protected the pup after the death of his mama. We believe they were mates."

The women passed the vase around, looked closely at the animals, and exchanged comments. The meaning became clear to them. When they gave it back to me, Eve continued her story.

"Though I seemed to be by myself then, Jehovah was near. He sent those animals to safeguard me. He watched over the orphaned pup and drew Adam and Absalom toward the pup and his mama. We are never alone. Jehovah sends assistance in the form of animals, men, or another woman."

The women in the green nodded silently.

I resumed the challenge of teaching. "Jehovah created women with tenderness and love, enough to support one another. Look what you offered to Ora." I swept my hand in Ora's direction. She now sat in a protective circle of women. "Each of us desires this kind of love. We all require attention and support at times. None is exempt. Not even Eve." I glanced her way. "Even Eve needs love and support from the women of Home Valley."

The crescendo of voices joined their applause. Those who sat close to Eve reached out, touching her in concern and love. She wore a smile broader than I remembered ever seeing.

"For now," I continued, waving my hands toward individuals across the crowd, "watch over the women who live on either side of you and those across from you. Be particularly aware of those whose men are gone and those who are about to giving birth. Do we need formal assignments?"

"No!" the women called.

"That settles it. Support the women who live near you. Love and help each one. Give service. Assign your children to assist in giving needed service."

Nodding and agreement permeated the green.

"It is time to return to your homes, your husbands, and your families. Do not forget this sacred responsibility to watch and care for the women who live near you."

Little knots of chattering women stood and left. The green emptied. I heard women telling those around them they would not be forgotten. A son or daughter would come over in the morning to check on them or a woman would stop by later to be certain all was well. I looked down, startled to see Enos sleeping through all the noise.

"I think that went well," I said.

Eve started at the sound of my voice. "Yes, Ganet, it did. Thank you for taking leadership."

I picked up Enos and carried him as we walked in warm companionship to Eve's home, deep in discussion.

Chapter Twenty-Seven

Ministering Sisters

D ays later, Adam joined the women in the tabernacle. The men cared for our little ones. Seth had returned, and stayed home with Enos. Eve sat near me as her sweetheart spoke to us.

"Jehovah agrees it is time to organize women." He looked about the room. "He is pleased with your organization. However, He has a better way. You will be organized under the Priesthood."

A low hum filled the space. Adam allowed them to talk a few moments before raising his hands to quiet them.

"Jehovah desires for you to help and support one another. He loves His daughters and longs for the best for them. He has chosen Ganet to be your first leader. Ganet, please come forward."

The night before, Adam came to our home to ask me to take on this new responsibility. I wondered then how the women would accept it. They now questioned in an excited hum.

"Ganet? Not Eve?"

"Why not Eve?"

"Why Ganet?"

Eve smiled turned and smiled toward the group, then returned her gaze to Adam and me in front of the group.

"I hear your concerns for Eve. I understand your belief that she should be your leader. Jehovah chose Ganet. We must trust Him in all things."

The women began to nod. The questioning ended.

Adam continued once more. "If you can support Ganet as the first leader of this organization, show it by raising your hand."

Hands raised, some slowly, until they saw Eve holding hers high.

"Ganet asked Eve and Zilpah to be her assistants. Can you agree to this?"

All hands lifted high. Zilpah and Eve joined me on the chairs set in front of the others.

"Ganet, please take over. This is now your responsibility." Adam sat beside Eve and took her hand.

"Women, I suggest we begin by agreeing to call one another sisters, for are we not all daughters of Jehovah and daughters of Adam and Eve? Are there any comments?"

Ora stood. "After our last meeting, I felt love from the women who aided me. My little Dan," she lifted the babe for all to see, "was born with the help of these wonderful sisters. It is right we address one another sister."

Others stood, sharing experiences of love and assistance during the days since our last gathering. Everyone supported the suggestion. I asked for a vote. The vote carried unanimously.

I next turned to the question of a name for the organization. "What shall we name ourselves?" I asked.

Sisters called out suggestions. Zilpah wrote them on a thin sheet of velum in front of the room for all to see.

"Women's Aid Society."

"Aid of Sisters."

"Sisters in Love."

"Sister's Relief"

"Ministering Sisters"

"Sister's Society."

"Society of Loving Sisters."

"Great ideas." I agreed when the names slowed. "Which is right for us? Turn to those around you and discuss these possible names."

Anticipation and excitement filled the room. Voices buzzed as the sisters discussed. I watched as they shared. When the discussion calmed, I brought the meeting to order and asked for recommendations. Each group recommended 'Ministering Sisters.' We had a name.

We completed other business, in a similar manner.

"Sisters, remember," I concluded, "you are Ministering Sisters. Treat your sisters and their families with love. Be there for each other. We will support you in your needs. We are here for you. Go forth in joy and service."

Women stood to leave and fell into each other's arms in heartfelt embraces. I watched them file slowly out of the room as sisters.

~

I directed the efforts of the Ministering Sisters over the next years. We met frequently to share the gospel and teach of Jehovah. We organized the sisters into pairs and gave them assignments. In this way, we ensured each sister in the village had a pair who cared and watched over her. Sisters cared for Eve and me, as well. They visited and checked on our health and happiness. These improved the feeling of sisterhood and love among us.

In time, Enos grew old enough to be left with one of his sisters, mama, or Eve while I made short trips with Seth. He was our last child. No longer would my body carry a babe. No more came to us. In some ways, it saddened. In others, I was relieved. I feared the difficulty and danger of carrying another within me.

We journeyed to those communities we taught over the first years of our marriage. I wanted to visit my friends there, again, and teach them of this new love Jehovah offered to women. In each village, Seth called a sister to be leader. I shared my experiences and trained the new leader.

When we passed by Geber, we noticed an air of emptiness and desertion. The once neatly tended fields lay fallow and clogged with weeds. We stared at the falling roofs.

"What happened here?" Though not prosperous all those years ago, when we first passed through it, I struggled to understand why it now languished in neglect.

Seth could only shake his head in wonder.

"Can we see if anyone still lives here? Ask what happened? Would Jehovah allow it?"

Seth signaled a halt and sat contemplating the village. At last he nodded. "We are allowed."

Seth guided the bullocks into the village. The houses on the outer edges were empty. Doors hung open and askew. A large rat scampered through one. They were obviously empty. We stared at them in awe.

It did not take long to reach the small village square. A cool wind tore at our clothes, enforcing the suggestion of vacancy. A door opened expelling a filthy stack of robes. It stumbled in our direction until I could see a grubby, dirt encrusted face. It coughed up a gob of phlegm and spat. It landed near the lead bullock's feet, causing it to lash its tail and low. Seth called out gentle words to soothe them.

"You 'er tol yer not welcome in Geber. Did ya come to laugh at me, like ta other 'uns?"

Gemin. He had not changed. Grumpy and rude. Shrunken from his previous bulk.

"What happened to Geber?" Seth asked.

"Like you'da not know. Your fault. You cursed us."

"I cursed you? How?"

"You cursed us wi' drought. The rains did not come to water our plantin'. Our fields withered. Our children starved. Ev'ry'un left, all but me. My goddess and I stay. She promises better days. I wait."

"Ah." Seth brushed his beard out. "I remember now. Jehovah warned you to repent. You have not. Can we help—"

"Nor will I," Gemin shouted. "Go away. Your pity is unwanted."

Seth called to the bullocks and we slowly passed the pile of rags enclosing Gemin, and trekked on.

In Lib, Seth chose Marta to lead their local group of Ministering Sisters. In Laish, he chose Hana. Though the wives of the village leaders followed Jehovah, He chose other, humble women. We spent the dark days of snow and ice in Laish with Lilah, sharing with our friends in companionship and love. Jehovah warned us not to travel anywhere close to Quillon. We returned to the other villages often. Over the years, we met with sisters in many villages, answering questions and helping resolve problems.

As we journeyed, we watched for Zamir, always hoping he had repented. I felt compelled to share my forgiveness with him. We never saw him.

Back in Home Valley, we discovered Enos had continued to grow tall and strong, sober, thoughtful, and obedient. He followed in his papa's footsteps, obeying the commandments of Jehovah. We joined Eve and Adam in praying that he would continue to follow his papa and be the one to receive the High Priesthood.

In time, Enos received the lower priesthood and the right to baptize. Adam took Enos with him on his trips to other villages, teaching and training him in the responsibilities of the priesthood. They stopped in villages not called by Seth. One had not been visited, even by Adam, in the many long years since they chose to follow the Destroyer.

Enos bubbled with the news when they came home. In their travels, they met with Adam's sons, Davud, Jed, and Mathis, and their families. These uncles felt the sorrow of their disobedience and returned to the light of Jehovah. These became a righteous, happy people.

Seth worked in the fields and Enos could not wait for him to tell his news.

He hugged me and leaned back to stare at me. "Mama. You cannot imagine how special it was to visit with Papa's brothers and have them listen to me, a boy! They leaned forward, listening to what I had to say."

"And you helped baptize them?" I asked.

"Grandpapa requested that I baptize the younger ones. I baptized the daughters and sons my age and younger. They had such confidence and trust in me, mama. It was exciting."

Later, when Seth came home, Enos ran to share his news with him. We all fell to our knees in gratitude to Jehovah.

Enos traveled often with Adam after then. Adam learned much of Enos's spirit and believed him to be the one to prepare to succeed in Seth's place, sometime in the future.

During those years, he became friends with a beautiful young woman, Rebecca. Her kindness to me and Seth impressed us. She brought Enos and Seth treats and helped me around the house. We all loved her.

One afternoon, Enos found us at home. Both young people glowed.

"Mama, Papa," Seth said. "Grandpapa agreed to marry Rebecca and me on the fifteenth day of the next moon."

"Congratulations, Enos and Rebecca." Seth and I spoke together.

"We are happy for you," I said. "This is a surprise."

"No, it is not," Rebecca said. "You knew it was coming."

"Yes, I did."

Grandpapa Adam performed the beautiful ceremony, the same one he performed for Seth and me. We sat across from Eve and Adam during the celebratory dinner. Eve questioned them about their plans.

"Enos received a commission from Jehovah." Rebecca brushed her long red hair back and patted Enos's arm. "He is to travel among those who have not yet heard of Jehovah. We leave next week, two days after the Sabbath. Enos needs to participate in the Sabbath and sacrifice once more before we leave."

Enos beamed at her. "We journey south and west to preach repentance to those who have been without Jehovah's light and truth."

"It is past time for a circuit south and west," Adam said. "It is a good direction for you to go teach."

Enos and Rebecca stayed in a guest house on the edge of the village until they departed. I missed them both. Now I understood how mama and Grandmama Eve felt when we were gone.

Chapter Twenty-Eight

Forgiveness

The time came for Seth and me to leave Home Valley once more. We departed to meet with the people we loved in the villages we taught earlier. We were allowed to travel to Axelston. There we discovered Elpis. We had not seen her in all the years since we left her with her mama, Rivka. Elpis still could not hear, but had learned to watch our lips.

"What happened to your mama?" Seth asked careful hold his face so she could look into it.

"She returned to Gemin after you left us. He used her. When she argued, he beat her. Once, he beat her until she fell against the corner of the table. She fell to the ground and never moved again."

"Gemin killed her?" My voice rose in pitch, my eyes opened wide.

She slowly nodded.

Seth lay his hand on my shoulder. "What happened to you and Ayab?"

"Gemin tried to use me. Ayab hit him. When he fell, Ayab grabbed me and we ran. We took horses, I guess you would say we stole those horses from Gemin, but he owed us, and rode into the night. We rode many days until we found our Grandmama and Grandpapa, who cared for us."

"And Gemin?" I asked, even though I knew the answer to that.

"I do not know if Gemin lives. I do not care. He used my mama up and killed her. If he died, he deserved it." Her hard voice grated.

I nodded. I could not fault her for this. "Where is Ayab now?"

"He left Axelston years ago. I have not seen him since. I think he still lives."

"What about you, Elpis? Are you happy now?" I hugged her.

She stepped back to see me speak. "Oh, yes. I have a loving husband and seven children. We live in a house near Grandmama and Grandpapa. Chadad taught us more of Jehovah. We always remembered what you did for us and the things you told us. I live in the light of Jehovah."

It was joyous to have made a difference in her life.

Aviv found me one day, surprising me. I thought she continued to live in Megid.

"No. Kadir came upon me there. He helped me learn not all men will hurt you. I married him and returned home. We are happy together with a small family of boys. For Axelston, boys are a blessing. Since your first visit, we regained an equal number of men and women. Axelston is a good place to live once more."

I held her in an embrace, grateful she had succeeded like Elpis.

Our visit to Seedar was not as happy. Some fell from the light of Jehovah, turning to the darkness of the Destroyer. Even some couples whose wives came from Axelston capitulated to evil. None welcomed us. I sorrowed to discover the great change in these beloved people.

We avoided Quillon, traveling far from that wicked place. Wicked men claimed the few buildings not destroyed by the shaking earth. Zil continued to reign there. I never heard if the serpent who represents Zil is as huge as the one that tried to consume me. I refuse to go there to find out.

We traveled on to Lib, staying with Elam and Tora. They welcomed us in friendship. I appreciated their kindness, especially after Seedar. Seth spent time with the men. I joined the women in weaving. The ugliness of the day so many years ago had been forgotten. I settled down and enjoyed being with them.

One afternoon, I departed from the town hall where the women were weaving, earlier than the others. I did not feel well and needed to rest before dinner and the meetings of the evening. The path led me near to the edge of the village. I allowed my feet to carry me along toward Tora's home, thinking only of the bed that awaited me there.

A hand reached from the bushes, grabbing my arm.

"What?" I cried out. Strong hands turned me and forced me to face into Lib. My heart pounded in my ears.

"Silence!" a man's voice hissed.

It sounded vaguely familiar. Male. I searched my memory for a name to match it.

"You ruined my life," the man growled in my ear, "now I will ruin yours."

The name clicked in my memory, the nightmare returned.

"Zamir?" His grip tightened. "It is you, Zamir. How are you doing? Not so good?"

"No, Ganet. Not so good. Vered left me after you told those lies about me. You know you wanted me. Why did you say otherwise?"

"Me? Want you?" I struggled to gain of control my voice. I wanted to laugh, but knew he would hurt me if I did. "What makes you think I wanted you? I never indicated in any way an interest in you, beyond the friendship I held for all citizens of Lib."

"You smiled in a secret way. I saw your desire in your eyes and in the way you walked away from me." He clutched tighter.

"Desire for you? Did you glance behind you? Did you not see Seth standing there in back of you? All my attentions and 'special smiles' focused on Seth. I loved him since we were small. You were a nice-looking man," I prevaricated, "I suppose you still are, though I have not seen you yet. But all my desires are concentrated on Seth."

"Seth," he spat, "always Seth. What does he have that I do not have?"

"Besides my love and the Priesthood of God? We have twenty-one children together. Good and bad experiences draw us close. Seth never gives me a reason to fear for his love. I trust him." I waited for his hold on me to loosen so I could break away.

Zamir pulled me tight against his body, his hot breath brushed the back of my neck. "Trust. Bah. Trust is not all you suggest."

"Perhaps not for you, but it is everything for me. Seth trusts me and I trust him. He never questioned my behavior or my love after our last meeting."

"Never?" Confusion and disbelief clogged his voice.

His grip loosened a bit. I twisted away and turned toward him, my hands behind me and out of his way. I stared at him. Any masculinity and handsomeness of his earlier years had disappeared. He shrunk into himself. His skin hung on his face. He appeared to have survived months without enough food.

"Do not pity me," Zamir growled.

I dropped my eyes, watching his hands. "It is difficult not to be concerned for you. When did you last have enough to eat?"

"Enough to eat?" he cackled. I worried for his mind. "As if you care about me." He cackled again, eerily high.

"I fear for your health. Come with me. I will be sure you are fed." I reached for his arm.

He balked and drew back from me, horrified. "I cannot go into Lib, especially not with you. I am no longer welcome."

"Do you believe in repentance? Do you believe in forgiveness? I have forgiven you."

"I cannot enter Lib without permission from the leader." He gripped his elbows and began to shiver.

"Stay here, then. I will speak with Lechish." I turned to leave.

"No! Not Lechish. He hates me!" Zamir grabbed at my arm and missed.

"Lechish hates no man. I will talk with Seth. Stay here."

Zamir stepped into the brush beside the path. I forgot my own illness as I rushed to the fields, searching for the men and Seth. I found him in the farthest oat field, helping the others harvest. I waited at the edge, aware of the dangerous sharp scythes.

Seth saw me as he swung his scythe across the grains in the field. At the end of the row, he dropped his arms and joined me, lifting his water bag to his lips.

"Do you feel better?" He leaned down to kiss my hot forehead.

"No, not really, but I need you to come with me."

Concern suffused his face and he glanced at the other men. "Let me tell Lechish I am leaving."

"Tell him to follow us in a few minutes. He will be needed."

Seth scrunched his eyebrows close before nodding. He made his way across the field toward Lechish. I appreciated his trust, the trust I spoke of when I talked to Zamir.

"What is this about?" He grasped my elbows to propped me up as we tromped down the hill from the fields.

"Zamir."

"Zamir? What is he doing here?" He spoke quietly, with an impatient edge.

"Starving. He looks as if he has not eaten a meal in months. His bones poke out sharply beneath the rags he wears as clothing."

"That bad? I have not thought of him for years. I heard he went to Nod to live. Perhaps he was not welcomed even there?"

"He did not say." I told Seth of my confrontation with Zamir. "I forgave him long ago, the fears long gone. I admit to a racing heart when he first grabbed me."

Seth reached over and touched my cheek. "You are a treasure, Ganet. Few women would have the compassion you show."

~

"I did not think you would come back," Zamir moaned when Seth and I found him at last, hiding under a bush. He struggled to scramble to his feet.

"I told you I would bring Seth." I heard the pout in my voice and brightened it. "I do what I say I will do."

"Ganet says you are hungry. When did you last eat?" Seth asked. "Looks like a long while."

"It has been a long time. Few want to feed a dirty, scrawny beggar like me. Some beat me away from their homes."

"That is wrong," Seth said. "Come with us. We will be sure you get food to eat."

"You had me banned from Lib all those years ago. Why would you help me now?" Zamir pulled himself erect with a groan.

"We forgave you long ago," I said. "It does me no good to be angry with you. It only injures me. We watched for you in all our travels, hoping to find you once more."

"We cannot be forgiven by Jehovah if we do not forgive others," Seth added. "Ganet did forgive you."

"I cannot enter Lib without permission from Lechish. And he hates me," Zamir grated.

"Who do I hate?" Lechish stepped of the path into the glen where we stood. "Zamir! Where have you been?"

"You banned me from Lib. Vered and I traveled as far as Nod. She stayed there. I could not. I remembered the things Seth taught. I dreamed of the hope and forgiveness he spoke of, and made my way west." His voice cracked.

Seth pulled his water skin from his shoulder and handed it to Zamir. He took a long drink.

"The ban was not permanent! I am sorry you did not stay long enough to hear. Come with us. Eat some food. You can tell us about your adventures after you have eaten and rested."

Seth and Lechish balanced Zamir between them and helped him into the village. I trailed behind as they helped him to Lechish's home.

"You will be comfortable here," Lechish said as they set him on the long seat. "Rest here, while I find food."

Lechish left to search the kitchen. Ora still wove with the women.

"You two really forgive me?" Wonder permeated Zamir's voice and tears glistened in his eyes, threatening to fall.

"Of course, we do," I said. "You more than paid any price for what you did."

"I have," Zamir whispered, looking at his hands.

Lechish returned with a platter of cold, sliced mutton, a slab of bread, and a bunch of grapes.

"I hope this will help to fill your empty stomach. Be careful. Do not eat too much at once. Ganet is right," he glanced at me, "you have paid more than necessary for your actions. I will introduce you to the village tonight during our evening meeting. I am certain the rest will welcome you. Now, eat, but eat slowly."

Lechish accompanied Seth and me outside. "Go home, take care of your wife. I will need your support tonight when I reintroduce Zamir. Some here still hold a grudge against him."

"We nodded and turned for Elam's house. I had heard negative comments earlier about Zamir from some of the women. This may be a major challenge. I slept. The heat left me and I felt able to attend the evening meeting.

"How can you forgive that man," Tora asked later as we walked together toward the village green.

"Forgiveness was easier than the headaches I suffered. Since I forgave him, they disappeared. I discovered a peace beyond understanding when I could honestly let the pain, all of it, go. He damaged my reputation, for a time. He only attempted to injure me, without success. However, he has been hurt far more than I ever was. You will know what I mean when you see him."

She shook her head, unwilling to believe he had changed. I knew my friend would think differently when she saw him. She was a charitable woman.

I heard a similar conversation between Seth and Elam behind us.

Lechish conducted the business of the meeting, as usual, discussing crops and the need for all to participate in the coming threshing. As everyone began to shuffle in readiness to leave, he signaled for Seth to help bring Zamir into the room.

"I have one final piece of business. Zamir has returned."

A clamor overflowed the green as they looked on Zamir. He had taken a bath and wore cleaner clothing than when we left him, but his starvation and sorrow clung to him like an old, wet robe.

"I move that we allow Zamir to become a member of our community once more." Lechish's voice rose among the clamor.

I stepped next to Seth, waiting for the commotion to settle. The merciless emotions expressed surprised me. Seth lifted his hands in the air, requesting silence.

"We do not live here. We are but visitors. Yet, we have a part in this. We believe you should hear what we have to say."

A few shouted out against Zamir, but were hushed by their neighbors.

"My wife, Ganet, and I were wronged by this man. He attempted to injure Ganet and take her virtue. Then he lied about it. But, this happened many years in the past. Although his actions damaged our reputations here, Zamir has suffered much more than we have." Seth waved toward Zamir. "Vered left him, choosing to live in Nod. He chose the greater honor, refusing to become a part of them. You can see he has suffered. We ask for you to forgive him. We did years ago."

"Has he really changed his ways?" Danel called. "Will he willingly participate in the work expected of men in Lib? He cannot stay if he does not work."

All eyes turned to Zamir. Danel was right. If Zamir was allowed to stay, he would be required to fully participate. Had he changed enough?

"I will not shirk my duties." Zamir's eyes stayed locked on Danel's. "I will be on the threshing floor tomorrow. I will do more than my share."

"In your condition?" Seth asked. "Is that wise?"

"It is required of me." Zamir stared at the group. "I shirked in those past days. I believed myself too good to work with you. I took without giving. My travels proved me wrong, so very wrong. I will join you on the threshing floor. I will do my part … if you will allow me to be a part of this village again." He lowered his head, waiting for the sentence.

Opinions buzzed through the crowd; some angry, many of the others were compassionate.

Danel's voice rose above the cacophony, "Let us accept him on a provisional basis. He is welcome—so long as he keeps his word, as long as he is a productive member of our community. Give the man a chance. Seth and Ganet forgave him. They had more to forgive than we do. Let us learn if he truly repented."

Others agreed, shouting:

"Yes, let us see if he speaks the truth."

"We will see if he joins us, tomorrow."

"We can wait and see."

Lechish raised his hands, gaining their attention. "Is this the will of the people of Lib? Shall we accept Zamir, with the requirement of his willingness to participate?"

"Yes." The roar echoed through the square. No one raised their voice in disagreement.

"Zamir, you are a member of our village, with the precondition of participation. Do you agree to this requirement?"

Zamir lifted his head and stared into the crowd. "I do."

Many of the assembly surrounded him, welcoming him back to the community.

Seth and I joined in the work the next morning. Zamir began before anyone else arrived, scattering grain on the stone floor, lifting and scattering the chaff. Danel and Adad pounded him on his back, welcoming him to Lib and the threshing floor. At midday, Zamir joined the men, eating large portions of the food provided by the women. They shook his hand and offered appreciation for his hard work at the end of the long day, though he struggled to keep up at the end. He was well on his way to acceptance.

Epilogue

"**S**eth and I continued our travels. We visited and lived in many villages. We returned often to Laish to visit Lilah and her family. Though bullocks pulled our wagons, traveling through the snow was always difficult. We came back to settle here in Home Valley, near Grandmama Eve and Grandpapa Adam, grateful for their continued love. Enos and Rebecca returned often, sharing their joys and sorrows. Many of our children and grandchildren are here. The life story continues."

The crowd of women and children stretched and stirred, coming out of the trance of a good story.

"Who shares her story tomorrow?" Ruth called out.

"That is easy." Eve glanced around the group, her eyes settling on Rebecca. "We need to hear about Rebecca's adventures. Ganet has heard many of them, as have I. These women should hear her story."

All eyes turned toward Rebecca, who shrugged her shoulders.

"Gather your thoughts and get ready, Rebecca," Ganet called. "Tomorrow is your turn."

The other women agreed. Those around Ganet and Rebecca patted their backs and hugged them. They gathered their blankets, bags, and children moving toward the center of the village, where food awaited them and their families. As they walked, they chatted about Ganet's story, looking forward to the next day and Rebecca's tale.

Extra Information

A Note:

You may have noticed the formal language in this and other books in the Ancient Matriarchs series. I purposefully did not use contractions, except in scenes where the people were less educated and had lived away from Eve's influence for many years.

I believe that the language was pure, undefiled by jargon and contractions. Only later, within the past two or three centuries, has that changed. For that reason, I carefully omitted contractions.

Did You Enjoy This Book?

If you did, will you do something for me?

I'm and independent author, publishing my books without the backing of a major publisher. That means no six-figure advances and no advertising budget. This makes it difficult to promote my novels and put them in places new readers can find them. But you can help me.

Honest reviews and genuine "word-of-mouth" advertising makes all the difference. I'm not asking for one of those awful book reports I used to try not to sleep through, that you did in school. What will help me is if you would leave an honest star rating and a couple of sentences on Amazon or Goodreads. Or a short review on your blog. Or tell your friends about it on Facebook or Twitter.

Let people know what you liked about this book and why they might like it, too. And, if there was something you didn't like, you can say that, as well. Constructive criticism helps me write a better book next time.

But, please. *No spoilers!*

Thanks for reading.

Would You Like More?

If you enjoyed this story, you may enjoy a Free Micro Story, written about Eve in her travels with Adam, later in their lives. Eve, mother to us all, and wife of the first man, and she is forced to save him ...

While traveling together, later in life, Adam is captured. Fearing the captures will take his life, Eve has to find a way to get him away.

Avenging Angel, a rich micro-story of historical fiction, continues the story of Eve found in Eve, Ancient Matriarch with compelling feminine perspectives and courage.

Avenging Angel is free and only available when you subscribe to my Weekly Musings.

Go to: http://www.AngeliqueCongerAuthor.com to get your free copy.

Ancient Matriarchs: Avenging Angel

Other Books by Angelique Conger

ABOUT THE AUTHOR

Angelique Conger discovered the wonders of writing books later in her life. Books, however, have always been important to her. As a little girl in a small town, she was given her own library card at the tender age of five, highly unusual in those days. She remembers walking to the few blocks to the library on her own to choose the maximum number of books, four, and took them back three or four days later for four more. As she got older and she occasionally returned the books a day or two past the limit of two weeks. The librarians allowed her to straighten the shelves to pay off her fines.

Angelique reads a book, or three at once, much of the time. She reads most genres of books and until recently only toyed with writing them. Since then, she has spent many hours each day learning the craft of writing and editing.

The stories and mystery of the lives of ancient women enticed Angelique. Little is known about the first patriarchs, beyond their names, and little or nothing is known of their wives. While little is written about our mother Eve, not even the names are known of the other women who supported their patriarch husbands. How then, can she write their stories? They are a work of fiction, though she believes they sat beside her, whispering their stories into her ear. Read their stories in the series Ancient Matriarchs.

Angelique received her BEd (education) from the University of Hawaii and her MS from Utah State University. She taught elementary school for 14 years in Utah after following her husband around the world as he served in the United States Navy. She strived to do her best to obey the command given to Eve to replenish the earth. She has five children and nine grandchildren, so far. Her goal is to be a noble matriarch like Eve.

Angelique lives in southern Nevada with her husband, love bird, and two turtles. She enjoys the visits of her grandchildren—and their parents.

Made in the USA
Columbia, SC
07 September 2021